Nice and Noir

Books by Richard B. Schwartz

Samuel Johnson and the New Science

Samuel Johnson and the Problem of Evil

Boswell's Johnson: A Preface to the LIFE

Daily Life in Johnson's London

After the Death of Literature

Nice and Noir: Contemporary American Crime Fiction

Frozen Stare (novel)

The Last Voice You Hear (novel)

After the Fall (novel)

The Biggest City in America: A Fifties Boyhood in Ohio (memoir/stories)

Ed. *The Plays of Arthur Murphy,* 4 vols.

Ed. *Theory and Tradition in Eighteenth-Century Studies*

Nice and Noir

Contemporary American Crime Fiction

Richard B. Schwartz

UNIVERSITY OF MISSOURI PRESS
COLUMBIA AND LONDON

Library of Congress Cataloging-in-Publication Data

Schwartz, Richard B.
  Nice and noir : contemporary American crime fiction / Richard B. Schwartz.
    p. cm.
  Includes bibliographical references and index.
  ISBN 0-8262-1393-6 (alk. paper)
  1. Detective and mystery stories, American—History and criticism.
2.   American fiction—20th century—History and criticism.   3. Crime in
literature.   I. Title.

PS374.D4 S39 2002
813'.087209—dc21   2002017956

Designer: Jennifer Cropp
Typesetter: The Composing Room of Michigan, Inc.
Printer and binder: The Maple-Vail Book Manufacturing Group
Typefaces: Nicolas Cochin, Palatino

For Judith Alexis
always there and never doubting

When a book, any sort of book, reaches a certain intensity of artistic performance, it becomes literature. That intensity may be a matter of style, situation, character, emotional tone, or idea, or half a dozen other things. It may also be a perfection of control over the movement of a story similar to the control a great pitcher has over the ball. That is to me what you have more than anything else and more than anyone else. . . .

The character that lasts is an ordinary guy with some extraordinary qualities. Perry Mason is the perfect detective because he has the intellectual approach of the juridical mind and at the same time the restless quality of the adventurer who won't stay put. I think he is just about perfect. So let's not have any more of that phooey about "as literature my stuff still stinks." Who says so—William Dean Howells?

Raymond Chandler to Erle Stanley Gardner, 1946

Contents

Acknowledgments

In a book entitled *After the Death of Literature* (1997) I articulated my views of Romanticism, popular culture, and the position of genre fiction therein. That book included some specific discussions of genre fiction that have been well received, and the response of readers has encouraged me to attempt the current project. Some of the material on *The Great Gatsby* in Chapter I appeared in *Text and Teaching: Reflections on Art and Literature,* edited by Michael J. Collins (1995); an earlier version of some of the material on *The Silence of the Lambs* in Chapter VIII originally appeared in an article entitled "The Moral of the Story," with Jonathan F. Schwartz, that appeared in *Notre Dame Magazine* (1993).

I would like to thank my wife, Judith, for her always acute advice and for her unfailing encouragement and our son, Jonathan, for his insights and suggestions, particularly with regard to film and television. I would like to thank both my literary history and creative writing students for their tolerance and wakefulness and for reminding me—by their presence—that literary history and creative writing should be as closely aligned everywhere as they are at the University of Missouri–Columbia. Finally, I would like to thank the press readers who offered comments that I found very helpful and my editor, Bev Jarrett, who always offers a firm and experienced hand with a supportive, light touch. Jane Lago, managing editor of the press, copyedited the manuscript in a most expert fashion. I (and my readers) are in her debt.

Nice and Noir

Introduction

Owners of mystery bookshops will tell you that there are several sorts of buyers: those who drift in and buy on impulse or whim, genre addicts who buy paperbacks by the week and by the armful, and, finally, the hard core—those who have caught up on canonical texts and buy new novels by select authors in hardcover. The hardcover hard core all have their favorite writers and they all watch publication dates, leading lives of quiet anticipation. Amazon has increased that anticipation by listing upcoming titles by month on the Mystery and Thriller section of its website. At some points—Thomas Harris's *Hannibal* is a good example—Amazon has gone so far as to release "reviews" by readers who have not actually seen the book but are so overwhelmed by their anticipation of it that they are driven to share tentative judgments.

As a member of the hard core I have my own favorites. These include approximately seventy writers whose careers I watch and the vast majority of whose work I read. I cannot pretend that my favorite writers are the best writers on some absolute scale, for (a) such scales are questionable, (b) the field is simply too vast, and (c) my own tastes are just that, my own. I can say, however, that most of the writers I regularly read command broad audiences and broad critical attention.

Since my perspective has been shaped by some thirty-five years of college-level English teaching I can say that I demand good writing (sentence by sentence as well as book by book) from the writers I read, and as a sometime practitioner of the fiction writer's trade I have a special love of craft that is rooted in both admiration and envy.

Whether or not the work of my own favorite writers constitutes the best that is being done these days, it is certainly representative of

1

the best that is being done. Because the broad category of crime writing is fluid but not open-ended, a consideration of several dozen writers who have attained success and prominence in the field should at least be indicative of the general state of the art and its interests and concerns.

Mickey Spillane once said that the first sentence of a novel sells the book and the last sentence sells the next book. Whether true or not, that is how I read and decide. Once I have found an author whose work I admire, I stay with him or her until one of us loses interest. In discovering new authors I apply the Spillane test. No matter how interesting the plot or the characters, I refuse to read bad prose. There are many writers who can plot like wizards but not write an effective sentence. I cannot read their work. The writers discussed in this book then, are effective stylists whose work I recommend to all serious readers.

The book is an examination of repeating themes. While it highlights the careers and current work of specific crime writers, it is neither a formal history of their genre nor a formal summary of its most recent developments. The first chapter is designed to place the chapters that follow within a larger literary and cultural context, and the themes highlighted there reappear in the succeeding material, so that the writers and books discussed constitute exemplars and illustrations. My concern here is to examine cultural patterns (including literary patterns), and my intention is to draw inferences from the examples adduced. Crime writing as a form is particularly responsive to contemporary interests and anxieties, and it is those interests and anxieties (exemplified in skillful and thoughtful writing) that are my subject.

My reading in this area is unsystematic in the Johnsonian sense of the term. It is driven by curiosity and passion rather than by obligation. Hence, my own readers should not expect the sort of reference apparatus one might normally supply in a scholarly monograph. Much of the most interesting material in this field is to be found in fanzine and internet interviews, documentary television programming, signing chats, booksellers' anecdotes, and agents' and editors' lore. I have appended some bibliographic material at the end of the study for those desiring a bit more structure and direction.

Tzvetan Todorov distinguishes between two types of criticism. One he calls *logical*, the other *narrative*. "Narrative criticism," he writes, "follows a horizontal line, it proceeds from theme to theme, stopping at a more or less arbitrary moment; each of these themes is as non-abstract as the next, they constitute an endless chain, and the critic—here similar to the narrator—chooses almost at random the beginning and the end of his narrative." While this is not a precise description of what I have tried to do, it is a relatively good one. The issues and motifs that draw my attention are generally connected, if not in an endless chain, at least in ways that are sometimes striking and often instructive. The connections are far more important than the order in which they are approached, and the breadth and insistence of the connections is the study's conclusion, not some all-encompassing claim or adjustment to a theoretical construct.

One would, of course, expect commonalities and connections in any body of genre fiction, but while each genre establishes a template and a set of expectations, serious genre writing (as opposed, for example, to work where the format is prescribed absolutely by the mass-market publisher) invites practitioners to expand the genre within a given set of constraints or transcend it without losing a recognizable relationship to the base. In most cases the best work in category fiction (my subject here) enlarges our sense of the category, sometimes to the point of shattering it. Nevertheless, the thematic motifs continue to appear, despite the innovative narratives in which they are embedded.

Not unexpectedly, the writer who stretches or shatters his or her genre is also capable of stretching or shattering our response in the process, with regard both to the arc and texture of the narrative and to the themes addressed therein. (An excellent example is James Ellroy's just-released *The Cold Six Thousand,* discussed below.) Thus, the very best genre writing shapes some perceptions while confirming others. It speaks to our needs and desires as a society but may challenge as well as satisfy them. It redirects at the same time that it reflects. It destabilizes at the same time that it assures.

If I were to summarize the themes discussed in the chapters that follow, the overarching story would be something like the following. Contemporary crime writers continue to take their essential inspiration from Chandler's vision of a society corrupted by the actions of large institutions, institutions motivated by the most banal and violent of self-interests and blithely capable of crushing the purest and bravest of individuals. The hostile landscape that such individuals enter is characterized by lines of division that invite even as they threaten, and the investigations and crusades that individuals undertake therein rarely lead to final, tidy resolutions.

The paucity of justice in these landscapes encourages the emergence of the vigilante as well as partnerships in the wasteland that bridge not only gender but, particularly, racial lines. The absentee God who once presided over this space is now revealed rarely, and then generally through angels of justice and vengeance with dirty faces rather than white wings.

At times the absurdity of our plight plunges us into a comic world that would not be unfamiliar to a Pynchon or a Beckett, and the landscapes in which these many actions are situated take on the importance of a major player or major theme. In confronting the broad strokes of narrative we may laugh or cry; in confronting the details that anchor that narrative we find a source of instruction that we eventually come to demand.

Finally, this most serious of diversions plays out in an art form whose terms are prescribed but whose boundaries are actively crossed. We thus find reassurance and reality both in the author's faithfulness to those terms and in his active desire to extend and even shatter them.

In the chapters that follow, all of these themes and ideas will be explored in greater depth, and in a way that I hope will make this volume as engaging as the books discussed herein.

Frontiers and Borders

While crime and mystery fiction broadly conceived represent approximately one-third of the contemporary fiction market, the genealogies of these most successful of novelistic works are to be found in prenovelistic forms. English mysteries or cozies, as they are sometimes termed by the trade, are traceable to the ethos and plot arcs of classic comedy, while crime fiction of the hard- and soft-boiled variety finds its principal anticipations and topoi in romance.

English mysteries (often set in American locales) are not my subject here, but it is useful, for purposes of contrast, to examine their roots. In Northrop Frye's well-known schema, comedy is recognized as, essentially, a conservative form. It assumes the existence of a once-happy society under challenge by evil (or at least, reactionary) forces that, we are assured, will not finally prevail. That assurance is foundational to the form and its atmospherics. The course of the narrative is to chart the actions of the perpetrators who have overturned or are at least threatening the status quo, block or blunt them, and, ultimately, exile them, so that the society they are undermining or obstructing can be returned to its previous, happy condition.

At the most basic plot level, comedies often deal with courtship, a courtship opposed by individuals who, we are assured, will not be permitted to participate in the culminating wedding or dance, which will represent the larger social unity of which this final plot element is a part. Comedy assumes a world that makes moral, political, and cultural sense, a world whose structures and values are generally acceptable to us, a world whose coherence we seek to preserve and extend.

On the other hand, tragedy (a writer such as L. J. Potts will argue) is an *interim* reading of life. It flourishes when we are between satisfactory worldviews. It is no coincidence that it enjoyed great success

5

in a period and place such as Jacobean England, where the dominance of the church and the aristocracy was under serious challenge, where science was in the process of displacing a theology and philosophy based on authority rather than reason, where civil war was imminent, where multiple regnal changes were on the horizon, and where the traditional alignments of patriarchy and family were shifting; this was a time when putative ignorance was being replaced by new or resurgent knowledge, an economy based on land was being displaced by an economy based on trade and capitalism, and new literary forms were being developed to serve the needs, slake the curiosities, and expand the imaginations of a burgeoning reading public.

It is not difficult to see Frye's classic form and ethos in such works as *Twelfth Night* or *As You Like It* or even in such late romances as *The Tempest*. (We can have both great tragedy and great comedy in the same period, since we must face the demands of new thought and experience at the same time that we long for a period of greater stability.) The far later works of a signature writer such as Agatha Christie are close cousins to these Elizabethan and Jacobean models. The stable society in the Christie mystery often reveals itself as populated by types harkening back to the characters of Jonsonian drama (with its backdrop of humor theory underwriting its seemingly simplistic psychology) or the characters of Charles Dickens (underwritten by the realities of English life and society, if one believes George Santayana). Type characters assume a predictable society— that is, one that will yield predictable individuals with predictable behaviors and predictable values.

It is a world not unlike that of the children's book, with butchers, bakers, candlestick makers, and other craftspersons plying their trades under sunny skies, in lanes punctuated by moving vehicles operated by smiling drivers and accented by parks, gardens, and private rose arbors. Into this world, however, there comes a figure or figures of violence with the result that society itself, and not just the individuals most immediately affected by the intruder's actions, comes under attack.

The crime is solved and the criminal brought to justice by a figure embodying patience, courage, and that most middle class of values, rationality. In John Cawelti's view, this assertion of the claims of reason is part of a far larger cultural pattern. The creation of the detective story in the nineteenth century (with Wilkie Collins, Edgar Allan Poe, and—shortly thereafter—Arthur Conan Doyle) is, in Cawelti's judgment, an attempt by the middle class to use one of its self-created forms, the novel, to both assert its cultural position and protect its flanks from rearguard operations by the clergy and aristocracy or open revolts on the part of the proletariat.

In literature this is anticipated by the earlier prominence of gothicism at the end of the eighteenth and beginning of the nineteenth centuries. Gothicism examines the power of the middle class (imagined symbolically as the virtue of middle-class womanhood) under the assault of lascivious monks and libidinous noblemen. As the century progresses and revolutions in thought are paralleled by revolutions in the streets, the middle class turns (in search of a stable defense) to rationality, the preeminently egalitarian virtue, least subject to the manipulations of the church, the decaying and thus doubly desperate aristocracy, or the mob.

The belief that crimes actually can be solved and criminals brought to justice provides emotional reassurance as well as the lineaments of a larger worldview, a middle-class reading of life that will not be an interim one, but rather an eternal one, as stable as the societies it is designed to preserve.

Hard-boiled writing, or crime writing (noir writing, to the industry), also finds its roots in England, not just in romance (on which more later) but in other prenovelistic or early novelistic forms. Truman Capote's *In Cold Blood* can be described plausibly as a "nonfiction novel," but this book—in which much of contemporary "true crime" writing has found its inspiration—has a long list of post-Renaissance and Enlightenment progenitors. Henry Fielding did not call his book about the notorious criminal Jonathan Wild a novel; he called it a history. The tradition in which he located it is that most "true crime" of forms, the criminal biography, a form antedating *In Cold Blood* by hundreds of years.

While so-called hard-boiled writing concerns "hard-boiled" detectives and the crimes they attempt to solve, there are many crime novels in which the focus falls on the criminal rather than on the detective (if indeed there even are detectives in the story). One thinks, for example, of the works of James M. Cain or those of Jim Thompson. Such work shares the ethos and attitudes of hard-boiled writing far more than the ethos and attitudes of the English mystery and can thus be lumped under the general category of crime writing. It may, however, take its formal inspiration from the traditions of criminal biography rather than from the romance. The lines are not perfectly tidy, particularly when the creators of the narratives are attempting to innovate and/or transcend genre. In the spirit of Justice Potter Stewart's description of pornography, crime writing (as opposed to English mystery writing) can sometimes defy definition, but it is nonetheless easily recognized.

One of the most popular of eighteenth-century publications was a work called the *Newgate Calendar*, a collection of accounts of contemporary criminals—their crimes, atrocities, escapes, and final punishments. In its focus on sex and violence the *Newgate Calendar* is a form of pious pornography, though relatively mild by modern standards. It is also a form of true crime writing.

In this as in other quasi-historical works the line between fiction and nonfiction is consciously blurred. Novels purport to be true biographies in order to leverage the weight and appeal of historicity, and in many cases they are actually based on true stories. Before Robinson Crusoe there really was an Alexander Selkirk. In addition, the arc of what one can still recognize as the Aristotelian plot is common in both fictional and nonfictional forms, so that the narrative devices that are so beloved and so effective in fiction are leveraged in nonfiction as well.

This, of course, is true today, where the very best of true crime writing, for example Joseph Wambaugh's *The Blooding* or *The Onion Field* or Sydney Kirkpatrick's superb *A Cast of Killers*, "reads like a novel." In some cases the differences between the two forms are quite incidental. A Martian with an unsteady grasp of earthly biomedical history who stumbled across *The Blooding* (a true crime study of an investigation of rape/murders in an English village) might take all of Wambaugh's discussion of DNA testing to be part of the "novel's" atmospherics and consider the story to be utterly fictional.

This is, in many ways, to be expected. One of the defining elements of the novel in its earliest incarnations is its realism and its plausibility. The novelistic form, from the outset, was designed to appear to be historical. Similarly—to return to the world of contemporary crime fiction—when Joseph T. ("Cap") Shaw assumed the editorship of *Black Mask*, the pivotal, early organ of crime writing, he decreed that the magazine's stories would henceforth be "real in motive, character and action . . . [and they] must be plausible."

How do we link these practices (of 1927) with the world of the chivalric romance? Raymond Chandler's conception of crime fiction and its protagonist was not necessarily original (certainly it had been anticipated in practice), but it was definitive in its articulation. In his celebrated essay "The Simple Art of Murder," Chandler imagined what he had both long enjoyed and personally created, the story of a "man's adventure in search of a hidden truth."

This is, in a sense, the oldest of stories, perhaps the only story. (The ultimate origins of crime writing can thus be located in antiquity as well as in the more proximate seventeenth, eighteenth, and nineteenth centuries.) Chandler's primary example was Dashiell Hammett, but his narrative voice was influenced (he tells us) by Joseph Conrad's Marlow, and the ethos of his stories was anticipated (he tells us) by the creator of the *Morte d'Arthur,* Sir Thomas Malory. Both Malory's and Marlow's names lie behind (he tells us) the name of his own great protagonist.

He is not alone in consciously evoking these chivalric echoes. Ross Macdonald's protagonist is Lew *Archer* and Sam Spade's partner's name is Miles Archer. Robert Parker, who has "coauthored" *Poodle Springs* with Chandler by completing it and has written other Chandler-related material, calls the protagonist of his main series (Parker now has three series underway) Spenser. It is Edmund Spenser (Parker's Spenser often points out) who wrote the principal chivalric epic of Elizabethan England, *The Faerie Queene.* Parker himself holds a Ph.D. in English literature and is thoroughly aware of the traditions in which he is working.

The mean streets down which Chandler's hero must go are the urban version of the forest in chivalric romance. Again, to return to Frye, "romantic" poetry is principally characterized by the attempt to communicate private experience in the face of its ineffability. Samuel Taylor Coleridge's ancient mariner is the textbook example— a man who disrupts weddings by buttonholing guests and attempting to convey to them the depths of a personal story that can never be fully communicated.

The forest is a threshold symbol, beyond the city's protective walls, a locus for activities and adventures that are possible only when one has stepped beyond the comforting confines of civilization. Romantic poetry, however, as in Wordsworth, for example, often softens the edges of such experiences, associating itself with other forms—the georgic, for example, and the pastoral. For the medieval knight, however, the forest is not bucolic but dangerous; moreover, it is a place whose dangers can be temporarily contained but never completely overcome. Some beasts are occasionally slain, but others seem always to survive. That is because there are essential goods and evils within the aesthetic construct, and the continuation of the construct demands the continuation of its constituent elements.

Chandler conceives of his own world in similar terms. His life was shaped by strong events and strong forces, many of which are directly reflected in his fiction. Chandler's world is one of omnipresent, interrelated corruption, a corruption that inheres in large organizations: businesses, police forces, unions, governments, and, yes, churches. Set against these often overwhelming forces is the lone individual.

It is not surprising that Chandler's vision would develop along these lines. His Los Angeles was as corrupt as his fiction suggests; there really were gambling boats in Santa Monica Bay. His personal experience was very dark. Born in Chicago of English parents, he returned to England with his mother when his father abandoned them. As a reminder of his mother's dependency she was routinely skipped when the wine bottle was passed around his grandparents' dinner table, an experience that was not lost on her son.

Chandler attended Dulwich Academy (near Greenwich), where he received a classical education, something he always cherished, since he believed (and stated) that he needed such an education to protect himself from those who already had one. Dulwich's distinguished headmaster, A. H. Gilkes, also numbered among his students P. G. Wodehouse and C. S. Forester. Gilkes believed in the dignity and capacity of the common man and instilled this belief in his students. With Chandler, the lesson obviously took.

After serving in the war Chandler eventually landed in Los Angeles, where he worked as an oil company executive. When the business failed he turned to writing. "It is not a fragrant world," he says, reflecting on the cumulative evils of society in the famous peroration of "The Simple Art of Murder," "but it is the world you live in."

It is interesting that an Englishman should be so firmly associated with so American a literary form as the hard-boiled detective novel. In their large, statistical outlines, the classic mystery novel is English, the crime novel American. The English mystery as a form is owned by women writers (one thinks of Christie, Ngaio Marsh, Mary Roberts Rinehart, Dorothy Sayers, and—in our own day— P. D. James and Ruth Rendell), while men predominate in the writing of more hard-boiled fiction. The English mystery is bigger on the East Coast, the crime novel on the West.

Having said that, we all immediately turn to counter examples. Crime fiction is extremely popular in England, the more violent the better, and it is interesting to observe the English taste for American regional fiction as well as successful attempts by English authors (most recently, for example, by Tim Willocks) to locate their best crime writing in an American setting.

Some of the most successful women writers operate in the so-called soft-boiled tradition of Ross Macdonald (Sara Paretsky, for example, or Sue Grafton), and there are ambidextrous writers such as Sandra Scoppettone who write strong crime fiction (under the pseudonym of Jack Early) as well as other forms—in her case adolescent fiction and, most recently, soft-boiled fiction with a lesbian protagonist.

While Chandler was English, his fellow contributors to *Black Mask* were largely American; thus his work stands out in a preexisting tradition whose prime practitioner (for Chandler) was Hammett. While *Black Mask*'s history seems quite local and accidental (a middlebrow market opportunity arising from the ashes of H. L. Mencken and George Jean Nathan's magazine, *Smart Set*), the fact is that the larger patterns of American fiction provided fertile soil for the growth and development of the crime novel.

Assuming the reliability of the evolutionary biology model and commonalities of DNA, every modern country, more or less, is a nation of immigrants, with large groups of citizens descended from a small handful of original mothers, but the immigrant model is particularly applicable to the United States, a country with a short history, a long literature, multiple ethnicities, and a vast and highly varied landmass. The physical and psychological frontiers and borders that mark every society are particularly striking facts of life here, not just because of the physical dimensions of the country, but because its history is so present to contemporary memory.

The frontier hypothesis of Frederick Jackson Turner conceptualizes the nation in terms of a receding frontier, one that stretches capability and defines character, where the lines between immigrants, invaders, and natives are ever more sharply drawn. Ditto the line between black and white, since we took nearly a century longer than Britain to abolish slavery. The impact of these realities on our culture, it goes without saying, is incalculable. The works of William Faulkner, for example, cannot exist without them.

The geographic and cultural lines of Mason and Dixon (Thomas Pynchon's most recent subject) and the battle lines of the Civil War are ever present within our consciousness and national life. The sheer size of our remaining wilderness areas is striking and attractive to Europeans, and the interstate highway system and availability of inexpensive gasoline yield a populace that is uncommonly mobile at ground and eye level. A series of cultural divides can be experienced in a brief period of time and a number of our cities consciously position themselves for convention market share through specific cultural definition.

New Orleans is a second home for American conventioneers and, like Las Vegas, a popular setting for crime fiction. It is no accident that Las Vegas is the fastest growing city in America. The strip is a subject for endless architectural theorizing, from the ruminations of Robert Venturi to the thoughts of the popular press. It ends and the desert begins, with dust and detritus in the foreground of billion-dollar plasticity. Its casinos putatively encompass much of human history and architecture in their artifices, blurring the divisions between night and day with their darkened glass and the divisions between hours of the day with their conscious elimination of clocks. Offering instant wealth or instant poverty (like the information technology industry), they also blur the distinctions of class even as they reassert them in a single promising, or devastating, stroke.

Las Vegas lays bare our aspirations and our drives. A city of nearly legalized prostitution, it is also the site for endless wedding chapels. Its array of Elvis impersonators blurs the line between life and death; its Liberace museum blurs the line between treasure and trash. Now that the mob has largely departed for other opportunities, it once again offers the expected contrast of putative suburban safety and imminent urban violence.

As a literary form, crime fiction explores (and thrives on) the border between good and evil, madness and sanity, war and peace, and guilt and innocence. Most recently it has fixed upon the contrast between hopelessness and redemption. It both commingles and separates the ethnic segments of our society and takes those alignments and divisions as one of its prime subjects. It takes the eternal relationships between men and women and individuals and societies and sets them in stark contrast.

It lives, aesthetically, on the border between high art and broad popular culture. In effect it takes William Wordsworth's conception of the poet as a man speaking to men to a new level while remaining equally stylized. As Chandler put it, Hammett's readers "thought they were getting a good meaty melodrama written in the kind of lingo they imagined they spoke themselves. It was, in a sense, but it was much more. All language begins with speech, and the speech of common men at that, but when it develops to the point of becoming a literary medium it only looks like speech." From the beginning this literary medium was highly advanced, so that the relation between the best work in the form and the masterpieces of American literature is often a close one.

Some have pointed to the work of James Fenimore Cooper as an early influence on one important subgenre of the form, the police procedural. The Mohicans' attention to detail and their ability to read and interpret the most minor of natural phenomena or the disturbance thereof is seen as an anticipation of the work of contemporary crime-fiction detectives. Actually, the cooperation and collaboration of red men with white in a dangerous wilderness is a far more important facet of Cooper's fiction for later writers. We will return to that subject in Chapter V.

Henry David Thoreau's *Walden* has had a greater impact on peacemakers than on students of crime, but in its outlines its influence is clear. Thoreau leaves the city to understand himself and his society, retreating to the wilderness (or at least the woods) in search of private experience that might somehow be generalized. The shores of Walden Pond are thus, as Sherman Paul long ago suggested, the shores of America, and in his refusal to pay his poll tax and in his willingness to accept that action's consequences Thoreau set himself as an individual in opposition to what he perceived to be a corrupt and immoral state structure. In the sixties it was said that there is a point at which the left and the right converge in their mutual opposition to oppressive large structures. Thoreau stands at that point of libertarian overlap, influencing Mahatma Gandhi and Martin Luther King on the one hand and, at the same time, underwriting the ethos and values of the Chandler construct on the other. With what appears to be a relatively small subject and narrow focus, Thoreau wrote one of the most comprehensive and important studies of America.

Thoreau's I/Them vision is mirrored in Herman Melville's *Moby-Dick*, a romance rather than a novel, and a study of obsession that balances on the knife edge between single-minded heroism and the madness that leads to violent death. These are the stuff and substance of horror and suspense fiction. Thoreau regrets the fact that his countrymen lead lives of quiet desperation, while Ahab pursues a life that is its equally desperate opposite.

At the same time, Melville is a student of the fine line between light and darkness, evil and innocence, life and decay. One of the favorite literary anecdotes of bibliographers is F. O. Matthiessen's overreading of a typo in *White Jacket*, in which Melville is imagined referring to a "soiled" (actually *coiled*) fish of the sea. Only Melville, who could contemplate the sepulchral white of the bleached bones in *Typee* or make his murderous and vengeful sperm whale stark white—the argument goes—could imagine a soiled fish in a great ocean. True enough, though not in that particular case.

The sea, like the wilderness, is a setting for private experience, and men went down to it together—black, white, red—in ways that conventional society would not yet permit. The struggle of such men against nature, Camille Paglia has argued, differentiates them from the 52 percent of humankind who, in their very physical makeup, embody the nature that men vainly attempt to control. Women are at peace with that against which men eternally struggle, and this is why the latter develop organized games and commit what profilers term organized murders. This is why, Paglia argues, there are so few great women composers and no great women serial killers. Whether she is correct or not, it is clear that it is a far shorter step from *Moby-Dick* to *The Silence of the Lambs* than it is from *Pride and Prejudice* or *Middlemarch*.

Nathaniel Hawthorne takes a related tack. Moving between the romance form and its shorter version, usually termed the *tale,* Hawthorne imagines a rigid society with sharp demarcations between good and evil and past and present; between European influence and American reality. Philip Rahv's celebrated essay "Paleface and Redskin" traces the lineaments of two traditions within American letters. The "paleface" is haunted by guilt, the past, and the heritage of old Europe. Hawthorne is the traditional exemplar, Robert Lowell the most recent incarnation. These writers are northeastern in orientation and carry the burdens of a past marked by religious intolerance, slavery, and the inability to detach from the old world, a fallen world that stands in stark contrast to the world of new possibility exemplified in the American dream.

The "redskin," on the other hand, looks to the West, to broad horizons that represent what Eliot would have called the objective correlative of open souls and open imaginations. The exemplar here is Walt Whitman, singing of America and its opportunities.

Crime writers have often been half-breeds here—locating their narratives in the West but identifying, exposing, and studying the serpents in the sun-soaked garden. The American dream imagines the country as a second chance for mankind, as an opportunity to throw off the sins and shackles of Europe and embrace individual possibilities as broad as the land itself. Unfortunately, it doesn't always work out that way. The characteristics of the land and the society that engender opportunity bring with them violent side effects. Chandler's summary in *The Long Goodbye* remains unsurpassed:

> "We don't have mobs and crime syndicates and goon squads because we have crooked politicians and their stooges in the City Hall and the legislatures. Crime isn't a disease, it's a symptom. Cops are like a doctor that gives you aspirin for a brain tumor, except that the cop would rather cure it with a blackjack. We're a big rough rich wild people and crime is the price we pay for it, and organized crime is the price we pay for organization. We'll have it with us a long time. Organized crime is just the dirty side of the sharp dollar."
> "What's the clean side?"
> "I never saw it. . . ."

James Ellroy refers to the Chandler tradition as that of tragic realism. The formulation is a very useful one. Chandler's vision of society as a network of finely interrelated corruption is that reverse of paranoia we call realism. The larger forces really are combined to get you. Since the novel, from its inception, depended on realistic narrative as a defining characteristic, and since Cap Shaw, as editor of *Black Mask,* demanded plausibility from his writers, crime readers have seen a number of forms of realism result.

There is the *realism of assessment* in Chandler's vision, the belief that he, finally, is right. This truly *is* the way things are. There is also the *stylistic realism* that he worked so hard to achieve. This is, finally, the way people of a certain sort talk. There is the *realism of detail,* which combines with those dimensions of the novel that associate it—in its very name—with that which is new, the subject of the newswriter's efforts. Thus, crime novelists often take on contemporary subjects and explain them while they are depicting them: the day-to-day details of the life of a crack dealer (Richard Price's *Clockers*), the plight of illegal aliens who live in mortgaged servitude (Robert B. Parker's *Walking Shadow*), the levels of social organization within a maximum-security prison (Mitchell Smith's *Stone City*), contemporary genomics, robotics, and nanotechnology and their criminal possibilities (Steve Martini's *The Jury*), the cultural ethos of Los Angeles gangs (Robert Crais's *Stalking the Angel*), and so on.

Thus, writers employ research assistants to help them get things right, since their readership is unforgiving with regard to accuracy and detail. They also struggle to be the first to identify subjects of emerging interest, subjects that then create mini-genres ("women in distress" books, for example).

There is the realism that might be associated with *simple honesty.* In all human life there are elements of experience whose importance is in direct proportion to their sensitivity and in inverse proportion to the exposure they receive in more mainstream art. Crime fiction often seizes on these "sensitive" issues (sexuality, violence, madness, obsession) and explores them with (honest) relish. When such issues are faced directly, the crime narrative approaches gothicism, as in the writings of David Martin or Joe R. Lansdale. When they are handled indirectly, as in Chandler, for example, the crime narrative approaches the novel of manners, where we assess the level of sexuality by observing the positions of fingers around a teacup or the color of a dress worn at a certain time of the day.

Finally, there is the *realism of subject.* For Gustave Flaubert, to turn to the art novel for a moment, realism consists in part in stressing the ordinary aspects of experience and life's more ordinary participants. The novel, unlike the romance, for example, chose to take common individuals as its protagonists and demonstrated the fact that their lives were no less compelling than those of members of the so-called nobility. This is because the novel (unlike the drama, where honesty generally comes only through such stilted devices as asides and soliloquies) could enter the minds of its characters at will and reveal whatever was to be found there.

Hence the novel's "invisible man" character; it allowed readers to pass among other people of both sexes unseen (in any and all situations) but it also—through its narrative devices—played to the primal human fantasy of finally understanding what others were actually thinking. It is no coincidence that the novel arose at the confluence of a series of cultural events all of which focused on the realization that the interior life of any human being could be of immense interest: the rise of the revelatory essay tradition of Montaigne, the mind/body dualism of René Descartes, the Protestant focus on individual scriptural interpretation as opposed to the more authoritarian "tradition" of Catholicism, the shift to private, affective relationships as the basis for marriage from the clan-centered desire to acquire new land in a pre-industrial-capitalist society, the rise of an epistemology of skepticism that privileged the individual perspective, and the erosion of the power of the church and nobility in societies of emerging democracy. The watershed here is the seventeenth century, the ethos from which the novel directly arose.

The central subject matter of the novel—the characters themselves and the choices they make—is of particular interest for the writer of crime fiction, who focuses on those individuals often overlooked by writers of mainstream narrative. The historical dimensions of this issue are interesting.

When Wordsworth thought of poetry as an act involving a man speaking to men he was consciously distancing himself from some of the central aspects of Romanticism. In its attempt to focus on unique, private experience, Romanticism was offering an aesthetic sea change, consciously separating itself from one of the central tenets of the eighteenth century, the notion that we should seek the universal in the concrete example.

The truly *unique*—for the eighteenth century—would be of little interest since it could not be generalized and thus applied to the lives of all readers. Hence Samuel Johnson's finding no interest in the biographical fact of Joseph Addison's irregular pulse. To make this subject of interest one would have to talk about the commonness of irregularities and their implications for human experience. The Romantics, on the other hand, often take greater interest in that which cannot be generalized. At its heights, poetry with such a focus can be magnificent, but it runs the constant risk of obfuscation, opaqueness, and degeneration into abstraction and private vocabularies. In short, it becomes academic, the language of private, small coteries, whose desire is to narrow rather than expand the privileged circle of responsive readers. In a sense it is also aristocratic, for though the aristocracy to which it aspires to belong is that of the mind, it recalls the practice of Renaissance noblemen who circulated their poetry in manuscript among their friends and eschewed publication as a practice wanting in dignity.

The eighteenth century had contributed two great forms—the novel and the periodical essay—to the English tradition, and both were decidedly middle class. Coterie Romanticism was thus a reaction against the rapid expansion of the reading public in the Renaissance and Enlightenment, a harkening back to the reactionary views of the Tory satirists, Jonathan Swift and Alexander Pope, with their fears of mass culture, and an anticipation of some of the academic poetry of postwar America. T. E. Hulme and others had expected Romanticism to run its full course by the early twentieth century, but the expansion of universities—and their willingness to provide havens for *academic* poets (writing, in a reversal of Wordsworth, for other academic poets)—expanded Romanticism's reach until the movement reached its end point in extreme poststructuralist theory, which, in many of its manifestations, reached the apogee of necessarily elitist, impenetrable writing.

A number of strains in late-eighteenth- and early-nineteenth-century verse either anticipated or allied themselves with Wordsworth and his focus on uncommon communication in common language for common men. Oliver Goldsmith and Thomas Gray are important figures here, and George Crabbe is a particularly important one. Each writes about rural, common individuals and consciously differentiates them from their nobler, richer, and generally more urban counterparts (concentrating, very often, on their nobility of character rather than of class). They write, in short, about what we in America would now term blue-collar figures.

It is the novel, however, that forms the principal bridge between the Renaissance, the Enlightenment, and the contemporary period, maintaining and expanding its contacts with a wide reading public both as consumers and as possible subjects. The novel of the nineteenth century does not succumb to the blandishments of Romanticism, and neither does that of the twentieth or twenty-first. (Poetry, cut off from its broad public, nearly dies, and its impulses displace into rock, pop, rap, and country music lyrics.)

The popular entertainments of our time, in fact, directly reflect the plot-driven art that Aristotle would instantly recognize and replicate the Aristotelian structure across cultural levels. Pynchon's *Vineland*, for example, is shaped very much like an episode of *Frasier*. Contemporary popular writers step right in—oblivious to the impulses of Romanticism and academic art and theory—and connect directly with the values of pre-Kantian literary theory and the practices of both highbrow and popular literary art from antiquity through the eighteenth century. They seek to instruct and please (as Horace recommended), and they seek ever new opportunities to impart eternal verities in new ways (as Johnson advised).

Crime fiction functions in an interesting way in this setting, for it takes as its subject the actions of criminals, those who in more traditional art forms would appear more often as subjects of humor or targets of satire than as protagonists or principal antagonists. The crime novelist takes these characters at the cultural border and moves them to the center of the narrative. Thus, we get blue-collar grifters named Cody or Roy and dangerous waitresses named Fay. We get the red-necked figures of Stephen Hunter and Joe R. Lansdale, the Boston lowlifes of Dennis Lehane, the Hell's Kitchen barflies of Lawrence Block, the dark predators of Andrew Vachss, and the Damon Runyonesque villains of Elmore Leonard.

Crabbe wrote brief poetic sketches of the populace of the local village, and Gray penned their elegy. Writers of English mysteries turn these characters into sentimental types, while crime fiction writers eschew sentiment for realism. Roger Wade, the historical novelist whose story occupies the second act of *The Long Goodbye*, notes that he would lose his audience if he depicted his characters realistically.

In real life, he says, these people didn't bathe and they had stale gravy beneath their fingernails. The English mystery writer situates them at the tea table, while the crime writer opts for the stale gravy, along with some grit and a little blood.

But where is the tragedy in Ellroy's tragic realism? The tragedy occurs with the discovery of the serpent in the garden—the realization that America is not so much a second chance for mankind as an ongoing reprise of *Paradise Lost*. The tragedy comes with the full realization that in leaving Europe we have brought our past with us. When Satan offers his soliloquy on Mount Niphates in book IV of *Paradise Lost* he realizes that he has not really escaped hell and replaced it with paradise. He can never escape hell, because he carries hell with him. "Which way I fly is Hell; myself am Hell," he says.

While John Milton may offer the hope of a "paradise within" to Adam and Eve, a psychological paradise that will follow their loss of a physical, localized paradise, the writers of American crime fiction are far less optimistic. The most they will offer—in the spirit of the romance—is a temporary victory over evil. At other points they will offer tragedy. The American novel that makes this point most clearly, one that should be directly associated with the crime fiction tradition but seldom is, is *The Great Gatsby*.

F. Scott Fitzgerald himself said that "the whole idea of Gatsby is the unfairness of a poor young man not being able to marry a girl with money. This theme comes up again and again because I lived it." This is a very curious statement, since it is clear that in America a young man without money can most certainly marry a woman of wealth. This has, in fact, long been an established part of American history as well as an important part of American mythography. The point is made again and again by the most popular nineteenth-century American writer, Horatio Alger, and it was even possible in old England. William Hogarth, for example, married *his* master's daughter and portrayed the archetypal pattern in his Industry and Idleness series (1747) in which Mr. Goodchild, a dutiful Christian and industrious apprentice, marries his master's daughter, becomes rich, and then, successively, sheriff, alderman, and lord mayor of the City of London.

The Great Gatsby is not about poor men and rich women; it is not even about wealth per se. Gatsby's quest for Daisy is only the proximate occasion for his and Nick's discoveries. "Show me a hero and

I'll write you a tragedy," Fitzgerald once said. The tragedy of Gatsby runs far deeper than his inability to win Daisy Fay. The tragedy of Gatsby is the tragedy of discovery, and the quest is not for Daisy. The quest is for America.

The green light at the end of Daisy's dock, the green light of hope on which Gatsby fixates, is the color of Vineland, an earlier name for America, as Thomas Pynchon has recently reminded us. It is a land of vines and tendrils as well as milk and honey. They lure us like their metallic, false counterparts in Spenser's Bower of Bliss, in that passage of *The Faerie Queene* which overwhelmed Milton and led him to characterize its author as a greater moral teacher than Scotus or Aquinas. Their putative temptation is sexual, their real purpose the destruction of one's humanity. They recall Kurt Weill's description of Hollywood as the City of Nets—nets that lure and capture and, finally, enslave us.

Gatsby ends with Nick's reflection on the history of Long Island:

> the old island here that flowered once for Dutch sailors' eyes—a fresh, green breast of the new world. Its vanished trees, the trees that had made way for Gatsby's house, had once pandered in whispers to the last and greatest of all human dreams: for a transitory enchanted moment man must have held his breath in the presence of this continent, compelled into an aesthetic contemplation he neither understood nor desired, face to face for the last time in history with something commensurate to his capacity for wonder.

Gatsby believed in the green light, Nick tells us, a belief Nick considers ennobling, even as he realizes that the belief was lethal— lethal for Gatsby, lethal for George Wilson, and lethal for Myrtle, whose body is torn apart by what Michaelis at first considers a light green death car driven by Daisy, leaving her left breast—we are told—swinging loose like a flap.

It is not, however, beauty that kills Jimmy Gatz, the midwestern boy who came to call himself Jay Gatsby. Nor is it a misguided sense of chivalry, the bestowal of love on the undeserving Daisy. Gatsby is dead long before Daisy strikes Myrtle and he takes the fall for it, the purest anticipation of film noir one might desire. Gatsby dies at the Plaza, a signature American setting—the one piece of his empire that Donald Trump will not, apparently, surrender. He dies when Daisy chooses Tom's money over his.

Gatsby's money (like Joe Kennedy's) comes from liquor, but, despite the size of his fortune, his money lacks what should never matter in America—*age*. And thus Daisy chooses Tom. He is also, of course, the father of her child, but that is really not a matter of any consequence. He was noticeably absent at the time of her birth, and when the child does appear, she is a doll-like, pasteboard figure whom Daisy addresses in syrupy baby talk before exiling her, with her nurse, so that Daisy and her guests can get on with the far more serious business of cooling themselves down with a tray of gin rickeys.

Tom Buchanan, Daisy's choice, is a racist adulterer who batters his mistress and humiliates her husband; a perpetual adolescent who believes women exist for the purchasing, whether the tender be pearls and polo ponies or puppies purchased from street vendors. After his honeymoon in the south seas, Jordan Baker sees Tom in Santa Barbara, his head in Daisy's lap as she rubs her fingers over his eyes. Daisy is, by then, carrying Tom's child. A week after Jordan leaves, Tom—driving south toward Ventura—runs into a wagon and rips a wheel from his car. His passenger, a chambermaid from a Santa Barbara hotel, suffers a broken arm. There are no reports on the driver (or hauler) of the wagon.

It is true that (so far as we know) Tom's money has not been acquired through criminal behavior, assuming that selling liquor during prohibition (but not before or after) makes one a criminal. There is more than a little bit of casuistry here; one could, for example, make and sell altar wine during prohibition, but not table wine. And what is it that makes a criminal? Are not robber barons still robbers, even though they do not suffer the penalties imposed on common thieves? And what of Tom? From the evidence in the novel he could be indicted for (at least) assault, battery, reckless endangerment, conspiracy, obstruction of justice, and, probably, driving under the influence. We are not told what it was that forced him to leave Chicago, but it must have been serious. Tom Buchanan is the purest form of Chandlerian antagonist, a criminal who is somehow above the law.

Daisy chooses this bit of scum with old money over Jay Gatsby and leaves Nick to sort through the emotional detritus left in her wake. After Myrtle's death, Nick sees Tom and Daisy at their kitchen table, conspiring over a plate of cold fried chicken and two bottles of ale—picnic food. "They were careless people," Nick says. "They smashed up things and creatures and then retreated back into their money or their vast carelessness, or whatever it was that kept them together, and let other people clean up the mess they had made." Owl-eyes is left to pronounce Gatsby's epitaph: "the poor son-of-a-bitch."

In leaving Europe, whether because of religious persecution or economic deprivation, Americans hoped to find not just a new land but a new Eden. A succession of public events, including the Lindbergh kidnapping (purportedly by a German) and the Sacco and Vanzetti trial, reconfirmed, in the public mind, the still-looming presence of Europe—aged, fallen, evil, and dangerous.

Crossing the Queensboro Bridge, entering Manhattan (a place where he sees Elysian Fields and John D. Rockefeller look-alikes), Nick observes a hearse followed by two carriages with drawn blinds and a set of carriages for friends. "The friends looked out at us with the tragic eyes and short upper lips of southeastern Europe." Manhattan is the future, Europe the past. Manhattan is life, Europe is death. Manhattan is, for Americans, a place for hopes and dreams and parties. Europeans leave it, crossing the threshold symbol of a bridge, on their way to a funeral.

But of course this is not true. As vivid as the imagery and mythography might be in the imaginations of American dreamers like Nick and Jimmy Gatz, the realities are quite different. We have *not* escaped the past; we have not peopled a new Garden of Eden. We have instead created new aristocracies and new systems with barriers of race and class. One embodiment of that fallen world is Tom Buchanan, a man who reads racist books and fears the overrunning of the "Nordics," as he terms them, by the "colored empires." Racial purity is apparently the only variety of purity in which he seems to be interested.

So what is it that Gatsby finds in the Plaza when Daisy rejects him for Tom? What is it that Nick finds when he sees his cousin betraying his friend and conspiring with her faithless husband? The serpent in the garden? Yes, and the serpent in the human heart as well. He finds more than that, however. He finds that wealth, particularly old wealth, is still a great insulator and that, at bottom, our society is as class-ridden as that from which he thought we had escaped. He should, of course, have known it all along. The Carraway family line—we are told on the second page of the novel—was founded by

Nick's grandfather's brother, who came to America in 1851 and sent a substitute in his place to fight the Civil War, so that he could start the wholesale hardware business that Nick's father carries on today.

Nick, like Gatsby, polarizes the country into East and West (or better, East and Midwest, since Gatsby terms San Francisco part of the Midwest). The East—always so much closer to Europe, always so much more ethnically diverse (at least in the cultural imagination)—is the site of evil, the locus for what we continue to term the eastern establishment, a body that relies on pedigree and connections rather than honesty and hard work, still the seat of American private education and still the nation's financial center.

But East and West or the East and Midwest are symbols; it is the money that is real. Iry Paret, the narrator of James Lee Burke's novel *The Lost Get-Back Boogie*, says that a "human being's life is not shaped so much by what he is or what he pretends to be or even by the compulsions that he tries to root out and burn away; instead it can be just a matter of a wrong turn in an angry moment and disregard for its consequences."

Such moments, as Iry Paret learns, are far more serious for the poor than for the rich and, as Jimmy Gatz learns, far more serious for the newly rich than for those with old money. Essentially there are those for whom the laws do not much matter and those who can be crushed by the slightest error or mistake. There are those who contribute to an economy and those who bleed it dry, those who pay taxes and those who have accountants who see to it that they need not do so, those who go to war and those who (like Nick's grandfather's brother) send others to fight wars for them, those who commit a single act in a desperate moment and pay for it forever and those who lie to Congress, send tens of thousands to their deaths in war, and themselves batten on foundation presidencies, college professorships, and $10,000 speaking engagements.

Here is the fracture at the heart of the democracy—the existence of a persistent aristocracy. As with all such aristocracies, it is a society based on money and bluff. The working and middle classes, as Jürgen Habermas argues, labor and produce. The aristocracy simply *is*. Its function is to *act like* the aristocracy. That it persists in America—despite the best efforts of the novelist, the writer of that most middle class of forms, to expose it—testifies to its tenacity and durability. Still worse is the wannabe aristocracy, that collection of individuals who aspire to be above the many and above the law. Mark Twain once commented that America has no native criminal class except Congress—a cheap shot to some extent, but not one with a nonexistent target. Until very recently, the nation's lawmakers did, after all, consciously and openly exempt themselves from the regulatory requirements they imposed on others, a textbook instance of the attitude.

"It is not a fragrant world," Chandler says, "but it is the world you live in." The tragedy lies in the fact that it is not inevitably so. There are always glimmers of hope and bona fide instances of the persistence of the dream and its possibilities.

If *The Great Gatsby* (like all of the works by our greatest living novelist, Thomas Pynchon) is, at bottom, a search for America, there have been earlier examples to which we might attend. Meriwether Lewis was sent by Thomas Jefferson to literally search for America, a country whose size had suddenly doubled but whose plains and mountains and rivers and harbors and peoples were largely uncharted and often unknown or misunderstood.

When the members of the Corps of Discovery reached the Pacific they faced a choice. Where should they winter? Where would they find food? Where were they most likely to survive? The captains, who had maintained strict military discipline throughout the expedition, took the profound and unprecedented step of putting the question to a vote, a vote in which both York, Clark's slave, and Sacagawea fully participated. This was, as Stephen Ambrose notes, the first vote held in the Pacific Northwest. It was the first time in all of American history that a black slave had been asked to vote and the first time that a woman had been asked to vote, in this case one with a considerable prior claim to her American-ness.

So it can happen. America can be found. And when so noble a dream is broken, indeed broken with some regularity, the crime novelist enters to realistically trace the outlines of the tragedy.

Eternal Vigilance

There are few more prominent figures in American popular film and crime writing than the vigilante. In some respects this is traceable to the violence and wildness of the society, characteristics to which Chandler refers and which he associates with sharp business practices. With shifting borders as late as the nineteenth century, large wilderness areas (both urban and rural), and an expansive and complex federal and local bureaucracy, jurisdictions shift, overlap, and are contested. The vigilante functions in ways that are cognate with the activities of the entrepreneur, entering areas with unmet needs as well as areas of hyperactivity where confusion, white noise, and entropy in effect create open opportunities. Vigilantes thrive, in short, in areas without judges and in areas with judges with overburdened dockets, some overburdened by laws and politics, some by the limitations of time and resources, most by both. In each case justice delayed creates opportunities for those who do not wish to see justice denied, and while few support the actual practice of vigilantism most seek swift, sure, and authentic justice. Hence our sense of ambiguity with regard to the vigilante's role.

A figure who operates outside the law in the interest of justice is also a close kin to all of those individuals who seek freedom from social and cultural constraints. The crime writer Robert Ferrigno speaks of having "lived without paper" for a time, that is, living without social security cards, insurance forms, and W-2s. As the only major country that does not require its citizens to carry identification cards (the social security card is, explicitly, not to be used for identification purposes), the United States has developed a culture in which the notion of seeking new identities and throwing off old ones is a signature element, one that permeates our folklore and fiction.

This juncture of the life of the individual with a morning-in-America vision is often associated with western migration (both individual and collective), the West being the place to which one traditionally goes when one wishes to escape the past and its representatives. Thus, we often think of vigilantes as culturally inhabiting the West (the word *vigilante* itself being borrowed from the Spanish and associated with the earlier property of the King of Spain), though they can appear in places as distant as New York subways. Paul Kersey, Charles Bronson's repeating character in the *Death Wish* series, for example, is a New York architect, and the initial film's tagline is "Vigilante, City Style."

The vigilante is different from his cultural cousins living beyond the system, because in his world the system of justice upon which society depends has become inoperable and requires his services in order to reassert its claims. He is not simply beyond the establishment's reach; he has set himself the task of reestablishing justice underneath the very noses of the constituents of the establishment. This figure repeats throughout our popular culture and has been noticeably visible of late, an indication of the contemporary American concern with regard to the effectiveness of the justice system. Judges are lax, public defenders overextended, police corrupt, juries incompetent. This was Chandler's observation, an observation that often squares with public perception. At the same time that we thirst for (sometimes extreme) alternatives, we realize the perils that we risk. Thus, our responses to the vigilante's brand of justice are heavily nuanced and at times explicitly ambivalent.

Two of the great vigilantes of our culture have been adopted from earlier texts and earlier times: Robin Hood and Zorro. Each has appeared and reappeared on countless occasions, including recent ones. Leslie Fiedler's notion that the most lasting of literary characters are those whose stories can be told in totally different forms (children's books, cartoons, television series, serious narratives) certainly applies to these individuals, as it applies, for example, to Don Quixote, Robinson Crusoe, Lemuel Gulliver, Dracula, and the Frankenstein monster.

In each case the vigilante enterprise is notably muted and qualified. Robin Hood, for example, is far more "merry" than obsessive, and his operations often verge on pranks. He plays a temporary role to which he is not finally wedded, for when King Richard returns, Robin falls back into the role of vassal to his lord in an instant. It is

interesting that the more "serious" incarnation of Robin, the Kevin
Costner vehicle (*Robin Hood: Prince of Thieves*, directed by Kevin Reynolds, 1991), features an oddly comic performance by Alan Rickman
as the sheriff of Nottingham, as if the narrative tradition's demands
are too strong for this version to contain. The Michael Curtiz version
(1938) remains definitive, not just because of the performance of Errol Flynn, but because of the unctuously nasty Claude Raines and
Basil Rathbone in the roles of the usurper and his functionary. Robin
can be merry, but he requires serious antagonists or we are plunged
quickly into parody (as Mel Brooks realized, with his *Robin Hood:
Men in Tights*, 1993).

Rathbone reappears in the definitive *Mark of Zorro* (directed by
Rouben Mamoulian, 1940) opposite Tyrone Power, who plays the
role with a merriness that sometimes verges on androgyny. The Antonio Banderas incarnation, as the student of the actual, aging Zorro (*The Mask of Zorro*, directed by Martin Campbell, 1998), combines
seriousness with clownishness and ends with a thoroughly domesticated figure with paternal and husbandly duties. Zorro can always
come out of retirement, presumably, but the point is that vigilantism
is a temporary activity, not a lifelong vocation. In both the Robin
Hood and the Zorro stories the rule of law under official auspices is
to be preferred.

In that regard, the stories are more comic than romantic, despite
the chivalry and swordplay in each. Each assumes a stable society
that has been taken over by an unjust individual. The treasure at the
end of the narrative arc is the replacement of the unjust ruler with a
just one and, coincidentally, the marriage of the protagonist with the
woman he has courted in the story's subplot.

The case is altered with Batman, an individual whose vocation in
pursuit of justice arises directly from an act of violence that orphans
him and haunts his memory. Functioning as a kind of ally of the
Gotham City government, Batman stands ready to help on all occasions, and the ongoing need for his services suggests that the conventional forces of justice are inadequate in the face of more serious
challenges. Thus, Batman enters, as needed, to reinforce the system.
His function is comparable to that of the Lone Ranger (another survivor of a massacre), who cooperates with the local officials and also
leaves when his work is done. Coincidentally, the Lone Ranger also
has significant financial resources on which to draw (in his case a sil-

ver mine) so that his moral, spiritual, and physical efforts are underwritten, like Batman's, by hard dollars.

Each of these figures functions in a role that I will later describe as that of the avenging angel and all—with their identities blurred and their faces, in some cases, masked—are often accused of being part of the criminal class. This speaks to the ambiguity of their position, both within their societies and in our own conception of the vigilante in ours.

One of the classic articulations of our ambivalence with regard to the issue of justice and vigilantism is the John Ford film *The Man Who Shot Liberty Valance* (1962). It is also a prime example of the manner in which the issue is conceptualized in terms of frontiers and borders. The territorial town of Shinbone is terrorized by an outlaw and his gang. Shinbone's sheriff, Link Appleyard, is more interested in his diet than in the lawlessness besetting his jurisdiction. The editor of the *Shinbone Star*, Dutton Peabody, takes the proper stands—when both in and out of his cups—but he is helpless in the face of violence. Into this mess comes an eastern-trained lawyer, Ransom Stoddard, who takes it upon himself to civilize Shinbone. That entails a gunfight with Valance, which Stoddard unexpectedly wins. He is elected to represent the territory in its efforts to attain statehood and eventually becomes a congressman in Washington. Shinbone becomes, in short, an official part of America; the law and the press win out over violence; the East, in effect, is brought to the West, and the days of Valance and his gang fade into the past.

The problem is that the inevitability of civilization is bittersweet. Stoddard did not shoot Valance; Valance was shot by another man, Tom Doniphon, who was standing in the shadows on the opposite side of the street, protecting Stoddard, who was unaware of his presence. Doniphon is a man of the West, and the rule of law could not have come without his courage and skill. Hence, the passing of the West underlines the tradeoffs of civilization and the realization of the beauty and strength of the wilderness that existed side by side with its lawlessness. The iconic casting of the film reinforces its themes, with Stoddard played by James Stewart and Doniphon by John Wayne. This is all further reinforced by the plot, which brings Stoddard back to Shinbone for Doniphon's funeral. Doniphon has become an anachronism and Stoddard something of a prig, with arrogance around the edges and a career made possible by a funda-

mental act of duplicity. He also gets the girl, now reduced to a dig-
nified fixture on a political arm, who remembers Doniphon as a man
who also loved her and who burned down his house (which he had
prepared for her as his potential bride) when he saw that she would
choose Stoddard.

The America found at the end of the film is duller but safer. The
law is a leveler, sweeping away heroes as well as villains. The government in Washington offers stability but exacts its tribute in the
form of faded dreams as well as tax dollars. Hence the conclusion of
the film is muted rather than celebratory, and we mourn the passing
of the West with the passing of Tom Doniphon. We sacrifice our
dreams on the altar of civilization. A few years later those dreams
would return, in darker form, with the films of Sergio Leone.

Clint Eastwood is a signature figure in our culture's collective ruminations on the role of the vigilante, for the man-with-no-name
films in which he was featured were succeeded by Don Siegel's *Dirty
Harry* (1971). In the Leone westerns the law is virtually nonexistent
and justice comes with a heavy and bloody price tag. In the seventies
and eighties, with Harry Callahan, we are in contemporary America
and the Eastwood figure operates within the law, but just barely.

The most interesting Dirty Harry film with regard to the vigilante
theme is *Magnum Force* (directed by Ted Post, 1973), in which a series of very bad men are being dispatched by some unknown figure.
Actually, there are three vigilante figures, all policemen, who are being directed by a police lieutenant, played by the usually avuncular
Hal Holbrook. They have given up on the law and its standard procedures and have opted instead to dispense their own form of justice. Harry is invited to join forces with them and chooses instead to
take them down, thus making the point that no matter how un-
orthodox or edgy his methods, Harry Callahan always remembers
the side on which he is ultimately operating.

The films make clear that justice is always in short supply and that
standard methods generally fall short; hence the related and contin-
uing crime-fiction topos of the private detective who was once a police officer but refused to continue playing the game by the system's
rules. The theme of *Magnum Force* concerns self-awareness and the
proper sense of boundaries. "A man's got to know his limitations,"
Harry says, as he wraps the case in a fiery explosion, but those limitations also concern the line in the sand that separates the legal from

the ultimately illegal. Harry knows those limits, even as he operates at their border, and our love of his success and sometimes grudging recognition of the importance of his methods demonstrates our own ambivalence with regard to vigilantism and the law.

All of these films and stories emerge from the tradition of chivalric romance, with heroes—sometimes smudged heroes—operating in the wilderness on behalf of the otherwise unprotected. In contemporary crime fiction one writer stands at the forefront of this tradition.

Andrew Vachss is a New York attorney who specializes in the abuse of children. He lists a colorful range of pre-lawyer activities on his dust-jacket résumé: probation officer, fruit picker, furniture mover, cab driver, credit collection agent, gambler, advertising copywriter, and photographer. His wife, Alice S. Vachss, is also an attorney. She spent ten years in law enforcement, working as a prosecutor and as chief of the Special Victims Bureau in the Queens district attorney's office, where her specialties included rape, incest, and child sexual abuse. Her experiences are summarized in her controversial book, *Sex Crimes: Ten Years on the Front Lines Prosecuting Rapists and Confronting Their Collaborators* (1993).

In the face of the horrors they confront daily, Vachss and his wife have decided to remain childless. As an outgrowth of his legal work (he systematically declines to represent defendants in abuse cases, despite his expertise in this area), he launched a writing career in 1985 with his debut novel, *Flood*. His novels are extensions of his legal work in that they generally focus on abuse and other sexual enormities affecting the helpless.

What is particularly interesting in Vachss's case is the range of genres in which he operates. In addition to nonfiction books, including books written for young readers, he has done collections of short stories, graphic (that is, "comic") stories, and dramatic works, at least one of which has played in London's West End. The subject is always the same: predators and prey and the manner in which the justice system fails the latter.

In place of that system—in his novels—Vachss offers a series character who is among the most haunting in contemporary crime fiction. His name is Burke; we do not know his first name, and neither does he. We know that his early life involved the child "protective" service system (his earliest identification was, simply, Baby

Burke), and that this system has left its scars. We know that he has spent time in prison. We know that his life has been changed forever by his contact with a person of consummate evil whose name was Wesley. We know that he lives on the lower east side of Manhattan. We know that he drives a sleeper Plymouth that looks like a junker but is equipped for heavy and fast duty. If Batman lived on the lower east side, this is what he would drive.

Burke has a dog named Pansy, a fearsome Neapolitan mastiff, whose toilet is the roof of Burke's building. Pansy is trained to respond to contradictory commands so that no one can poison her or employ her in the attack. (She is killed off in Vachss's most recent novel, *Dead and Gone*, her choke chain serving as the novel's cover art. Advance notices concerning the novel revealed that Burke's "partner" would die in this book—an apt description of Pansy.) Burke lives without paper. He pays no rent. His utilities are all paid by others, often unintentionally. There is no official record of his existence; he works through a set of aliases and pays no taxes.

Burke earns his living through two principal occupations. The first consists of the cheating of predators and fools, to whom he sends off-the-shelf materials on weapons, soldier-of-fortune careers, and so on, for highly inflated prices. His second activity is to serve as an unlicensed investigator in the kinds of cases for which no one else is likely to have the stomach or the skill. Many of these cases involve predators, to whom he dispenses justice, or victims for whom he creates the conditions in which justice can be dispensed. In these activities he is as ruthless as he is accomplished.

His family consists of a crew that began to form when he was in prison. First among them is a black man known as the Prof (for prophet, not professor), a watcher who knows the streets and always speaks in rhyme. Second is a Jew known as the Mole, an electronics and explosives expert who lives in an underground home in a junkyard, protected by a pack of attack dogs. Burke's love interest is a transvestite hooker named Michelle who is saving money for sexual reassignment surgery; Michelle and the Mole mutually care for a young boy who is a survivor of events in the "normal" world. Burke's principal partner is a Mongolian deaf-mute named Max the Silent, a martial arts expert who is related to a woman named Mama Wong, who operates a Chinese restaurant that is a front for other operations and serves as a home base, mail drop, and answering service for Burke.

This ensemble cast repeats throughout the Burke series. As over-the-top as they sound when described straightforwardly, the individual members of Burke's crew are sufficiently well developed in the narratives to attain plausibility and compel interest. Once we become familiar with them we begin to see their alternative world as one that, in its strange ways, offers the love, fidelity, and support that the "normal" world somehow denies. It is a world of guardian angels with very dirty faces and, often, very bloody hands. With the occasional exception of a sympathetic lawyer, they are the victims' only recourse.

Burke's universe is divided into three groups: his family/crew, the world of the "citizens," and the world of the "freaks." His family sees life as it is; citizens walk in a dream state, unaware of the evil with which they are surrounded; and the freaks live in a world of sexual fantasy and desire that is slaked by preying on the citizens' innocence. Burke's role is to prevent the freaks from doing so or to terminate their activities once they have begun.

It is a stark vision and a stark world, and it is not one that supports the aspirations of the tourist bureau of Manhattan. In that connection, the greatest threat to Vachss's urban setting may be Rudolph Giuliani, for Vachss has chronicled endlessly the sinks and pits and fleshpots of the city to the point that its perceived threats serve as direct projections of the freaks' desires. As the jungle increasingly becomes a garden or, at least, comfortable urban space, Vachss will find himself in the position of the espionage writers who must ply their trade in a post–evil empire world.

Several interesting aspects of Vachss's work should be noted. The first is its political dimension. Vachss is very open with regard to his purposes. His novels and stories and plays are propagandistic in their purpose, though—he believes—true at their core. He writes to influence, to persuade, and to change, and he does so relentlessly. While this is often countenanced on the left and institutionalized within much politicized academic criticism, Vachss offers the solutions of the right to the victims in his novels. He has little or no faith in government programs or versions of sensitivity training. Freaks exploit the helpless for their pleasure. They do so consciously, and they enjoy what they do. Hence the only real solution available to us is to stop them.

This leads Vachss to taking stands that seem to some to be extreme, though for him they are anchored in personal experience. He has said, for example, that many abusers were themselves abused and that the cycle of abuse is so difficult to break that it would sometimes have been better—for society—if the original abuse had resulted in death rather than psychic wounds that continue forever and echo, in their results, down through the generations.

Perhaps most interesting, Vachss articulates his views in such balanced and mainstream forums as *The Oprah Winfrey Show,* where he is a frequent guest and where he is taken quite seriously and viewed quite sympathetically. This is so for a number of reasons. First, he is knowledgeable. Second, he is skilled. Third, he walks the walk in his own life and behavior. Finally, he is a serious man whose actions do not appear to be motivated by self-interest, a man who is, finally, a bona fide crusader.

He is also a man who inhabits a world of nightmare even as he is creating such a world in his fictional narratives. In 1996 Vachss took his crusade a step further, a step that was a cultural long jump, when he published *Batman—The Ultimate Evil.* Vachss was not the first to take this major cultural icon in a new direction. Frank Miller's graphic novel *Batman: The Dark Knight Returns,* now in a tenth-anniversary edition (1997), introduces a Bruce Wayne who has come out of a ten-year retirement to face a world in violent decay, the world that Tim Burton attempted to capture cinematically in his gothic imagining of Gotham City.

Bruce carries the weight of years and is physically battered in the course of Miller's narrative. The new Robin is a young girl, who uses such expressions as "It doesn't suck" when describing her role and feats. Miller's graphics are stunning; if a poll were taken on the greatest graphic novel ever produced, this would be a likely candidate for first place. Essentially, Miller's heavily stylized conception is also extremely realistic. We hear the creaking joints and the heavier breathing. The most interesting touch is a showdown battle between Batman and Superman, the latter now little more than a government flunky, a characterization that makes Batman appear to be much more of an outsider than the person who used to be called a strange visitor from another planet.

The book is a meditation on death and aging and cultural decay. As such, it is a significant departure from the traditional imagery surrounding Batman and the polar opposite of the silly Adam West television series with its self-conscious comic slapstick. While Miller's book is compelling on aesthetic grounds, it is equally interesting in terms of cultural history, particularly if we think of the manner in which cultural mainstays are consciously protected (consider, for example, the guidelines one must follow—absolutely—if one attempts to write a Star Trek novel).

Batman, after all, goes back a long way in the memories of our society. He was even pressed into service in the interest of wartime propaganda with the 1943 serial *The Batman* (directed by Lambert Hillyer), which was reissued in 1966, principally for its value as camp. The serial featured what later reviewers called "veteran overactor" J. Carrol Naish as a Japanese agent (Dr. Tito Daka), whose headquarters are in an American amusement park (whole new vistas for cultural-studies monographs appear on the skyline). Dr. Daka has developed a device that turns men into zombies (more vistas open), and the dissolution of his operation requires the skills and energies of no less than Batman. Cheesy in the extreme, with such weird touches as gangster cars with devices for repainting themselves, so that chases are foiled, the serial still illustrates the enduring power of the Batman image and the fact that it is close to our cultural heart.

Vachss's take on Batman is as interesting a departure as Miller's, for Batman is adopted as a complete representative of Vachss's vision and a central player in his project. In the course of the novel we learn the real facts behind the murder of Bruce Wayne's parents. It was not an act of random violence, a petty robbery that turned lethal. The real truth is that Bruce's mother, Martha, had paved the way for his own career. Masquerading as a quiet housewife, Martha Wayne was actually investigating (and closing in on) a network within the world of child pornography and abuse. Hence her murder. Moreover, we learn that the principal subject of her investigation has a relative who is still alive, operating a child prostitution/enslavement ring in Asia. In the course of the story Bruce goes to the country in Asia, "Udon Khai," introduces those operating the ring to the values and methods of the Batman, and cleans house. He thus shows that he is indeed his mother's son and, in effect, takes his anticrime operation international. This fits precisely with his vigilante role, since the country of Udon Khai flourishes as a sex/tourism venue because of its permissive legal system. It is, in effect, beyond civilized law (and hence, justice) by design.

Vachss goes much further, however. He has Bruce investigate the accuracy of his mother's belief that the ultimate truth behind the practice of abuse is behavioral and not genetic. "You are what you *do*. Children are born with different genetic allotments, from the color of their eyes to their intellectual capacity, but the rest is what they themselves contribute." He learns that it "is *absolutely* true" that "there is no biogenetic code for criminality." This balances some of Vachss's public musings on the notion that it would be better for some victims of abuse to die rather than survive, since the cycle of abuse would then end, for not all go on to abuse their own children. "There is *always* a choice," Bruce Wayne is told. As we learn, Batman learns.

The novel ends, and it is followed by an essay by David Hechler on child sex tourism, thus removing any doubts that the reader might have concerning the veracity of the novel's premises and subject. This is reminiscent of the Steven Seagal film *On Deadly Ground* (1994), which ends, literally, with a lecture by Steven Seagal on the real-world challenges to the environment that have been touched upon in the film. Two millennia ago, Horace argued that art should teach as well as please, but the heavy-handedness of this instruction is something that few would have anticipated. Seagal, interestingly, was criticized more than Vachss, though both environmental degradation and child abuse are compelling and important subjects. The answer probably lies in the fact that Seagal is expected to make escapist froth, while Vachss is a known crusader with a following that both accepts and appreciates the seriousness of purpose that he brings to his task.

All of Vachss's works carry a heavy message, but they do so with a relatively light narrative touch. The pacing is extremely swift. Industry lore suggests that successful genre fiction should consist of at least 40 percent dialogue. This quickens the read and amplifies the conflict and suspense by engaging us—the listeners who re-create the staccato, urgent voices in our own heads.

Vachss's novels are heavy on dialogue, and many, particularly some of the earlier ones in the Burke series, have extremely brief chapters, some no more than a paragraph in length, some little more than a sentence. If comic violence is muted by the distance between the reader / observer and the individual who suffers and if realistic violence is stylized by rapidity of narrative (consider, for example, the muted violence of Voltaire's *Candide*), then Vachss camouflages the heavy-handedness of his themes and conclusions by embedding them in breathless narratives. He makes his points, always, but his books are crime fiction, not sermons. The skill of the narratives enlarges his audience and, as a result, extends the reach of his messages.

English departments are now fond of exploring the issue of cultural hegemony and the manner in which power and authority are reinforced by cultural products. The expansion of the traditional canon has as its subtext the expansion of the cultural authority of the hitherto forgotten or overlooked groups who have found themselves at the social and cultural margins because of the structures that have solidified the positions of those who have traditionally enjoyed both political and cultural dominance.

This political reorientation of the canon and curriculum has brought with it a degree of seriousness that adjusts Horace's balance between teaching and pleasing toward the former at the expense of, sometimes nearly to the exclusion of, the latter, as political and / or moral concerns marginalize aesthetic ones. There has even been a recent movement (at this late hour) to reassert the claims of art in literary study, though warnings have been issued that this process not be taken over by the cultural right.

In such an ethos, Andrew Vachss flourishes, but the message he inculcates—the necessity to protect the helpless by whatever means necessary—evokes the ethos of the chivalric tradition and envisions a world in which there is very real evil and against which we must launch very real crusades. The defense of helpless victims transcends the aesthetic concerns of art. Art, in effect, is put in direct service to society.

Because Vachss uses genre fiction for this purpose, there has been little or no mainstream debate about the issues he raises and the vehicle he uses. Genre fiction, in effect, is overlooked by the academy as escapist, mass-cult fluff. It is interesting to note, however, that no contemporary writer seems to have learned the lessons of the left-leaning academy better than Vachss, however its members might feel about the service to which he has put their principles. Presumably the debate would all come down to the manner in which one explains the fundamental basis for the personality and practices of the abuser and the solutions that would then be prescribed. Reeducation, understanding, and sensitivity training would be advocated by some, termination with extreme prejudice by others.

The issue is raised, in a slightly different context, in *The Silence of the Lambs.* Dr. Hannibal Lecter is angry at God for making him what he is, but when Clarice Starling is asked, "Is it true what they're sayin', he's some kinda vampire?" she replies, "They don't have a name for what he is." Thus, contemporary crime writing explores the new and current, in this case the conclusions of sociology, psychology, sociobiology, and neuroscience with regard to extreme behaviors, but sometimes it is forced to admit that it has reached an impasse. Vachss is surely correct in saying that abuse is heinous. If he is also correct in saying that abuse is the result of conscious choice in the interest of personal gratification, the dark knight's response to such evil takes on greater plausibility and might earn wider acceptance, particularly to the degree that the current systems of justice perpetuate the success of abusers rather than address the protection of their victims.

Our preference, of course, would be for a system that would protect the victim and authentically rehabilitate the criminal as part of the process of exacting justice. The fact that that is far easier said than done, combined with the urgency of our desires for provisional solutions in the face of intense and widespread human suffering, provides the cultural opportunity for Vachss's literary success. That success stands as an ongoing commentary on our current social and cultural condition.

The Never Ending Story

Chapter III

Toward the end of the first book of *The Faerie Queene* the Redcrosse Knight slays a particularly nasty dragon and is betrothed to the fair Una. In the course of the celebration the local children are sporting on the ground near the dragon's corpse and are struck with wonder at the sight:

> X
> Some feard and fledd; some feard, and well it faynd;
> One, that would wiser seeme then all the rest,
> Warnd him not touch, for yet perhaps remaynd
> Some lingring life within his hollow brest,
> Or in his wombe might lurke some hidden nest
> Of many dragonettes, his fruitfull seede;
> Another said, that in his eyes did rest
> Yet sparckling fyre, and badd thereof take heed;
> Another said, he saw him move his eyes indeed.
>
> XI
> One mother, whenas her foolehardy chyld
> Did come to neare, and with his talants play,
> Halfe dead through feare, her litle babe revyld,
> And to her gossibs gan in counsell say:
> 'How can I tell, but that his talants may
> Yet scratch my sonne, or rend his tender hand?'
> So diversly them selves in vaine they fray;
> Whiles some more bold, to measure him nigh stand,
> To prove how many acres he did spred of land.

This is Spenser at his best, adding human details that both anchor his allegorical narrative and reinforce its lessons. Within the world of chivalric romance, it is never beyond the reach of possibility that a putatively deceased dragon could contain viable dragonettes or,

39

indeed, revive and continue to make mischief. Evil may be temporarily contained, but it is never fully eradicated, for it is an ongoing feature of our world. The slaying of a dragon or solving of a crime merely brings a single battle to a close; the overarching war never really ends. Hence, the series character in crime fiction—the heir to the chivalric romance legacy—encounters a new form of evil or at least a new manifestation of evil in each new book, and it is not uncommon to have a repeating antagonist to reinforce the point. Holmes has his Moriarty, Nayland Smith his Fu Manchu—actually *Dr.* Fu Manchu, an educated antagonist like Professor Moriarty and his later incarnation, Dr. Hannibal Lecter.

The series character—often surrounded by an ensemble cast—participates in the genre fiction equivalent of the *roman fleuve,* the novelistic form that takes repeating characters through a multivolumed narrative. In some cases the series character does not age. Parker's Spenser goes through phases (his past breakup with Susan Silverman now serving as a repeating memory), but with regard to physical capacity, intellectual interests, and sexual appetite he is still more or less the same individual.

Any exception to this pattern would have to be done very gently. Readers are unlikely to tolerate an arthritic or impotent Spenser. Part of his appeal is the degree to which he is resistant to the changes that affect the rest of the world, just as part of his stories' appeal lies in the fact that their readers can be reasonably assured of happy, successful endings and a sense of justice and roundedness that they are often denied in their daily lives.

Other writers have taken other tacks. Steve Thayer, for example, moves between contemporary time and past time in gangster-ridden St. Paul. His first novel, *Saint Mudd,* focuses on a newsman, Grover Mudd, from the 1930s. His second novel, *The Weatherman,* bridges what has become an asynchronous trilogy and features a Vietnam vet whose face has been destroyed by napalm. This character, Rick Beanblossom, appears in his third novel, *Silent Snow,* which moves between the present and the 1930s and reintroduces Grover Mudd, Beanblossom's journalistic idol. Mudd had investigated the Lindbergh kidnapping, and the novel begins with the kidnapping of the child of Beanblossom, who looks for both answers and inspiration in the experience of Mudd.

This parallels the impressive effects that Sidney Kirkpatrick achieves in his masterful true crime narrative, *A Cast of Killers*. Kirkpatrick was writing a biography of the great director King Vidor when he was suddenly stymied by a break in Vidor's activities. Discovering a cache of Vidor's papers he simultaneously discovered what Vidor was doing. He was attempting to solve the second most celebrated (and also unsolved) murder in the history of Los Angeles, that of the actor/director William Desmond Taylor.

Kirkpatrick proceeded to interview all of the living individuals previously interviewed by Vidor and then constructed a narrative of Vidor's investigation of the case, an investigation that parallels his own. The result is a story that is simultaneously biography, autobiography, and reportage, a story that leverages the full effects of novelistic narrative while it operates on three time levels: Taylor's, Vidor's, and Kirkpatrick's. The result is a masterpiece of true crime writing on the level of Truman Capote's *In Cold Blood* and Joseph Wambaugh's *The Onion Field* and *The Blooding*, but also one that reinforces the point that reflections on crime are often, simultaneously, reflections on time.

The story is an archaeological dig, examining the layers of the city's past. It is interesting to note that the house of the actress Mary Miles Minter (her mother is a prime suspect in the murder case) has become a home for unwed mothers, while Taylor's fashionable bungalow on Alvarado Street has been removed and replaced by a rubble-strewn parking lot, both still replete with ghosts. It is equally interesting to point out that a recent A&E special, *Hollywood Confidential*, focusing on the Taylor murder—which happened directly in the wake of the Fatty Arbuckle trial—interviewed Kirkpatrick, scholars, historians, and an individual who conducts limousine tours of the crime scenes of Los Angeles, an array of individuals appropriate for what Mike Davis has called the "City of Quartz."

Two major writers have recently worked this territory. The first is Walter Mosley. Mosley is often dubbed an African American writer, since his father was African American. His mother, however, was Jewish, a point that is important for his life story (though not highlighted by publicists), for his father sought a wider world than the slums of Houston where he grew up. The father's eyes were opened by his military experience, and his marriage to a Jewish woman and departure from Houston for Los Angeles signaled his freedom. The breadth of his son's cultural inheritance is now mirrored in his life and in his writing, for Walter Mosley (long a New Yorker) has written mainstream fiction (*RL's Dream*) and science fiction (*Blue Light*) and made some sorties into essayistic work. In addition to the Easy Rawlins books for which he is best known, he has also started a second crime fiction series, this one featuring an ex-con (with a two-legged dog) named Socrates Fortlow, and a third featuring the title character of *Fearless Jones* (2001).

While the image of Mosley as the dedicated patron of the small, African American–owned publishing house (one of which published *Gone Fishin'*, the prequel to the Easy Rawlins series) and his image as the inheritor of the Chester Himes mantle may each be useful for sales, they are only a part of the Walter Mosley reality, for this Jewish/black writer who worked for a time in the computer industry is closer to the mainstream of a diverse, contemporary America than the characters of which he writes. This may, in fact, account for his success as a writer, one who bridges communities and acts as a translator and interpreter at their borders.

Walter Mosley's principal accomplishment to date is the creation of a fictional account of black Los Angeles, or at least one individual's take on it. Mosley's chief series concerns a character named Ezekiel ("Easy") Rawlins, and the five central books in the series take Easy from the 1940s to the 1960s. It was after completing these books that Mosley published *Gone Fishin'*, a coming-of-age book that charts the early relationship between Easy Rawlins and his friend Raymond ("Mouse") Alexander. One of the books, *Devil in a Blue Dress*, has been made into an exceptional film (directed by Carl Franklin, 1995), with Denzel Washington as Easy and the stunning Don Cheadle as Mouse. I will return to the latter character in the next chapter.

In the course of the series we watch Easy change and develop along with the city. Essentially he is a survivor, skirting the reach of the law, aiding where he can, and seeking some small measure of personal success and happiness. This is complicated by his friendship with Mouse, a character upon whom he depends but one he simultaneously fears. Their relationship is one of the most interesting in contemporary crime writing, for Mosley has merged a number of traditions in creating it. On the one hand Mouse is the avenging angel, the fierce figure upon whom one can rely in difficult times. He is also the accompanying figure to the protagonist, the man of color in the wilderness, a subject we will address in Chapter V. Here, of course, both men are of color and the lines between them—which fade as the threats rise—are psychological rather than racial. Mouse also plays to the gangsta stereotype as Easy plays to the shuck-and-jive stereotype. They are an interesting and complex pair, and their interactions shape both the plot and the subtext of discourse on the black experience.

Los Angeles also functions as a character in the narratives. Ross Macdonald's oft-quoted comment that Chandler "wrote like a slumming angel and invested the sun-blinded streets of Los Angeles with a romantic presence" comes to mind here, but there is nothing very romantic about Easy's world. On the contrary, Easy inhabits the historical and cultural space of the city that is often forgotten amid the sunshine, and Mosley brings it to life with great skill.

He does not, however, feel it and fear it like that other city son writing about it from afar, James Ellroy. Ellroy is one of the great crime writers of our time, and all of his writing begins with personal experience, a private history that he has made public and upon which he has built a writing career.

The son of divorced parents, Ellroy outraged his mother when he told her he preferred to live with his father, a Hollywood hanger-on behaving as much like a rowdy older brother as like a parent. While still a child, Ellroy lost his mother in an act of criminal violence that remains unsolved. This initiated a downward spiral—depicted in detail in Ellroy's *My Dark Places*—which involved drugs, burglary, dysfunctional sexuality, a faked nervous breakdown resulting in a military discharge, and homelessness. Eventually Ellroy secured a job as a caddy and began to put his life back in order. He read voraciously, sold a crime novel, *Brown's Requiem,* and began a writing career.

His career has fallen into three phases. The first consists of a series of six relatively conventional novels done well. Two were made into films: *Cop* (directed by James B. Harris, 1987), based on *Blood on the Moon* and featuring James Woods, and *Brown's Requiem* (directed by Jason Freeland, 1998). These were followed by a tetralogy that Ellroy terms the "L.A. Quartet": *The Black Dahlia, The Big Nowhere,* the masterful *L.A. Confidential,* and *White Jazz.* He is now engaged in writing a third set of novels, this group connected like the second, but played out on a wider canvas. The first, dealing with the events leading up to the Kennedy assassination, is entitled *American Tabloid*. The second, which has just appeared, is entitled *The Cold Six Thousand* and takes us up to the deaths of Martin Luther King and Robert Kennedy. In addition to the true crime autobiography *My Dark Places*, Ellroy has done edgy journalistic writing (particularly for *GQ*), short stories, and a true crime novella, *Dick Contino's Blues*.

The latter is particularly interesting. At the time of his mother's murder in June 1958, Ellroy and his father had watched Contino, the famous fifties accordion player, on television. Ellroy remembers seeing him play "Bumble Boogie." He also remembers his father saying that Contino was no good, because he was a draft dodger. A year or so later, Ellroy saw a B movie at the Admiral Theatre (*Daddy-O*, directed by Lou Place, 1959) featuring Contino. Years later, the film was released on tape; Ellroy ordered it, and as he watched it the memories came back in a rush. Determined to meet and interview Contino, he tracked him down in Las Vegas and persuaded him to permit him to write his story, one—exactly like Ellroy's—of, as he says, heavily compromised redemption. (Contino had been accused of draft evasion and cowardice for his actions with regard to the Korean War and took years rehabilitating his reputation.)

The success of the film adaptation of *L.A. Confidential* (directed by Curtis Hanson, 1997), which took two Academy Awards and was nominated for seven others, including best picture, is sparking new opportunities and projects. Ellroy's reputation is at its zenith. His very presence in Los Angeles (characteristically at the Pacific Dining Car as a base of operations) initiates a spate of rumors and second guesses. A film was recently issued that chronicles his experience: *James Ellroy: Demon Dog of American Crime Fiction* (directed by Jud Reinhard, 1998).

Ellroy's novelistic history of midcentury Los Angeles contains an implicit theory of history, one that squares nicely with Raymond Chandler's. In Section IX of *A Tale of a Tub*, Jonathan Swift suggests that the great events of human history often arise from putatively small causes. Dyspepsia and other physical ailments, sexual frustration, or inactivity can all affect the decisions of kings and princes and motivate consequential actions on the international stage. Ellroy's take is similar. He depicts what he has described as the actions of bad white men and is at pains to demonstrate the manner in which these individuals' personal needs and desires lead to actions that undermine the fabric of their societies.

These men are generally not positioned at the highest levels of society, but they are positioned high enough to do significant harm. They are often, as Chandler would have it, members of large organizations within society, particularly but not exclusively the LAPD. Lone individuals—for example, Sid Hudgens of the tabloid publication *Hush-Hush*, who figures prominently in *L.A. Confidential*—may yet stand for a multiplicity of individuals in a growth industry. The preeminent figure of evil in the "L.A. Quartet" is Dudley Liam Smith, the LAPD mastermind and éminence grise who is secretly and violently taking over all of Mickey Cohen's rackets. Surrounding Smith is an ensemble of individuals whose voices echo across the four novels of the tetralogy, some of them surviving, some not. We see them at various stages of their careers as we observe Los Angeles in various stages of its history, and what we see is generally not pretty.

Ellroy takes this all to the next level in *American Tabloid*, the first of a three-volume trilogy dubbed "Underworld, U.S.A." which is expected to move from the Kennedy assassination (volume 1) through 1968 (volume 2) to 1973 (volume 3). In *American Tabloid* he returns to the men in the background who manage to make history, what he has described as "bad men and the price they paid to secretly define their time." This is all very noir, very tabloid, and very conspiratorial (and, likely, very true or at least very plausible).

In *American Tabloid* the figures include Pete Bondurant, a former L.A. County deputy sheriff who works for Howard Hughes as a bagman, staffs *Hush-Hush* magazine, and eventually links up with Jimmy Hoffa. He is essentially a freelance shakedown artist. Kemper Boyd, an undercover FBI agent, a J. Edgar Hoover spy working for Bobby Kennedy, is as attracted to the Kennedys as Hoover is repulsed by them. A CIA agent provocateur, Boyd is JFK's double—a handsome charmer with no moral compass. Finally, there is Ward Littell, a protégé of Boyd's (who allows him to do some work for Bobby Kennedy). An FBI agent turned mob attorney, Littell is also a former Jesuit seminarian.

This covers Chandler's bases. We have big government, big law enforcement, big unions, big business, the media, and what their respective members call the Company: the Central Intelligence Agency and the Society of Jesus.

These fictional but plausible characters representing very real organizations are all involved in the events that ultimately lead to the grassy knoll at Dealey Plaza: the pursuit of Jimmy Hoffa, the debacle that became known as the Bay of Pigs, and the mob's loss of Cuba, the syndicate's prized cash cow. Reviewing *American Tabloid* for the *New York Times,* William Vollmann described it as "brilliantly unpleasant . . . a supremely controlled work of art." With the possible exception of Bobby Kennedy, all of the characters in the book are unlikable, "and yet these people, while unable to command our empathy on their own account, serve as dye markers to illustrate the vector trails of all the various evil forces that spring from that most capitalist force of all, self-interest."

Fundamentally, this book takes the ethos of the "L.A. Quartet" to the national and international level. Its final concern is human interaction and human deceit, and given the event at which the respective plot lines converge (the crime of the century, or at least a fair competitor for that designation) the book ultimately concerns nothing less than the loss of American innocence, the loss of political community, and, in effect, the loss of some important share of American society.

We now know the disparity between the hopes that were riding on JFK's administration and the realities that underpinned them. The monarch of this putative reincarnation of Camelot was actually an adulterous, compulsive womanizer (with a Mafia mistress) from a dysfunctional family who hid his Addison's disease from the electorate and gave us a cabinet at least one of whose members was eventually prepared to lie to Congress and plunge us ever more deeply into the bloody morass in Vietnam, a war that ultimately shattered our universities, set back our economy, destroyed our sense of trust, and sacrificed nearly sixty thousand American lives. There is no greater textbook example than the managing of the Vietnam War of a conspiracy against the public and a demonstration of the fact that there are two Americas, one that loyally fights wars and one that callously takes us into them.

Ellroy began this story with his accounts of Los Angeles, the endpoint of the American Dream, whether in the form of that dream's apex or its nadir, a city built on illusion—both in its creations in Hollywood and in its endless reselling of ever more expensive desert real estate, one of the great scams of our time, in Mike Davis's analysis, attracting weary ex-soldiers, struggling Okies, and steelworkers fleeing Johnstown. Ellroy has taken this story of ruined hopes and dreams east, and to tell it he has developed the perfect stylistic instrument.

It is a controversial instrument. There are those who see it as the culmination of his art and those who see it as an irritant and annoyance. The break came with the "L.A. Quartet," and some readers refer to the "old" versus the "new" Ellroy. It is interesting that the writer who has criticized Chandler's plots (fairly, I think) and labeled him as primarily a stylist should now himself be so associated with his own unique style. That style does not, however, involve a sacrifice of plot. The following is a sample:

> Press clippings on his corkboard: "Dope Crusader Wounded in Shootout"; "Actor Mitchum Seized in Marijuana Shack Raid." *Hush-Hush* articles, framed on his desk: "Hopheads Quake When Dope Scourge Cop Walks Tall"; "Actors Agree: *Badge of Honor* Owes Authenticity to Hard-hitting Technical Advisor." The *Badge* piece featured a photo: Sergeant Jack Vincennes with the show's star, Brett Chase. The piece did not feature dirt from the editor's private file: Brett Chase as a pedophile with three quashed sodomy beefs.
>
> Jack Vincennes glanced around the Narco pen—deserted, dark— just the light in his cubicle. Ten minutes short of midnight; he'd promised Dudley Smith he'd type up an organized crime report for Intelligence Division; he'd promised Lieutenant Frieling a case of booze for the station party—Hush-Hush Sid Hudgens was supposed to come across with rum but hadn't called. Dudley's report: a favor shot his way because he typed a hundred words a minute; a favor returned tomorrow: a meet with Dud and Ellis Loew, Pacific Dining Car lunch—work on the line, work to earn him juice with the D.A.'s Office. Jack lit a cigarette, read.
>
> (*L.A. Confidential*, chapter three)

James Joyce is reputed to have said that since he spent so much of his life writing *Finnegans Wake* his readers could spend a comparable part of theirs trying to make sense of it. Ellroy's writing is not that complex, but it is challenging. The passage above is comparatively straightforward, though it requires the reader to keep a long list of characters and plot lines straight and it assumes a knowledge of the City of the Angels that is consistently above tourist level.

There are echoes here of John Dos Passos, another writer who took the entire country as his subject—not so much in the staccato sentences but in the broad canvas, multiple characters, historical frame, and intercut citations from the contemporary press. There are also echoes of high modernism, though Ellroy characteristically substitutes a torrent of consciousness for his antecedents' stream. He has said that at times he has written as much as seven hundred pages and then boiled them down to one hundred.

The result is a phenomenological style (assuming a phenomenologist writing crime fiction on methamphetamine). There is a flood of facts and impressions, truths, half-truths, second guesses, and intuitions. In some cases the observations are literal ones: a man sits in a stakeout car, recording all that he sees. In other cases the observations come from memory or from reflections based on memories. Facts, ideas, and images tumble in the brain like rocks polished by heavy waves.

The medium is effective for a number of reasons. First, this form of intellection is quintessentially that of the detective: observing, recording, measuring, checking, cross-checking, selecting, and, finally, *seeing*. In Ellroy's world, however, the detectives are often more guilty than the putative criminals. Honest cops are searching out dishonest ones. Dishonest cops are lying to honest cops as well as to one another. Cops, like prosecuting attorneys, spend much of their time challenging the defendant's story, writing and rewriting it in search of the truth. Here they spend much of their time (like the best liars) keeping track of their own stories, keeping track of the stories they have told others, and keeping track of the stories that others have told them.

The rapid-fire, densely textured style goes hand in hand with multilayered plots of great complexity. Ellroy's *outline* for the last novel in the "L.A. Quartet," *White Jazz*, was 164 pages in length; the outline for *L.A. Confidential* was 211 pages.

The style and substance of these narratives make great demands on the reader, but together they constitute a superb instrument for depicting the world Ellroy seeks to represent. As in Barry Levinson's television program *Homicide: Life on the Streets*, the homicide detective (robbery/homicide in the LAPD) is the intellectual of law enforcement. That does not mean that he or she does not sometimes resort to violence or require weaponry, but it does mean that survival and success turn on a shrewd intelligence.

The moments in which the lies are revealed and the realizations set in are epiphanic (the film version of *L.A. Confidential* catches this brilliantly, with the "Rollo Tommasi" ploy). In the meantime the characters in the crime drama live in a world of facts, images, and stories that can lead, by turns, to success, salvation, or violent death. The stylistic medium conveys a sense of the urgency of events in this world, of the tenuous nature of the truth, of the nearly electric world of connections, impulses, and results. All of the goals of the writer of crime fiction—a sense of conflict; a sense of danger; a sense of curiosity, tension, resolution, and frustration; a sense of the unforgiving ticking of the clock; and most of all a sense of a society of shadows and borders that mirrors our own deepest fears and doubts—are served well by Ellroy's stylistic medium.

Ellroy himself is so personally immersed in this medium that he speaks its language with no sense of irony or anachronism. He speaks of hepcats and hopheads and is as likely to begin a sentence with "Dig . . . " as he is to say "Good evening." Chandler knew that language was central to crime fiction—the language putatively spoken on the American street, which became the language written on the literary page. In utilizing it so effectively he associated its tone and nuance with the events described and made their realities commensurate.

Now its realities are primarily literary ("crime fiction sounds like this"), but Ellroy has so imbibed that stylistic reality as to make it a part of his personal identity. He speaks as he writes, despite the fact that his writing is so stylized. At the same time he has added elements of realism that go beyond Chandler and his ultimately romantic roots in chivalric romance.

Ellroy is romantic in one crucial sense of romanticism—the desire to convey ultimately ineffable truths about the self. The later Ellroy, however, has little time for the ethos of chivalric romance. Chandler on the other hand is far sweeter and quainter in this regard, consciously combining the detective's search with the knight's quest: "The story [of crime fiction] is this man's adventure in search of a hidden truth, and it would be no adventure if it did not happen to a man fit for adventure."

The characters that populate Ellroy's novels are of a quite different sort, as are their quests. Their adventures involve a grubbing after power that is ultimately rooted in the most narrow self-interest. These are not nice people. These are the people that your history, traditions, entire genetic code, and mother warned you about. As Ellroy puts it in the preface to *American Tabloid*, "It's time to demythologize an era and build a new myth from the gutter to the stars. It's time to embrace bad men and the price they paid to secretly define their time."

This embrace is an extremely subtle one. Ellroy knows what Wayne Booth taught us a generation ago: the more we know about bad people the more we are likely to entertain sympathetic thoughts toward them, since we know them better than other characters in the narrative. If Thomas Harris can make a cannibal and Lawrence Block a hit man like John Keller sympathetic, Ellroy offers us an entire list of dramatis personae that ranges between evil and unpleasant, with a significant number tilting toward evil. When he does offer redemption (as in the Contino novella, for example), it is always, as noted, heavily compromised.

This is not too distant from Chandler; if government, business, unions, and the church are all corrupt, what is left? What is left is the lone individual, presumably, but what sorts of individuals, Ellroy implicitly asks, are eventually created by such a society?

Contemporary literary theorists, operating under the influence of the French Nietzscheans, attempt to generate images of society that might eventually bring what are perceived to be positive, liberating results. Ellroy depicts an alternate reality. Once we are cut free from the institutions that could offer support (as well as oppression), once we realize the constructedness of everything (or believe that we do), and once we see the reality of a universal will to power that can tilt in other directions than the creative, we do not end up with a happy world of mental play and *jouissance*, for humans have appetites as well as intellection. We end up with a horrific world in which bad men seek (as we are told in the epigraph to *L.A. Confidential*) "a glory that costs everything and means nothing."

More than anything else, Ellroy's world is a world of lies, and his medium is the perfect vehicle for representing such a world, a fact we might consider for a moment. In *Adventurer* number 50, Samuel Johnson writes:

The liar, and only the liar, is invariably and universally despised, abandoned, and disowned; he has no domestic consolations, which he can oppose to the censure of mankind; he can retire to no fraternity where his crimes may stand in the place of virtues; but is given up to the hisses of the multitude, without friend and without apologist. It is the peculiar condition of falsehood, to be equally detested by the good and bad: "The devils," says Sir Thomas Brown, "do not tell lies to one another; for truth is necessary to all societies; nor can the society of hell subsist without it."

The individuals in Ellroy's world, however, do tell lies to one another, and they do it routinely. They do it as a pivotal part of their modus operandi. If the deconstructionists are correct in their argument that signifiers really slide endlessly, we have a theoretical construct to underwrite the practices of such a world; since the truth cannot be agreed upon, we are left with something else—multiple truths presumably, but this has not proved to be a particularly propitious time to introduce a notion that can be so easily turned to other purposes.

In a world of newspeak and what Daniel Boorstin calls pseudo events, a world of puritanical euphemism and political correctness, plain talk is always in jeopardy. So too is honest talk. Much is said now concerning the breaking of the social contract in America. Individuals who offer an honest day's work for a fair wage can no longer count on a commitment of ongoing employment. Greed, piratical capitalism, the MBAification of society, disloyalty, and the sudden wealth (or poverty) that accompanies the economic and social distortions of the communications revolution are all contemporary facts of life, a multiplication, many times over, of the sharp business practices that Chandler saw as the flip side of the violence of our society.

Individuals now expect to have multiple careers, including periods of self-employment, and the pursuit of their own self-interest is an equal and opposite reaction to the pursuit of corporate self-interest, despite the human costs. This has resulted, to some degree at least, it is argued, in a shredding of the social contract.

Johnson's view (and Ellroy's) is more basic. For Johnson, civilized society depends on a fundamental sense of trust. Without it we face something beyond uncertainty or temporary indeterminacy; we face barbarity. When we reach a point in our national life that lying—at all levels but especially at the highest levels (or putative highest levels)—becomes a constant means to pursue the dreams of self-interest, we have created an ethos that is the end point of crime fiction.

We speak of it somewhat lightly because it is too horrible to contemplate directly. We speak of "spin" or of statements that are "no longer operative." We speak of a "noticeably unreliable memory" or a tendency to "remember things differently." There are moments, however, when we stare into the eyes of a president or priest (perhaps an individual playing both roles) and hear what we know is a self-conscious, willful lie. At that moment we confront barbarity.

A friend of mine was once giving a lay sermon and was commenting on the Twenty-third Psalm. He proposed a question concerning the location of the valley of the shadow of death and suggested that it was not really very difficult to find. It was just beyond the church door. It is fitting that our premier crime novelist should take such a locale for his subject. Johnson talks of a world of lies as one of barbarity; James Ellroy depicts it, and the world of lies that he depicts is one with no final victories, only temporary abatements. The never-ending story that he tells is all the more powerful in that it is one that has been lived by all of us and not simply woven from his novelistic imagination.

Ellroy is fond of quoting a passage from an Evan Hunter novel in which the question is asked, "When was the last time a private investigator solved a homicide case?" The answer: "Never." The point is that real private investigators handle relatively mundane, often grubby matters. It is the police who handle homicides, and it is the police department that is the real locus for the ongoing investigation of serious crime.

One of the most telling recent novels to explore this territory is Kent Anderson's *Night Dogs*. Anderson, like the protagonist of the novel, was a decorated member of the Special Forces in Vietnam as well as a former police officer in Portland. Like James Crumley, he has also written a mainstream novel about his experiences in Southeast Asia (*Sympathy for the Devil*), featuring the protagonist of *Night Dogs*, a man named Hanson.

Night Dogs is set in the north end of Portland, the most crime-ridden section of the city. Watchers of *Cops* will know of Portland's crime and criminals, the bisecting interstate serving, for example, as an important conduit for drugs, but for many, Portland will be thought of as a quieter, more idyllic setting, a good bit removed from the valley of the shadow of death. That, of course, only serves to reinforce the awareness of that valley's proximity.

The novel is a very impressive one, a more-than-five-hundred-page reflection on an urban hell and the interplay between the police and citizens therein. It is set in the mid-1970s, a time when the social and political fabric of the country often seemed to be little more than an open wound. There is no overarching plot other than the linked experiences of the protagonist. Three modest subplots (the actions of a rival, the actions of a Vietnam comrade in arms, and an uncertain romantic relationship) are decidedly *sub*plots. They intersect with Hanson's life but do not dominate it in the way that constant threats, constant violence, paperwork, and very imperfect resolutions of criminal situations do.

Night Dogs lays bare the essential conflict besetting the urban police officer: the need for courage, strength, and the capacity to absorb and inflict violence and the balancing need for a deep sensitivity to the plight of the victims of criminality as well as the perpetrators of it. Hanson must demonstrate a capacity to intimidate but also an awareness of when to pull back, when to choose allies, and when to issue thanks.

In one scene, for example, a retarded black child has accidentally stepped on an exploding cherry bomb during a Fourth of July celebration. His mother, who is incapable of caring for him because of her addictions, shouts at Hanson as he attempts to care for her son, going so far as to grab her son's leg when he is in excruciating pain and attempting to wrest him from Hanson's hold. Meanwhile, the crowd that surrounds him is hurling racial epithets and threatening violence. Hanson must be strong enough both to protect the child and to keep anyone from taking his gun and using it against him. At the same time, he must know when to surrender the child to a black man who intercedes on the child's behalf in the face of the actions of what is fast becoming a mob. All the while, the child—who has soiled his pants—is screaming in pain and unaware of the precise nature of the situation in which he finds himself.

There are dozens of such wrenching episodes in the book. One of the most telling is one in which Hanson remembers having endured a form of Special Forces training that involves the conscious infliction of wounds upon live dogs. The trainees are responsible for healing the wounds or at least ameliorating the effects of the trauma, the point of the training being to introduce them to the actual effects of bullets and shrapnel and the need to stay calm and follow proper medical protocols in the face of the dogs' terror and their own emotional involvement with them. After the dogs are healed they are sent to the pound, where most will be destroyed. When he confronts an angry crowd of demonstrators outside the training facility, Hanson approaches one, presses what money he has into her hand, and asks her to go to the pound and rescue the dog whose life he has been protecting.

Throughout the novel Hanson cares for a blind, aged dog that falls into his hands in the course of an investigation, this act contrasting with the periodic shooting of the packs of feral dogs (in which he does not participate) that give the novel its title.

This is a book of almost unrelieved suffering and violence depicting the strategies employed by the police to maintain peace, order, and some semblance of personal sanity and humanity. It reflects at length on questions of race and does so with alternating anger and sensitivity. There is no Aristotelian plot arc per se. On the one hand Hanson falls deeper into the pit; on the other he begins to realize the necessity for changing his life and climbing toward what little daylight might be found. Either way, the crime will continue. In focusing on the daily facts of such a life we stare momentarily into the abyss, grateful for the fact that we (at least) need not do so continually.

Aside from a small handful of human relationships, most of them dysfunctional, there is no relief here. The hell is beyond Dante's; the food is poisonous, the bodies diseased, the psyches fractured by violence, addiction, and desertion, the air filled with foul smells, the streets littered with rubbish and excrement.

This is not a book that one reads to wile away the time; it is a book that one reads to gain a sense of the enormity of urban suffering and its effects on the human beings (including the police) who populate such a landscape. In his foreword, James Crumley says that "*Night Dogs* is not just a fine book, it is an important book." It is not a book of complete despair, but it is a book that serves up certain forms of reality without remorse. It is a case study or slice-of-urban-life narrative, but one done on an epic scale—an epic with few heroes and those significantly compromised by their pasts, their present, and their likely future. It is, in effect, a fictional documentary with the solid ring of unbearable truth. It is a book of horror but not a horror novel. It is a crime novel that makes us grateful for the softer conventions and softer subjects we generally seek, but one that reminds us of the depth and recalcitrance of the recurring realities that undergird the form.

The Avenging Angel

Chapter IV

Sir Thomas Browne's aforementioned comment to the effect that the devils in hell do not lie to one another was made two decades before the publication of *Paradise Lost*. Milton chose to take a different course: his devils *do* lie to one another, and the fact that they lie ultimately results in their downfall. Satan, the father of lies, also lies to himself, and the title of Milton's poem, which refers to Satan's fall as well as to Adam and Eve's, suggests the cost of his sins.

In book V, Milton depicts the seduction of the soon-to-be-fallen angels by Satan. Only one individual stands up to oppose him, a member of the seraphim by the name of Abdiel. Abdiel, though created by Milton, is clearly one of Milton's greatest heroes, for Milton, standing exposed to his enemies after the fall of the Cromwellian government (in which he served as Latin secretary, justifying the regicide to a continental audience), associates himself with this figure: "His Loyalty he kept, his Love, his Zeal; / Nor number, nor example with him wrought / To swerve from truth, or change his constant mind / Though single."

When the heavenly battle ensues in book VI, Abdiel and Satan have a frank exchange of views and Abdiel strikes a blow that drives Satan to his knee. Satan's forces gasp, and Michael sounds the trumpet of war. The battle rages for about 550 lines of verse, covering two days of action, at which point God notes that the forces are so balanced that the war might go on forever.

But that is not God's plan. He turns now to his Son, who drives a fiery chariot conveyed by four four-faced cherubim and is accompanied by ten million angels. The Son utters some lines that are tantamount to "This is my fight . . . and since violence is all that they understand. . . ." The cherubim under the chariot spread their wings, the sky is darkened, the Son hurls ten thousand thunders, and the war comes to an instantaneous close. The rebellious angels are cast out of heaven and fall for nine days, through Chaos and into Hell. The lesson is clear: it is good to have an invincible individual on your side, particularly one who can defeat the rebel angels and only use half of his strength in the process.

Such a figure regularly appears in contemporary crime fiction. I call him the avenging angel, but I would suggest that part of our desire for his presence may imply a yearning not just for justice or vengeance but also for a greater sense of the presence of divinity.

Angels are interesting figures, particularly these days when there are entire bookshops devoted to their study. Medieval theologians exerted a great deal of effort in detailing the positioning of angels within the celestial hierarchy and in charting their capabilities and identifying their particular duties. Within the so-called Great Chain of Being, angels were placed between God and humans, our own position being closer to the angels prior to the Fall and closer to the animals beneath us after it. After the Fall that which might be characterized as bestial in our behavior becomes stronger and that which might associate us with the angelic weaker. It is not surprising that a literary form that often focuses on the bestial would simultaneously invoke the need for greater celestial assistance.

The concept of a guardian angel is an enduring aspect of Christianity, the guardian angel looking after us in a generalized way on an ongoing basis and stepping in, as necessary, during times of particular need. Guardian angels are common in both Christian children's books and in greeting-card iconography. They are also common in contemporary crime fiction.

Parker has blended this figure with the buddy-of-color figure (the subject of the next chapter) to great advantage. As a character, Hawk is central to Parker's narratives, but he has never gotten the attention that Parker's readers believe he deserves. In the fanzines and on the internet there is often criticism of Spenser's psychiatrist lover, Susan Silverman. Their dialogue is seen as mawkish and predictable, their meals of johnnycakes and afternoons of kissy face tedious. Hawk is a far more interesting companion than Susan. His advice is trenchant if far more terse than hers, and the necessity of his physical support in tight moments is an absolute.

When asked why he has not given Hawk greater prominence, Parker has responded that he knows Spenser better than he knows

Hawk, an interesting comment given the fact that he created both. Hawk did receive sufficient acclaim to justify a short-lived television series (1989), featuring Avery Brooks, who has found a more comfortable home on *Star Trek: Deep Space Nine.*

We know very little about Hawk. He is black. He is in peak physical condition. He enjoys champagne. He accepts jobs that require his unique services on either side of the law. He spars with Spenser. He likes to go to France. He is gentle with Susan and other women. If anything, he is hypercivilized. With male antagonists he is savage, though always very economical in his choice of words as well as in his application of force.

In the most recent Parker novel, *Hugger Mugger,* he is absent, a fact instantly noted—with disappointment—by reviewers. (He has accompanied a French professor to France.) Spenser is also called to Georgia for much of the novel, his task being the investigation of the shooting of race horses. Spenser is not locked into his Boston setting; one of the novels is set in California and another in Washington, but the Boston setting and the ensemble cast are part of the Spenser ethos. Only Susan appears at length in *Hugger Mugger.*

The book is still an effective one. Spenser has ample opportunity to exhibit his skill at irony and the wiseass apothegm. The dialogue is brisk and lively, the writing economical, the texture and layering applied with a light but highly skilled touch. If Parker has been accused of writing on autopilot he still delivers product both regularly and reliably. He currently has three series characters in motion— Jesse Stone, Sunny Randall (a character created for Helen Hunt), and Spenser, with some relatively recent re-creations/continuations of the works and days of Philip Marlowe.

But Spenser without Hawk? In some ways the two are inseparable. Their jokes about the racial divide between them are nearly always in the interest of demonstrating the ultimate absence of such a divide. They spar verbally as well as physically, defining each other in this mutual relationship, but they are finally different in capacity. Spenser is strong and shrewd, but he will bruise and bleed. He can face down most antagonists, but there are moments of final confrontation when he will not go in without Hawk. That is because Spenser, like all of Parker's readers, expects Hawk to be invincible, and in that invincibility lies one of the pivotal elements of much contemporary crime fiction—the hope, however certain, that a greater power will emerge to reassert the claims of justice. The possibility that such a power could actually be with us for the duration offers even greater hope and reassurance.

This invincible figure need not be conventionally strong. In Jonathan Kellerman's Alex Delaware novels, for example, the guardian is anything but conventional. Milo Sturgis is a gay member of the LAPD, with a partner named Scott and a goodly bit of personal baggage. He is above all, however, a detective with the physical as well as intellectual wherewithal to extricate Delaware, a child psychologist turned amateur detective, from difficult situations.

They play off one another nicely, the sometimes disheveled Milo both bracing the bad guys and dropping in unexpectedly at odd hours to raid Dr. Delaware's refrigerator. He serves as a foil to the scholarly and just-a-tad fussy Delaware—who is described reading his journals and feeding his koi—and also contrasts with Delaware's love interest, a comely luthier who dresses primly and smells of lacquer and varnish, in contrast to Milo, who can smell of any number of things, depending on his diet and the nature of his current caseload.

Milo's dependability (in the face of his unpredictability) is comforting for an additional reason. While noting that Milo has taken some abuse in the LAPD because of his sexual orientation, Kellerman is able to portray him as a complex and sometimes unusual individual while at the same time depicting him as the friendly policeman of common lore who really does have the community's best interest at heart and who really is there for us when we need him most. While he is not the physical specimen that Hawk is, he moves in and out of the narratives, appearing when he is most needed and always giving a good account of himself.

Another example of the avenging angel is the creation of Robert Crais (the name rhymes with *grace*). Crais, a Los Angeles screenwriter, appeared on the novelistic scene a decade ago with a striking paperback original entitled *The Monkey's Raincoat*. Since then he has written eight novels and slowly but surely built what is now a very large audience.

Crais's protagonist is a detective named Elvis Cole (twice the king, presumably). Cole is Spenser's West Coast counterpart. He has a tart tongue, a refined sense of irony, and little patience for fools. He is also capable of physical shtick that can undercut what seriousness he does possess and undermine the confidence of clients considering an investment in his services. Such individuals are never a favorite of the police, and the gulf between the PI and the establishment—overworked ground in the genre—still manages to work as a useful and even refreshing theme in Crais's narratives.

Cole's strong and largely silent partner is something else again. His name is Joe Pike, and the directness of his name (which certainly has a different ring than "Miles Archer") and the uses of the weapon to which it can refer are clearly designed to exist in apposition with one another. In *L.A. Requiem*, Crais's most recent novel but one, we see a great deal of Pike.

The novel takes a considerable risk. While Pike has generally appeared as a rare but menacing presence with both technical skill with weapons and consummate physicality, in *L.A. Requiem* he moves center stage. The action is precipitated by the discovery of Pike's former lover's dead body and the narrative explores his personal life in detail. Faced with the choice between the engaging inscrutability associated with a character like Parker's Hawk and the opportunity to exploit his audience's interest in such a character, Crais has chosen the latter, trusting that the plumbed depths will compensate for the loss of the magic that inheres in mystery.

I consider Crais's decision a mistake. Joe Pike is an ex-cop, and in *L.A. Requiem* his friend Elvis, and others, fear for his safety in prison, should he be convicted of the murder of his former lover. The endangered cop-in-prison, surrounded by those he has previously helped convict, is a genre cliché, and any fear for his safety reduces Pike's stature. He should be as dangerous and effective in prison as he is on the streets. There is also some exploration of the fact that he was abused as a child, another cliché and, again, one so debilitating as to reduce our sense of his stature. This is simply too sensitive and too touchy-feely for an individual who regularly functions in the role of terminator.

My view has not, however, been sustained by the responses of Crais's other readers (or by a far more experienced reader than I, Otto Penzler). *L.A. Requiem* is being described as a book transcending genre that takes Crais closer to the literary mainstream. Jacket notes always label a book the masterpiece to date, but in this case the publisher has been joined in that judgment by many readers. They have warmed to the notion of a kinder, gentler, suffering Joe Pike, despite the explicit betrayal of genre expectations.

In my judgment, readers come to a genre that is as finely etched as crime fiction expecting certain things. They expect clever variation within the constraints of the form, but they also expect the essential elements of the form to be sustained. Another recent novel has raised the same issue as *L.A. Requiem*.

I will have more to say about *The Silence of the Lambs* later, but we can pause here and look at the case of Dr. Hannibal Lecter, one of the great creations of contemporary crime writing. Lecter serves multiple functions in *The Silence of the Lambs*. One of his roles is an interesting variation of the avenging angel type. Lecter aids Clarice Starling at a crucial point in her career, and we have no doubt that he could easily solve the crime that she is investigating. We also have no doubt that he has the physical wherewithal to protect himself and her and inflict grievous suffering on anyone who stands in their way. His strength is represented principally through his intelligence and his tenacity, but there are conscious indications of the physical dangers he presents as well. We have no doubts concerning his capacity for vengeance and an equally strong set of assurances that he will make good on his promises and survive. He is just as dangerous in prison as he is beyond the prison's walls.

Harris's readers hungered for a sequel, and they had to wait for more than a decade to receive it. Harris chose to take the same route as Crais, moving Lecter to center stage in the sequel, *Hannibal*, and revealing things about him that were previously unknown. *The Silence of the Lambs* is quite explicit with regard to the mystery concerning Dr. Lecter's pathology. In *Hannibal* the curtains are parted and a goodly part of the truth revealed.

One great trick of the mystery writer's trade is to reveal the identity of the perpetrator or solve the mysteries attending the crime in such a way that the reader is given all of the necessary evidence but still fails to see the implications of that evidence. It must be done without trickery and in such a way that later revelations serve to confirm what has already been learned but not fully understood. The signature moment in this regard in *The Silence of the Lambs* comes directly after Lecter's discourse on Marcus Aurelius: "The Emperor counsels simplicity. First principles. Of each particular thing, ask:

'What is it in itself, in its own constitution? What is its causal nature?'"

Clarice, functioning as a Jamesian central consciousness in the third-person narration, speaks the official line (that is, our response as sympathetic readers): "That doesn't mean anything to me." Lecter continues, brilliantly:

> "What does he do, the man you want?"
> "He kills—"
> "Ah—" . . . "That's incidental. What is the first and principal thing he does, what need does he serve by killing?"
> "Anger, social resentment, sexual frus-"
> "No."
> "What, then?"
> "He covets. In fact, he covets being the very thing you are. It's his nature to covet. How do we begin to covet, Clarice. . . . We begin by coveting what we see every day. Don't you feel eyes moving over you every day, Clarice, in chance encounters? I hardly see how you could not. And don't your eyes move over things?"

While Lecter is as explicit with regard to the perpetrator as the genre permits, he is far more guarded about himself. "A census taker tried to quantify me once. I ate his liver with some fava beans and a big Amarone." We learn a few things. Lecter collects instances of divine acts that appear to punish the faithful, such as church collapses. He is outraged over the facts of his own nature and carries a grudge against God. What we do not learn is the etiology of his pathology. The secret is preserved, and he stands as the embodiment of, simultaneously, a hypertrophied civility and savage brutality, red in tooth and claw but specifying the Gould rendition of Bach's Goldberg Variations.

In *Hannibal* this all changes. The mystery is, more or less, revealed and we get to know Dr. Lecter up close and personal. I consider this a mistake, and in this case a significant number of Harris's readers have agreed with me. *Hannibal* has brought polarized responses, ranging from the gravely disappointed to the warmly enthusiastic.

Part of the problem resulted from the anticipation and the expectations the book raised. Websites were posting "reviews" of it before it appeared, the reviews consisting of statements to the effect that "it has to be great, it just has to be great." Much of the book's notoriety focuses on its ending, which I consider inevitable and appropriate, for reasons I will explain later, but there are significant changes from Harris's text in the cinematic version, while *The Silence of the Lambs* was reproduced perfectly in Ted Tally's screenplay, with only a few elements excised because of the constraints of time. Like Brian Helgeland's script for *L.A. Confidential*, the authentic feel of the book and the central plot lines were all preserved.

This is not to suggest that *Hannibal* the novel was a failure or that *Hannibal* the film is a mishmash. (The cinematic ending provides for the possibility of sequels of a different nature from those envisioned by the book.) There are great books with weak plot elements (for example, *The Big Sleep*), but it is an expectation of the genre that shadowy avengers will retain some significant portion of their mystery and inscrutability, and any violation of that expectation is a perilous step. A cognate example here would be Vachss's revelations about Bruce Wayne's family experiences, including the efforts of his mother as crusader, in *Batman—The Ultimate Evil.*

The problem is that the avenger finds his strength in his superhuman or at least exceptional qualities. To the extent that he or she becomes human or unexceptional the role is diluted of its force. Given the fact that the role is so common in crime fiction there is also, implicitly, a betrayal of the genre and the reader's expectations.

Such modifications of the role are possible, but they are difficult. In Walter Mosley's *Gone Fishin'*, the challenge is met in an interesting way. *Gone Fishin'* is a prequel to the Easy Rawlins series, taking Easy and Mouse (Raymond Alexander) back to their youth. Mouse is Easy's violent, homicidal guardian angel. The more risk-averse Easy fears that his association with Mouse will get him in serious trouble, but he also relies on Mouse for help in tight moments. Though gentle with Easy, Mouse is essentially a stone killer. In *Gone Fishin'*, however, we see them at an earlier stage of their lives, and Mosley dodges the problems of genre by presenting their youthful experience in a coming-of-age book rather than a crime narrative. There are some crossover elements, but the pace, setting, tone, and details are all those of the mainstream novel, so that expectations are shifted and not betrayed. Mosley, who has lately been writing science fiction, is attuned to the demands of genre and adjusts accordingly. Harris's narratives (unlike Vachss's, for example) have a great many crossover dimensions, but the central elements involve crime, procedure, and suspense, which are variations on a basic theme, not departures as dramatic as those in *Gone Fishin'*.

Another interesting, though heavily compromised, figure who plays the avenger role is Clinton Tyree, the former governor of Florida who appears in Carl Hiaasen's novels. Tyree simply walked out of office one day and retreated to the wilderness of the everglades (and beyond), where he subsists on whatever he can find, including roadkill. He enters the narratives at various points, helping the afflicted and bedeviling the guilty. He is capable of violence that verges on the irrational, but his values are good (they are principally environmental, in the face of the despoiling of the state by greedy developers and their fellow travelers). Hiaasen presents him as a form of natural man, someone frighteningly real in a plastic world. He is often barely dressed. He has a bad artificial eye, which he has a tendency to remove at inappropriate moments, and he often lives in trees, descending to the ground in unexpected, unanticipated ways. The echoes of Tarzan are conscious, both in his appearance and in his desire to achieve a harmonious rather than exploitative relationship with the natural environment.

Vachss's vision is too dark to permit the existence of an intervening angel. While Max the Silent has physical gifts beyond Burke's and is often available for crucial help, Burke needs the Prof, the Mole, and the other members of his crew to function effectively. Vachss underlines the bleakness of his moral landscape by investing antagonists with the types of powers usually reserved for the avenging angel. Max is strong, but in Vachss's novel *Blue Belle* we are introduced to a character named Mortay, against whose powers Max's are ultimately inadequate. Arching over all of the Burke novels is the memory of a character named Wesley, a pitiless, remorseless figure from Burke's youth who shocks and staggers even Burke's imagination. Wesley is the subject of Vachss's hitherto unpublished first novel, *A Bomb Built in Hell*. Fortunately, that book is now becoming available on the internet.

Let me provide a final example of the avenging angel character, one that has remained compelling and intact. Dennis Lehane is a Boston writer who has produced five crime novels to date. His work is among the most exceptional on the market. Each of his novels is deeply imagined, heavily textured, nicely plotted, and rich in char-

acter and incident. He is often compared favorably with the more famous Boston novelist Robert Parker, the implication being that their
novels have a great deal in common. This is not really the case. Parker is far more soft-boiled than Lehane when their respective novels
are placed side by side.

Spenser often turns up in hotel bars on the Common, gazing into
Susan Silverman's eyes and enjoying a favorite potable. He is easily
imagined rowing on the Charles or spending a sunny afternoon vis-
iting the north coast. Dennis Lehane writes of the other Boston, the
Boston of slums and violence, of racial gulfs and clogged traffic
lanes, of the homeless in a world of inflated house prices and the
drunk in a world of prim matrons; a place with high taxes, bad
weather, and plentiful political corruption—a place in significant de-
nial that curiously calls itself the hub of the universe.

Lehane's protagonist is a man named Patrick Kenzie, a private investigator whose partner, Angela Gennaro, is a lost love. Angie is
married to another man for part of the series, a man who abuses her.
Patrick's responses to this situation add sexual tension, jealousy, and
anger to the successive narratives and provide an effective undercurrent. Angie's family is mob-related, which adds yet another dimension to the stories.

The role of avenging angel is played by one Bubba Rogowski. The
name is off-putting, though it is nice to have a Bubba in Beantown.
Rogowski is an old school chum. Described in the jacket notes of
Prayers for Rain as "lethally unbalanced," Rogowski is physically for-
midable and intellectually unpredictable. I imagine him as something like wrestling's George "the animal" Steele with better muscle
tone and another seventy-five pounds of weight.

Bubba is a functioning and successful criminal, one of his specialties being arms dealing, but he has a soft, warm spot in his heart for
Patrick and Angie, and he appears on their behalf whenever he is
needed. When he is sent to prison (relatively briefly) he treats it as
a form of summer camp; there is never any thought of his being
abused or exploited there. Lehane presents us with villains of the
vilest variety who enjoy the basest forms of violence, but they all
back off in Bubba's presence.

Superman has his fortress of solitude and Batman has his batcave.
Bubba has a house that is wired throughout with explosives, so that
any intruder who does not know which slabs, steps, and slats are

safe will be transformed into red vapor before he reaches Bubba's inner sanctum. This is a nice touch. It recalls the use of uneven steps in darkened English stairwells where the stumbling of an intruder is a first-alert form of alarm. It also adds tension to any scene occurring in Bubba's home. The only residence in contemporary crime writing with more interesting dimensions is Burke's apartment in the Vachss novels.

John Cawelti argues that the mystery novel arose in the nineteenth century as a middle-class response to the twin threats of mass proletarian movements and the final efforts exerted (often against virginal middle-class women) by the clergy (usually Italian) or the aristocracy in its death throes. In the face of hysteria and numbers on the one hand and arbitrary or inherited authority on the other, the mystery novel offers us as an alternative the detective—the paragon of science and common sense, the objective weaponry that is part of the preserve of the middle class.

However, between the nineteenth century and the late twentieth falls the shadow of Freud and the realization that balanced, common sense is sometimes in short supply, while madness or the capacity for bouts of it is seething just beneath the surface of our lives and our society. The nearly constant warfare that characterized the twentieth century has served to confirm that belief. The likes of a Raymond Alexander, a Hannibal Lecter, or a Bubba Rogowski may not seem particularly angelic, but as they say in the army, there are circumstances in which you need people who are "mission oriented." There are tasks that more rational spirits will hesitate to undertake, and you need those who will undertake them at your side.

It is fair to ask why this figure recurs so frequently in contemporary crime writing. Part of the answer is traceable to the development of the genre. Chandler envisioned a central presence who was less than a superhero in both experience and capacity. This character, who will bruise and bleed, who is often compromised and in search of redemption (another ongoing, quasi-religious theme in this literature), cannot achieve justice alone.

Of course, sometimes there is no justice. Ellroy, for example, does not give us guardian angels, and neither does Charles Willeford. The template for this form of genre fiction calls for either a happy ending or a sad ending that offers a learning experience, where the curricular focus is the fundamental evil inhering in a great deal of human life. When the writer seeks an ending that is happier or at least satisfying in a different way, the guardian angel can deliver the strength and firepower required for such a resolution of events.

This offers us a taste of justice, and we would not seek such justice in our fiction to the degree that we do if we did not believe that it was in increasingly short supply in our daily lives. The presence of these characters may, however, speak to a deeper need.

Justice is promised in the beatitudes to those who hunger and thirst for its sake, but that thirst often goes unslaked in the sublunary world. In T. Jefferson Parker's newest novel, *Red Light*, his heroine, Merci Rayborn (her given name suggesting gratitude for that which she seeks?), finds herself alone at the end of the novel. She has worked the evidence that results in the arrest of her lover, then finds the counterevidence to exonerate him, only to lose him and his trust in the process. Her partner has seen the treatment for his wife's brain tumor lead to paralysis, coma, and eventual death. Her father, who helps her take care of her son (whose father has died in a previous novel), is found to be implicated in the crime whose details ultimately exonerate her current, but soon-to-be-lost, lover. When Merci falls back on prayer she does so realizing, as Parker puts it, that God is not there to answer all of the time. There is no avenging angel available to Merci. She must face the killer alone and take two bullets in justice's name.

This vision is ultimately Manichaean, the Church-labeled heresy with which Augustine flirted for a time. The Manichaeans imagine a dualist universe in which God is not omnipotent, but is rather met with an equal and opposite reaction from the powers of darkness. In *Paradise Lost* Satan is a deluded Manichaean. "He trusted to have equall'd the most High" (book I, line 40). Unfortunately for Satan, Milton's God does not share this theological orientation. Satan's revolt is crushed, and his later attempts to destroy God's creation are redirected.

Satan was unhappy with the terms of the cosmic arrangement and hoped to be able to change it by changing his personal view of it. ("The mind is its own place, and in itself / Can make a Heav'n of Hell, a Hell of Heav'n.") This proves to be ironic casuistry, for Satan will learn that he has in fact made a hell of heaven by disobeying God; thus he will carry hell with him wherever he goes. His Manichaean hopes and strategies of mental control will prove empty. Nevertheless, the promises of Milton's God with regard to his eventual triumphs have not proved to be sufficiently reassuring to contemporary crime writers and, presumably, the members of the enormous audience they have attracted. They return again and again to the problem of evil, since evil is one of their central subjects. If God is good why would he permit evil? If he is omnipotent why would he not prevent it?

Milton's answer is that without freedom of choice humans would be either puppets or automata. Hence our moral stature comes from good choices, and evil is the price we pay for our liberty. That does not, however, satisfactorily address the question of justice. Assuming that some will make bad choices, why are they then permitted to prosper, and why are the good allowed to become their victims? Is the value and importance of what Milton would call Christian liberty sufficient to counter the cataclysmic effects that the choices of those who are evil have on the innocent? The depth and extent of the injustice with which we all must conjure suggests (in narrative practice if not theological fact) that God's powers are limited and that he is unable to listen or act all of the time.

Some writers (Vachss, for example) offer us a vision of a trash-heap world in which the faint degree of justice that is eked out is the result of actions by individuals prepared to meet evil on its own terms and level. Others offer us some measure of hope that the justicers are still above and that an agent acting on their behalf will intervene from time to time.

The absence of justice is not a new issue. Jesus asked, from the cross, why he had been forsaken. It is the prevalence and insistence of the issue now which is so telling, suggesting a near total erosion of our trust in those institutions that have been established to insure justice's presence. Swift worried about the same thing two hundred and fifty years before Raymond Chandler, as he beheld the diminution of the church's authority, the continuance of old exploitative economic systems and the rise of new ones, and the progressive expansion of mass culture. He was particularly taken with the fact that the growing number of lawyers seemed to exacerbate rather than ameliorate the problem, and he was struck by the ease with which the church became complicit in political machinations that either distracted it from its central values or indeed ran counter to them.

He saw luxury displace morality or truth as the summum bonum. He saw academicians vainly turning inward in the face of enormities and atrocities, and he saw the flagrant lie become the principal currency of public discourse. He is not, perhaps, as distant from us as we might sometimes assume.

Together in the Wilderness

Chapter V

Lawrence Block is a highly skilled professional writer who is currently working on two principal crime novel series. The first is a revival of his earlier Burglar books, the Bernie Rhodenbarr stories. Rhodenbarr is a New York bookseller who moonlights as a burglar. In the course of these illicit activities he is drawn into the scenes of other peoples' crimes, which he must solve. The series is light in tone and subject, closer generically to the English mystery. One volume in particular, *The Burglar in the Library,* is a direct spoof of that form.

Block's more hard-boiled series features an investigator named Matt Scudder. Scudder, a reformed alcoholic, spends much of his time looking for churches and A.A. meetings. He tithes at the former, though he does not appear to belong to any particular denomination. In reviewing his personal experience he is vague on the origin of his practice of tithing. It is simply something that he has come to do.

This motif of the church-as-haven that runs through the Scudder novels recalls the medieval practice of the church's providing sanctuary during times of political upheaval and injustice. In these novels, however, religion exists as what the deconstructionists would call a *trace.* There is the memory of meaning, but little more than that. The church exists as an entity from the past whose connections to our experience seem benevolent but remain shadowy. The church as physical and sacramental structure is a doorway on a set of mean streets, offering a positive but still vague alternative to the harsh world in which it is embedded. From time to time Scudder attends the butchers' mass in early-morning Manhattan, and we see him there standing amid men in bloody aprons listening quietly to the sounds of formulaic prayers. The image says it all.

(John Woo is also fond of the use of churches as settings, but his churches are less often loci for redemption or remembrance than places for violence and revenge. His practice recalls Mircea Eliade's concept of the church as symbolic center of the universe, with heaven above and hell below and the reenactment of a sacrifice as the pivotal event.)

Scudder is sometimes involved with lovers, with friends, with bartenders, and even with mobsters, but he enters the urban wilderness essentially alone. He lives in Hell's Kitchen hotels or small apartments and quietly plies his trade. The Scudder novels are relatively free of extreme violence. It is the grayness of his tasks and his world, the destructive lure of omnipresent gin mills, and the faint, former promises held out by churches that one most remembers. It is also a largely enclosed world, with rare trips beyond a single borough, a motif developed with great skill by Jonathan Lethem in his recent novel *Motherless Brooklyn*.

There is an inverse tradition in crime fiction and a much more common one, a tradition in which the protagonist finds himself in an alien, largely enclosed universe—a wilderness—but a wilderness in which he is not alone; instead he is accompanied by a partner, often a partner of color. The multiple associations and permutations with regard to this motif form a deep tradition in American letters, one that transcends genre fiction. It was described many years ago by Leslie Fiedler.

I do not have the space here to look at this motif in all of its richness, but a few Fiedlerian suggestions can be offered. The cultural backdrop of this motif consists of a number of elements. One is the deep resonance and influence of specific cultural artifacts whose effects have been palpable. In terms of literary art, for example, Fiedler would point to the deep impression made on European and American letters by Richardson's novel *Clarissa*, an epistolary narrative whose subject is the tangled set of possible relationships between the sexes and the manner in which they are affected by parental meddling, self-delusion, social climbing, and predatory sexuality. A second novel with a deep impact on our culture, one that examines the relationships between the "races," is Harriet Beecher Stowe's *Uncle Tom's Cabin*. In the first case a man is attempting to understand the experiences of women by writing an extended narrative concerning them; in the second a white woman is trying to understand the experience of black men by constructing a narrative and, in the process, achieving a deeper sense of that experience. (Fiedler refers to Rich-

ardson as a "female impersonator," to Stowe as a "black impersonator.")

The novel, it should be noted, is an extremely "personal" form.
While verse and drama are presented publicly, fictional narrative is
largely experienced in private (though the Victorians often read to
one another in small groups, a practice replicated to some degree by
books on tape). We re-create the voices of novelistic narrators in our
own heads and *possess* the texts in special ways. We carry novels
around with us, reading as time permits. We display them on the ta-
bles beside our beds and consult them in moments of quiet reflection. They thus carry some of the functions once served by such
important and private texts as diaries and commonplace books.

This type of narrative, combined with the deep sense of empathy
that attaches to the form (a point stressed by Samuel Johnson), makes
the novel a powerful moral instrument, one that helps to prepare the
way for social change and sometimes even effect it. Hence, narratives have become generational property (Goethe's *Werther*, for example, or Salinger's *Catcher in the Rye*) and have been said to both
shape and reflect their times.

There are two overarching cultural corollaries here: America's
long struggle with issues of race and its struggle with issues of interpersonal sexual maturation. Both, Fiedler argues, are reflected in
popular cultural artifacts. What is interesting is the manner in which
the two issues interlace, particularly in crime fiction.

Put baldly, Fiedler argues, Americans have had a great deal of difficulty in achieving mature heterosexual relationships. The etiology
of the problem (certainly Puritanism and the configuration of the
American landscape bear some portion of the responsibility) is not
as obvious as its cultural representations. One recurring motif in this
regard is the ongoing attempt by the American husband to escape
the constraints of the household and achieve some greater degree of
individual freedom. Classic examples from Melville, Washington
Irving, Thoreau, and Twain with their retreating male figures come
immediately to mind, but so too do examples from popular culture,
with Jiggs continually attempting to "step out" on Maggie, Wilbur
Post (à la Lemuel Gulliver) escaping the house and hearth for a chat
with his talking horse, Mr. Ed, and Dagwood Bumstead congenital-
ly avoiding work and escaping the job jar of his wife, Blondie, for the

happier prospect of a nap on the couch, a hot bath, or a game of poker in Herb Woodley's garage.

Jane Tompkins has seen the emergence of the western—a form closely related to crime fiction with the romance functioning as a common ancestor—as part of a male attempt to wrest cultural control from the successful hands of post–Civil War women writers. The writers of westerns offered an alternative to the largely religious, pro-temperance view of the world offered by such writers. For the quiet but constraining setting of more civil society the writers of westerns substituted the open spaces of the American landscape. For the privacy of home and hearth they substituted the public spaces of the saloon, jail, and livery stable. For the peace, faith, and mutual support of the pious, married household, they substituted moldering bodies on the open plains. While women are sometimes valued as companions in this ethos, their role is decidedly subsidiary to that of men. These are not stories of brave pioneers. They are stories of male survival in the face of evil and violence.

Just as our cultural artifacts often represent American men following the urge to set out for the wilderness, that is, to leave behind the constraints of civilization and the mundane duties attending it (an opportunity largely denied them in the everyday world), those same artifacts often represent such men joining with men of color in an attempt to understand one another and achieve a degree of brotherhood that seems difficult or even impossible to achieve in daily life.

This tendency does not always end in an idyll of male bonding. More often, it is merged with the notion of the wilderness as threshold symbol, a locus for intense and, to a degree, private experience of the sort associated with romance and Romanticism. In leaving civilization we logically encounter the uncivilized; we may find adventure there, of course, but we may as well find violent death, whether in the recognizable wilderness of Cooper's novels or Faulkner's or in other wild places such as the sea (as in Melville) or its contemporary analogue, "outer" space, "the final frontier."

The correlation with crime fiction comes naturally as the urban "jungle" is conceptualized as disputed, untamed territory. Pathfinders, seamen, and frontiersmen find their contemporary counterparts among the police and private investigators who populate the crime narrative.

The pairing of white men with men of color in the wilderness extends from classic narrative to popular culture. In the nineteenth century we have such famous pairs as Cooper's Leatherstocking and Chingachgook, Twain's Huck Finn and Jim, and Melville's Ishmael and Queequeg. Among the pop culture archetypes there are the Lone Ranger and Tonto and the Green Hornet and Kato. Robert Culp and Bill Cosby (as Kelly Robinson and Alexander Scott) extended the tradition to the world of espionage in *I Spy*, preparing the way for such television icons as Tenspeed and Brownshoe (Ben Vereen and Jeff Goldblum), *Hill Street Blues*'s Bobby Hill and Andy Renko (Michael Warren and Charles Haid), *Miami Vice*'s Sonny Crockett and Ricardo Tubbs (Don Johnson and Philip Michael Thomas), and the preeminent cinematic pair, *Lethal Weapon*'s Martin Riggs and Roger Murtaugh (Mel Gibson and Danny Glover).

In some cases the characters are nearly interchangeable; in some cases they are opposites, often playing against stereotype. Martin Riggs, for example, lives in poverty in a trailer by the beach, mourning his lost wife. He is positioned at the margins of society as well as at the margins of sanity, though the latter is consciously exaggerated. Murtaugh, on the other hand, is the solid, conservative family man, whose home is so suburban and so middle class as to suggest a West Coast branch of the world of John Hughes.

In crime fiction the characters play a multiplicity of roles. Spenser and Hawk are close but not interchangeable. Their verbal sparring often includes racial stereotyping that is clearly designed to undercut the stereotypes by exaggerating them. Some of the characterization is against type. Spenser drinks beer or chichi wine. Lately he and Susan Silverman have been following their yuppie counterparts in exploring the joys of merlot. Hawk drinks champagne, as previously noted. Spenser might offer him a malt liquor as a joke, but Hawk would never drink it. At the same time, Hawk is the dark figure, literally and figuratively, whose past is even more mysterious than Spenser's. Stereotypically, he is very attractive to white women. All of this evaporates in moments of confrontation and violence. In one of the novels Hawk turns to an individual trying to drive a racial wedge between him and Spenser and says, "He isn't white, I'm not black, and you're not human."

In the Dave Robicheaux novels of James Lee Burke, Dave operates a fishing camp in the bayous of New Iberia. He employs a black man by the name of Batist. Batist is as vulnerable as Dave, but he holds up his end in violent moments. Since Dave's work in law enforcement takes him away from the camp, often as far as New Orleans and Baton Rouge, Batist maintains the camp in Dave's absence.

The portrayal is quite conservative. Unlike Hawk, Batist does not play the avenging angel. He is more an employee than a partner. Though not invisible, as a servant might be, he seldom comes center stage in the narratives. He is there, however, minding the shop and providing a certain degree of continuity in Dave's life. Though generally calm and measured, Dave—like most of Burke's protagonists—is extremely violent in those moments when control is lost. Batist counsels prudence and serves as a form of conscience, like an intervening god in classical epic, grasping a hero's arm in a moment of rash action. As such, his portrayal is somewhat Faulknerian, a black figure holding society together, though he may not be sufficiently rewarded or appreciated for his actions. A further, cognate example would be Woody Strode's character, Pompey, in *The Man Who Shot Liberty Valance.*

Batist's relationship to Dave says more about Dave than about Burke's racial views. An immensely private person with a difficult past, Dave treats Batist with affection and respect. He simply collapses into himself from time to time, and all of his personal relationships, save those with his wife and daughter, are strained and tenuous.

A somewhat similar relationship exists between Clinton Tyree ("Skink") and Jim Tile in the Carl Hiaasen novels. Tile is a police officer who worked as Tyree's bodyguard when Tyree served as governor. He continues in a similar role, but in a psychological capacity, after Tyree leaves office and heads for the trees. Tile attempts to be a counter to Tyree's impetuous and violent inclinations. He counsels reflection and moderation. His goal is to protect Tyree from himself and from jail or worse. His is a steady hand, like Batist's, Pompey's, or Roger Murtaugh's, and while Tyree is a largely comic figure he is still a dangerous one, a man who lives on the borders and in the twilight.

One is reminded of the role played by Sergeant Al Powell (Reginald VelJohnson) in John McTiernan's *Die Hard,* calming and guiding John McClane (Bruce Willis) as he takes on the terrorists / thieves within the skyscraper. Al Powell is cool and sage, and though he can wield a gun in McClane's defense, and does so, his more natural instrument is his voice, one that reassures the far more impulsive McClane.

The function is replicated in the *Mission Impossible* films with Ving Rhames playing Luther Stickell to Tom Cruise's Ethan Hunt. The immensely versatile Rhames, who could play a highly physical role, is here cast as a computer wizard who controls the operation—a voice in the darkness, counting seconds and giving directions. The only bow to stereotype is Luther's concern for his dress. In the John Woo sequel (2000) we first encounter Luther stepping out of a helicopter and into a pile of sheep manure, soiling his Guccis. Later, when his Versace shirt is torn by gunfire, his blood pressure rises and he returns fire aggressively.

The similarities in these portrayals are striking, but the portrayals themselves are not nearly as interesting as those in the top crime drama of the 1990s—Barry Levinson's *Homicide: Life on the Streets,* which, though primarily a television series, was based on a true crime book by David Simon.

There are two principal black/white pairs in the series: Meldrick Lewis (Clark Johnson) and Steve Crosetti (Jon Polito) and Tim Bayliss (Kyle Secor) and Frank Pembleton (André Braugher). Meldrick is one of the few characters who continued for all seven years of the series. Light-skinned, he is sensitive to the suffering of the African American community from which he himself came, but simultaneously suspicious of cant and posturing, no matter what its source might be. Uneasy and even innocent in his relationships with women, his most enduring relationship has been with his partner.

Crosetti, an eventual, unexplained suicide, haunts Meldrick's memory and imagination. In life their relationship was one of opposites exerting a powerful attraction. Meldrick is relatively quiet and detached, Crosetti loquacious. A recurring touch is Crosetti's fixation on the assassination of Abraham Lincoln. The actions of the conspirators is his single and constant subject of conversation, one that reaches its apogee in an episode that takes the two to Washington and permits them time for a memorable trip to Ford's Theatre.

Tim Bayliss, still the unit rookie after years of service, is highly skilled but deeply wounded. Uncertain in his sexuality, he is also haunted in his work, fixating on the unsolved murder of a young black woman, Edina Watson. Frank Pembleton is actually Francis

Xavier Pembleton, educated (very effectively) by the Jesuits. Frank is the most able of the homicide detectives, but his marriage is troubled; his spirituality varies between the conflicted and the absent, and his relationship with Bayliss is consistently uneasy.

A loner, Pembleton resists partnering, particularly with a rookie. The uncertainties of his relationship with Bayliss result in endless discussions, ranging from the mundane to the metaphysical, discussions that serve to underline both the nature of the occupation (homicide detectives are the least physical and most intellectual in the department) and the essential humanity of the partners.

These two relationships would be enough for any series, but the pièce de résistance is the delineation of the watch commander, Lieutenant Al Giardello. Played by Yaphet Kotto, the lieutenant is half Italian, half African American, and each part of his heritage plays out simultaneously with the other. In one signature episode the final dissolve finds Giardello sitting on a stoop on the border of the black and Italian communities, looking longingly at each and bridging what for him is an artificial divide.

Kotto's physical presence complicates and deepens the portrayal. Dark-skinned with broad features, Kotto is more easily imagined as Kananga / Mr. Big in Guy Hamilton's *Live and Let Die* (1973), his most prominent role before that of Giardello. His series son Mike (Giancarlo Esposito) has the kind of racially diverse physical presence associated with but not physically embodied by his father. Giardello must convey his African American and Italian sides through word and gesture, and he must do it to the degree that his features begin to disappear and his personality and deepest humanity come to the surface.

We are to see him, in short, as he is and not as he appears, and each time he struggles with his appearance (for example, in first encounters with women) the poignancy is clear. This is the whole point, of course. In his very being, Giardello brings together the usual dyad of the black and white partners, demonstrates their indissolubility in the face of physical appearance, and drives home all of the lessons one might wish to see inculcated. He is fundamentally good. He is fundamentally tolerant. He is fundamentally without irrational prejudice, but he has no illusions about human behavior and no illusions about the need for justice in a fallen world.

Simultaneously, his superiors within the department (both black and white) are sleazy time servers and sell-out politicians while the villains Giardello strives to bring to justice can as easily be white racists or black criminals. This clear-eyed view of the department-as-institution is a bow to Chandler, and the clear-eyed rendition of equal-opportunity criminality is a bow to realism, a realism that blends so sweetly and delicately with the stories' idealism. In another bow to Chandler, that idealism centers on personal, human relationships rather than on institutional ones. It is an idealism that shatters stereotypes at the same time that the stories' realism reinforces the existence of behaviors and phenomena that can undergird such stereotyping.

This is truly excellent work, pushing the current boundary of human perception with no sacrifice of authenticity or plausibility in the rendering of the violent ethos in which the human relationships are embedded. Few narratives approach the level of quality that one comes to expect in this series.

The depiction of the partners in the wilderness, one white, one of color, is now so common in our cultural narratives that we are likely to underestimate its effects. We are so accustomed to this representation that it has become a part of our cultural landscape and, as in the case of the physical landscape, is taken for granted by those who inhabit it daily. Its importance and uniqueness is brought home to us by foreign travelers.

In addition to DisneyWorld and Las Vegas, one of the favorite sites visited by British tourists is Monument Valley. The impact of the American western on the British sense of this country (as with the Japanese sense of it) is enormous, and the stories and figures we have often come to take for granted continue to exert a powerful influence on cultures other than our own.

When the Moody Blues received a platinum disc for their record *On the Threshold of a Dream* they were asked who they would like to have present their award to them. One might have expected them to request a noteworthy musician or representative of the recording industry. On the contrary, speaking for the group, the bassist, John Lodge, selected a somewhat unlikely individual who had had a profound influence on his personal life: Jay Silverheels.

Lodge has posted a remembrance of the event and, more particularly, of the person on his new website. He speaks about the discovery of Jay Silverheels (actually Harold J. Smith of Ontario, Canada) by the comedian Joe E. Brown and his early work as a stuntman. He describes his role in *Key Largo* and his multiple portrayals of Geronimo (1950, 1952, 1956), as well as other performances. He focuses on the Lone Ranger series, on the alleviation of stereotypes, the convergence of cultures, and the skill, goodness, loyalty, and integrity of the character Tonto. He recounts discussions of the band's hopes to put some of Jay Silverheels's quite expert poetry to music. The impact of their meeting thirty years ago is still extremely strong. It is not an exaggeration to say that Jay Silverheels's work as an actor helped to change John Lodge's view of Native Americans, his view of human culture, and his view of American society. The event was of sufficient importance to, finally, change his very life.

Jay Silverheels and Clayton Moore changed all of our lives, of course, but once our lives have been changed we tend to forget the attitudes that preceded our present ones. Crime writers can be credited with a pivotal role in this set of processes. In terms of literary theory, their practice has combined traditional method with contemporary material.

Crime writing has traditionally dealt with issues of contemporary importance. From floating gambling vessels in Santa Monica Bay to internet crime, the writer explains and describes issues of current interest. One could reconstruct a history of contemporary social and legal concerns from the books of crime writers, with, for example, Robert Crais writing of Los Angeles gangs, Robert Parker of illegal, exploited immigrants, Andrew Vachss of networked pedophiles, and Carl Hiaasen of environmental terrorism. Parker has his Hollywood book, his Washington book, his horse country book, and so on, as he moves about like a practicing journalist.

The underlying notion is that we want to learn about events and phenomena, but we want to do so through the reading of fiction rather than the reading of less engaging nonfiction. Tom Clancy is the leading practitioner of the "techno-thriller," a specialized form of crime/espionage writing that embodies the material of field manuals and blueprints in suspenseful narratives. It is, of course, a short step from Clancy's thrillers to actual manuals or nonfiction narratives, both of which he has produced. A nice hybrid would be a book such as Martin Cruz Smith's *Polar Star*, which features a Russian detective working on the "slime line" of a Russian fishing vessel in the Bering Sea.

This form of writing, expected both to entertain and to instruct, falls directly in line with what Meyer Abrams terms the "pragmatic" tradition of criticism that dominated the west from antiquity until the end of the eighteenth century and continues today in much popular writing. Horace, Philip Sidney, Johnson, and critics of their ilk speak of the writer's responsibility to both teach and please. The genre writer specializing in crime enjoys the ability to draw on the strengths of history, philosophy, journalism, and biography in the construction of literary narratives that inform the audience at the same time that they engage it in ways that manage to both satisfy and surprise.

With regard to questions of race and color the messages conveyed have been both radical and conservative. It can be argued—with Leslie Fiedler, for example—that we have been able to get along in our fictions much more effectively than in our everyday lives. Crime writing projects a vision of America that counters prejudice, sees the individual qua individual, and celebrates mutual help and mutual respect. As such, it has prepared us for a change of attitudes in our personal lives and an actual change in our behavior. Having seen, understood, and finally accepted the notion of equality and brotherhood in thousands of stories, books, television shows, and films, we are prepared for concrete changes in "real" life. This is particularly true for the novel, with its focus on character, its capacity for instilling a sense of empathy, and the fact that it is consumed in such a private, personal fashion. Once we have come to know individuals this deeply, the prejudices that we may have had are undermined and attenuated.

This putatively radical or at least progressive vision can also be seen as a conservative one. The identity politics of the 1990s, for example, struggles to see people as members of groups rather than as individuals. Identity politics focuses on the experiences of groups qua groups and seeks to celebrate differences over commonalities.

This is, of course, a very complex issue, for there are identifiable differences between groups. African Americans have more problems with high blood pressure, for example, than Irish Americans, and women can hear across a broader range of the sound spectrum than can men. At the same time, as Russell Jacoby has demonstrated at length, our society is far less "diverse" than it was at the turn of the century. Then the first-generation immigrant population represented a higher proportion of the whole than it does today. There were a multiplicity of foreign-language dailies published in the cities and far less intermarriage.

If California is the harbinger of the future, what one finds there is a succession of cultural exchanges that results in children with a blend of European, Asian, Latino, and African ancestry, children with names like Jennifer Wang or Sean Nakamora, who opt for black music, Italian food, and German cars—individuals who have "ethnic" names, yet whose speech is free of any hint of dialectical variation.

One of the internet reviewers of Marcel Montecino's *The Crosskiller* asks the question, "Whoever heard of a Jewish cop, in love with a black woman and hooked on Jazz?" The answer is, nearly anyone who reads a great deal of crime fiction. Jack Gold, the protagonist of the novel, also has a Latino partner who aspires to be an actor and who has to take time away from his job to meet Hollywood casting calls.

Thus, the form that has done so much to shatter stereotypes and represent the full and common humanity of individuals who are putatively different can also be seen as conservative by those seeking to perpetuate a perception of difference and of separateness. Some of this is consciously political, like the efforts to urge individuals of complex parentage to select a single racial designation on their census forms in order to achieve greater clout for a single group. Some is well-meaning and seeks to resist the loss of group experience that has been culturally consequential or to save individual voices from being lost in a homogenized popular culture.

Those whose job it is to sift evidence and root out lies and cant— the protagonists of crime narratives—are the creations of writers whose own perspectives are likely to be skeptical and realistic, with balanced measures of cynicism and idealism. Cutting through political spin and ideological posturing is their stock-in-trade. They are far more likely to judge individuals on the content of their character than on the nature of their pedigree and will celebrate that character as quickly as they will deflate pretense and pomposity. They are accustomed to finding high crimes among the upper reaches of society and to being lied to by representatives of large institutions and groups. Hence they are often apolitical, at least in their writings. They have something of the detachment of Joyce's God along with the skepticism of an eighteenth-century philosophe and the tenacity of the passionate investigator. They have little patience with lies and stupidity and realize that the truth is always in short supply. As such they bring a perspective to contemporary life that is both sorely needed and consistently appreciated.

A friend of mine commented once that the best commencement speakers are writers, since they are one of the few groups that are likely to actually speak the truth. This is true, but genre writers are less likely to be invited to such occasions than their more mainstream sisters and brothers, for they are even more likely to offer advice that might shock the pious or upset the pretentious. At one recent ceremony, held by a confident university, the genre writer / speaker invited the graduates to think through a mental list of all of those who had predicted earlier that they would fail and promptly call them, directing each of them to go to hell. One is not likely to see that engraved on a bronze tablet or reprinted in the university's alumni magazine, but it is nice to know that someone has articulated what many have thought but were too cautious to say.

It is not surprising that the political thrust of crime fiction in the area under current discussion remains in dispute. For the lunatic right, crime narratives focus excessively on interpersonal, interracial relationships and are too political; for the lunatic left, crime narratives offer a scenario that is excessively optimistic and too apolitical. The former have difficulty recognizing our common humanity; the latter have difficulty recognizing our essential individuality. Such writers often find themselves in the position of Mark Twain: the lunatic right finds Huck's friend Jim too sympathetic; the lunatic left cannot bear the appearance of the n word. Thus, both are prepared to censure and / or censor. The general acceptance of crime narratives, however, and more particularly of the motif of the brotherhood of the wilderness suggests that the attitudes embodied in such narratives are close enough to the heart of common opinion (or common desire) as to suggest that the authors of such narratives speak for the broad and sensible center of our society.

I once knew a student who prepared a master's thesis on the acculturation of dentists. She expected to discover that men would take one route, women another, and that they would end up with very different perspectives on their profession and very different approaches to its day-to-day practice. What she found instead was that the vast majority of the students pretty much ended up as dentists.

The army and the various police forces are fond of denying the existence of black and white in their ranks. There is only one color in their organization, they say: green (or blue). This can sometimes be a public relations piety, but it is also true that professions that involve cooperation in the face of mutual threat often strip away the incidental and focus on the essential. Graham Greene was not the first to describe life as a battlefield. To the extent that Greene's metaphor is apt, those who construct and those who populate crime fiction may come closest to delineating and embodying life's central issues and promulgating its central truths. In the case of interracial relationships they have certainly not hesitated to attempt to do so.

The Electric Mist

Classic discussions of the novel have tended to focus on character and plot and their interrelations while devoting significantly less attention to the third narrative leg: setting. In genre fiction, however, setting has always played a prominent role and been expected to do so by its readers. Science fiction, for example, which finds its roots in pastoral, is—like pastoral—often built upon the contrast between two societies. Where pastoral generally begins with the contrasts between the urban and the rural, science fiction often begins with the contrast between past and present, present and future, terrestrial and extraterrestrial, or developed and deserted. Crime fiction, like the western—which also finds its roots in romance—tends to focus on frontiers and borders, the dividing lines (and their threshold symbols) between good and evil, law and lawlessness, sanity and insanity, peace and violence, civility and barbarity.

Ecologists sometimes note that the greatest areas for environmental activity are those that adjoin natural frontiers and borders; it is certainly true that these dividing lines are often crucial determinants of character and plot in crime fiction. It is more than coincidental that the period in which genre writing began to develop and flower (the eighteenth century, with half-century shoulders in the seventeenth and nineteenth) was one in which violent, attritional warfare, shameless, colonial exploitation, and grisly blood sports stood side by side with such masterpieces of material culture as Palladian public and domestic architecture, Gibbons and Adam decorative pieces, "Capability" Brown's landscape architecture, Reynolds's portraiture, Wedgwood's pottery, and the furniture of Chippendale, Hepplewhite, and Sheraton. This period of debtors' prisons and highwaymen, of the gin madness and floating brothels on the Thames, coexisted with such aesthetic masterworks as the poetry of

Dryden, Pope, and Keats and the music of Bach, Haydn, Mozart, and Beethoven.

The image of unwashed bodies in handmade finery or the use of fine-tooled, ivory-handled "scratchers" to discourage body vermin make the point reinforced by crime fiction, namely that humans are to be located somewhere between angels and animals, with the Fall and its aftermath (according to the hierarchical notions attaching to the "great chain of being") pushing us ever farther south. The notion is reinforced very nicely in the recent Jake Scott film, *Plunkett & Macleane* (1999), an eighteenth-century period piece featuring two highwaymen, one of whom is an aristocrat. The line between an aristocracy based on rank and one based on ability is continually traced, with the ongoing lesson that, regardless of either rank or ability, one can still end up in prison among the lowest members of society.

In crime and mystery fiction, setting has played a foundational role in the formulation of the genres, with Chandler's West Coast contrasting with the English settings of the traditional mystery—far, far to the east. Chandler's purposes tilted toward realism; he is, in good measure, attempting to capture a sense of southern California *as it was*. He saw a great deal of it, of course, since he moved almost constantly, but he saw it as well through the perspective of a prosperous (for a time) oil executive and a struggling (for a time) writer, an individual born in what Carl Sandburg called the city of the big shoulders, but educated in an English public school. He knew what he was trying to do as a writer, and he knew the very real distinctions between the tradition he saw exemplified by Hammett—his tradition—and the quite different tradition exemplified by Agatha Christie.

The English mystery, which finds its inspirations in comedy rather than romance, is, interestingly, far more fanciful than it is realistic with regard to setting. Idealization replaces realism, civility triumphs over brutality, and order succeeds as the chaos represented by violence is discovered, rooted out, and expelled.

Of course, not all hard-boiled fiction is set in Los Angeles; nor are all English mysteries set in the Cotswolds, and modern conditions have had an impact on literary traditions, both reinforcing and sometimes redirecting them. Los Angeles is a major media market, and sales-conscious writers and publishers understand that narratives set in such locations have a greater chance of success than those that are not. The same is of course true of New York. The East was the original site of the film industry, and it is still the source of much of the film industry's funding. Studios and publishing houses are parts of common corporate families, all searching for top scripts. Thus, crime fiction is often set in a specific locale for commercial as well as aesthetic reasons, and large population centers enjoy the advantage of a large citizenry and, hence, potential audience. Readers, including readers for studios and publishers, like to read about their own towns. When an area of the country or the world is suddenly of cultural interest—Seattle for its coffee and computer industry, Bangkok for its sex/tourist trade, for example—crime writers may exploit the journalistic dimensions of their craft and set their books there. Moreover, the cost of travel has plummeted since Chandler's time and the personal familiarity of readers with individual sites and settings has increased markedly. We have second or third cultural homes as a result, and readers can read about where they are as well as where they would like to be, having personally experienced multiple locales.

English mysteries have long transported individuals to fantasy sites. Murder is far more likely to occur on the Nile or the Orient Express than in a more mundane location. Prior to the twentieth century many travel books contained significant fictional content. Since distant sites were rarely visited, authors could pitch their narratives to the fantasy lives of their readers, a practice often extended by genre fiction, particularly the mystery and the romance. That has changed somewhat with the onset of discounted air travel and the multiplicity of modestly priced hotel chains. Now, some of the fantasies, or at least the exotica, can continue, but be further enriched by direct experience. The Cotswolds remain charming and, at times, slightly unreal, but real readers have driven real cars and eaten real meals there. Stately homes above the tors of Cornwall can be visited in person as well as in the pages of a romance novel. What has been lost on the fantasy side has been gained on the personal, experiential side.

It is no accident, for example, that New Orleans is a popular setting for crime fiction since so many visit it for conventions and association meetings. It is now familiar to many, and as a result its visitors want to read about it. At the same time, the city consciously utilizes the PG- and R-rated venues of the Vieux Carré to project an aura of edginess, the promise of experience beyond the quotidian and ordinary. Harry Berger has argued that we seek both stimulation and reassurance in literary experience and that we find them particularly in genre fiction. The New Orleans setting meets those needs perfectly, with endless servings of comfort food in restaurants surrounded by dark alleys, odd smells, and strange people. *Easy* is a word that cuts in multiple directions.

New Orleans is, quintessentially, a city of frontiers and borders, with lines drawn between old and new, American and French, Creole and Cajun. Its legal system is unique in America, and the area is divided by parish rather than county. It is bisected by a great river, separating the "safer" New Orleans from the more ominous districts of Algiers and Gretna, the original Gretna Green being the Scottish border setting to which overheated young English couples or duplicitous fortune seekers eloped.

As readers develop greater knowledge of individual locales, and as they consume larger and larger amounts of fiction written by individuals with a passion for technical accuracy (and sometimes the research assistants to help them achieve it), they develop an expectation for such accuracy and are often pleased to be able to personally confirm it or dispute it. Hence, the authenticity of the portrayal of the setting and the attention to that setting's many details have become as important as the details of the techniques of murder or the details of investigative procedures. In short, crime writing has often merged with regional and travel writing to great mutual advantage, John Berendt's *Midnight in the Garden of Good and Evil* being perhaps the most successful example. Savannah is a tourist mecca, a very real and unique city, but also a city that plays to our fantasy lives. It is, after all, the hometown of Rhett Butler.

Writers have sometimes responded to this phenomenon in somewhat surprising and unexpected ways. Chandler, for example, whose work is so deeply associated with Los Angeles and environs, fictionalized his settings, writing of "Bay City," "Idle Valley," "Poodle Springs," and other locations. The same is true of Ed McBain (Evan Hunter). The master of police procedural writing (as well as ensemble writing) in his 87th Precinct series, McBain writes of a fictional city named Isola, not a real city named New York.

This provides a certain degree of leverage. All readers know that Chandler is writing of Los Angeles and McBain of New York, but the authors are free to add "inaccurate" details about their respective cities without being criticized for them. In some ways they are writing about literary space rather than geographic space. Most urban areas contain some common elements, so that the space being portrayed is largely generic. That is why urban films with putative U.S. settings can now regularly be shot in Toronto and why video games create setting through generic visual cues rather than through the use of what cineasts term "establishing shots" (narrow alleys and tipped garbage cans versus the top of the Chrysler building or the tower of the Embarcadero). *Hill Street Blues,* for example, is set in a fictional city that looks a bit like Philadelphia, a bit like Chicago, and a bit like New York. *NYPD Blue,* on the other hand, like *L.A. Law,* is more specifically located. The characters in *L.A. Law* could rally at Musso & Frank's for drinks and dinner, thus capitalizing on local color, tradition, and association.

The downside of a specific setting in time and place lies in the fact that it now raises high expectations of authenticity. The upper west side on *Seinfeld,* for example, is continually bathed in bright California sunlight. The streets are movie-set tidy, and key elements are somehow missing. One notices, for example, the very real differences between the *Seinfeld* streets and the forms of signage that one finds on the actual upper west side. (Makers of historical films now employ a gallery of historians, advisers, and consultants to insure period accuracy. The sight of a single vaccination scar on a gladiator, one industry insider recently remarked, can distract the audience for as long as twenty minutes.)

There is a sense in which *setting* is portable if *ethos* is sustained. For example, Chandler sees the sprawling urban setting of Los Angeles as one dominated by certain levels of institutional corruption. However, it is one of the mainstay plot strategies of both the western and the crime narrative to take the protagonist to a small, rural location in which the local authority is corrupt. The protagonist, as emissary of truth and justice, quickly finds that the "whole town" is against him and that he will have to work outside institutional channels if he is to be successful. If one looks at the arc of James Ellroy's writing career one finds that Ellroy is generalizing his setting, moving from Los Angeles to the entire United States, finding ever greater layers of evil and corruption as the canvas is expanded.

The nation's capital is, in short, bigger game. Since "Washington" is often understood to suggest, by metonymy, the country, it is a far better setting for crime, espionage, and thriller writing than for less violent regional writing, despite, for example, the truly unique ecological dimensions of the Chesapeake. By the same token, its metonymic associations with comic corruption have resulted in films like *D.C. Cab* (directed by Joel Schumacher, 1983).

Some novelists choose interesting settings but fail to exploit them fully. In 1999, for example, there was a great flood of hype over a debut novel by Mo Hayder entitled *Birdman*. London bookshops offered refunds to readers who did not find this serial killer novel about an individual who implants live birds in the chests of his (female) victims to be the equal of the works of Thomas Harris. *Birdman* is set in Greenwich, and while there is some development of the contrast between the gritty reality of the birdman's crimes and the blue-sky talk of the nearby Millennium Dome, the Greenwich location is never fully utilized.

Blackheath Common, for example, which figures briefly in the narrative, is replete with ghosts as the great historical site for the final organization of invasionary forces before their descent upon London. It was also the site, for example, of the organization of Wat Tyler's "peasant" rebels in the late fourteenth century before they moved on to the city proper. These associations run very deep, as do the Tudor associations with Greenwich, which include Henry VIII's palace there, Placentia. The *Gypsy Moth* is there, and the *Cutty Sark*, along with the architectural monuments to British naval history and the formerly active site of the Observatory. While contemporary families picnic on the celebratory lawns below, Blackheath looms above them, a dark and brooding fixture surrounded by highways with heavy and fast lorry traffic.

Looking across the Thames to the north the Greenwich visitor sees Canary Wharf, a living boom/bust/boom economic symbol, a site in which a crime/finance novelist like Paul Erdman or a social melodrama writer like Arthur Hailey would find delight. Looking toward the city there are great contrasts and associations: million-pound flats, Wapping Dock where pirates and mutineers were executed, Limehouse, and the haunts of the Ripper. There is tremendous cultural resonance here. Those who were in London in 1988 can testify that the anniversary of the Ripper (1888) dwarfed the impact of the anniversary of an event as important as the Glorious Revolution (1688), though the defeat of the Armada (1588)—commemorated at Greenwich—did come in a close second.

Very little is done with these elements in *Birdman;* a mystery writer would build an entire plot around one or more of them and would likely include the site in the title ("Millennium Doom"). There is also a scene in the novel on Tooley Street, by London Bridge, which is not fully exploited. Tooley Street is the site of the "London Dungeon," a gross-out commercial museum illustrating historical, British methods of torture and execution. The London reader might mentally connect all of these dots without formal prompting, but many foreign readers would not. For contrast, one might look at Harris's depiction of the dirty backwaters of the Licking River in *The Silence of the Lambs* or the more operatic treatment of Florence in *Hannibal* for a sense of the state of the art.

The master of setting in contemporary crime fiction is James Lee Burke. Jonathan Kellerman has called him the Faulkner of crime writing. Now one of the most successful crime writers in America, Burke began as a mainstream novelist and short story writer. In the course of his writing career he has focused on the landscape he knows best, that of Texas, Montana, and Louisiana, but he has made forays into other regions—for example, into Appalachia and southern Ohio for his novel *To the Bright and Shining Sun.*

Burke characteristically provides an exhaustive sense of the sights, sounds, and especially the smells of his subject's setting, with due attention to flora, fauna, and local foods. The following is the opening paragraph of his *In the Electric Mist with Confederate Dead* (1993):

> The sky had gone black at sunset, and the storm had churned inland from the Gulf and drenched New Iberia and littered East Main with leaves and tree branches from the long canopy of oaks that covered the street from the old brick post office to the drawbridge over Bayou Teche at the edge of town. The air was cool now, laced with light rain, heavy with the fecund smell of wet humus, night-blooming jasmine, roses, and new bamboo. I was about to stop my truck at Del's and pick up three crawfish dinners to go when a lavender Cadillac fishtailed out of a side street, caromed off a curb, bounced a hubcap up on a sidewalk, and left long serpentine lines of tire prints through the glazed pools of yellow light from the street lamps.

The damp, heavy atmosphere that is suddenly churned by a storm is a fair characterization of police officer Dave Robicheaux, the principal protagonist of one of Burke's series. Robicheaux is a slow moving and pensive man, capable of exploding in a rush of violence when the right stimulus is applied. If T. S. Eliot was right in suggesting that literature include some "objective correlative" for mental states (the distracted Lear standing on the heath in a storm, for example), Burke has learned the lesson well.

Readers homesick for Louisiana, Texas, or Montana can always get a quick fix through Burke's writing. In addition to his acute sensory perception of the land that he describes there is a parallel valuation of the land as a human good. The protection of the land and, by extension, the human and / or family history it embodies is one of Burke's favorite themes. In his mainstream masterpiece, *The Lost Get-Back Boogie*, Burke studies the experience of Iry Paret, an unjustly convicted individual who, when released from prison, moves from Louisiana to Montana in search of a life and a place. Forced to give up his share of his father's land in Louisiana, he finds the otherwise stunning landscape of Montana poisoned by smokestacks and corporate greed. The residents are too dependent on the local industry to oppose it, though Iry does, at a considerable price. The novel ends in a form of quietism, and Iry gains, as moral compensation, a small spread of land upon which he can begin to rebuild a life.

The novel echoes the signature speech of Joshua Chamberlain in Michael Shaara's novel of Gettysburg, *The Killer Angels*. Forced to take on mutineers from another Maine regiment, Chamberlain attempts to exhort his new troops by explaining to them why his unit is fighting. Chamberlain implicitly describes the often arbitrary, even absurd nature of human battle. A site is selected for defense and blood is spilled. The site is sought by one side, held by the other. The site itself is often irrelevant. What is relevant is the purpose of the battle. There is always more land, as Chamberlain notes. The fight is for human freedom and dignity, not an elevated, elongated strip of earth. The land offers an opportunity and an occasion. It offers a *setting* for a conflict that we desperately wish to see as moral. It is the stage on which the action proceeds, and we are positioned upon it, like Everyman in the medieval morality play, in the presence of God and in the presence of Death.

Burke is currently writing two series, one set in Texas featuring a former Texas Ranger and local attorney named Billy Bob Holland, the other set in New Iberia (and often New Orleans) featuring Robicheaux. The settings change (though the levels of description and the creation of rich atmospherics are constants), but the characters are often similar. The Burke hero, both in his crime fiction and in his mainstream narratives, is a decent, quiet individual with the capacity for sudden violence in the face of injustice or personal threat. He is tied to an uncompromising land that he nonetheless loves, and he devotes himself, in situ, to the cause of decency and justice.

Such simple but high-minded ideals come very close to melodramatic or formulaic pieties. They are possible only within a narrative that is both morally compelling and highly textured. In order to make you feel, Burke first makes you see and taste, touch, hear, and smell. The description serves to reify and reinforce the themes by situating them in a setting that is fully authentic because it is fully realized. Where science fiction writers create a world with new elements and a new taxonomy, all of which can correspond to items and issues in our more familiar world, the crime writer takes his reader into a world that is already there but not yet fully felt and perceived. In making that world more completely real, he makes the lessons learned there fresh and compelling.

The mainstream analogue to Burke's technique is that of Charles Frazier in his extremely successful first novel, *Cold Mountain*. Frazier's themes are commonplace, principally a farewell to arms and the longing for home. The narrative embeds these themes in a multilayered, heavily textured depiction of geography, flora, fauna, and, principally, the nature of hunger and the need for such essential edibles as grease. Although the plotline is thin, the novel is rich and the narrative compelling enough to survive the quite predictable but still jarring ending.

In *In the Electric Mist with Confederate Dead* James Lee Burke pushes his technique to the limit. In the course of the narrative Dave is drugged and starts having visions, encountering the Confederate general John Bell Hood in the mist of the bayou. If one set out to meet a Confederate general, one could do far worse than the romantic Hood, who lost the use of one of his arms as a result of the battle for Little Round Top, but Burke is here in the realm of magic realism, a commonplace in contemporary fiction, but not in contemporary crime fiction with its greater expectations of nonmagical realism. He is, perhaps, more comfortable with more conventional but no less interesting forms of description, such as his depiction of the lot of convicts at Louisiana's notorious Angola prison, where, as he describes in the opening paragraph of *The Lost Get-Back Boogie*, "our Clorox-faded, green-and-white-pinstripe trousers were stained at the knees with sweat and the sandy dirt from the river bottom, and the insects that boiled out of the grass stuck to our skin and burrowed into the wet creases of our necks."

It is sometimes said that good writing involves the skillful use of common words. Many have described the blood-streaked remains of freshly slapped insects lodged in the creases of sweaty necks, but few imagine them as having *boiled* out of the surrounding grass. Angola is legendary prison ground, and many have described it, but few have done so with such economy and point as Burke. In a single, brief chapter he portrays it more richly than, for example, the sum of the images of Angola in Oliver Stone's *JFK* (1991). Indeed, for all their considerable strengths, Burke gives us a more intense and precisely felt sense of prison life in a single chapter than we receive in the two great prison novels of our time, Mitchell Smith's *Stone City* (1990) and Tim Willocks's *Green River Rising* (1994).

It is always tempting, though seldom accurate, to argue that a writer's newest work is his best, but that is the growing consensus with regard to Burke's second most recent project. *Purple Cane Road*, his last-released Dave Robicheaux novel (2000), more than exceeds expectations and indeed takes readers and writers to an entirely new level. Michael Connelly's jacket blurb says as much, and his statement is no exaggeration. In *Purple Cane Road* Dave Robicheaux is thrown into the past by rumors of his mother's alleged career in prostitution and her murder at the hands of dirty LOPD cops. His uneasy relationship with her has already been anticipated in earlier books. Dave must reach back into his own as well as his parish's history to both solve the case and clear his own psyche. As such, this is Burke's fictional echo of James Ellroy's search for his mother's killer and for the lineaments of his own past in *My Dark Places*. Both books also draw heavily on the history of the settings in which the respective murders occurred.

In some ways, the novel is extremely conventional. Burke plays the familiar gender variation on the buddy-in-the-wilderness theme by pairing Dave with a woman detective, Helen Soileau. Clete Purcel, Dave's drunken but always dangerous friend, plays the wounded avenging angel who serves as both asset and liability. There is an out-of-town psychopath who tries to develop a relationship with Dave and his daughter, thus further personalizing a succession of public crimes; a scheduled execution that functions as a ticking clock beneath the narrative surface; corruption at the highest levels of government and law enforcement; and an undercurrent of racial strife, exploitation, and misunderstanding. There are even instances of child sexual abuse and, of course, the maximizing of setting. In this case we visit Baton Rouge, New Orleans, the bayous of New Iberia, and key points between.

While conventional on its face, the novel is executed with a skill and craft that are nearly heartbreaking in their effects. The signature descriptions of landscape and atmosphere are all there in heightened form, but they are also frequently coupled with descriptions of behavior and psychology (Johnson's "nature") that are unparalleled, many involving extensions of descriptions of physical nature (Eliot's "objective correlative"). Think of a writer coming into his maturity and achieving as yet unattained levels of craft. Then think of a writer who is already at his maturity, pausing a moment, and then taking all that he is capable of to a wholly new level. *Purple Cane Road* sets a standard for the establishment of setting against which other crime novels will now be measured.

Tim Willocks, the above-mentioned crime novelist, is, interestingly, an English writer working with American settings. His newest novel, *Bloodstained Kings* (1998), is set in Louisiana and Georgia, while his prison novel, *Green River Rising*, is set in Texas. (His debut novel, *Bad City Blues* [1991]—available only in the United Kingdom—is set in New Orleans.) When London physician/psychiatrists like Willocks write regional crime fiction set in America it is clear that the delineation of setting is seen as an epistemological enterprise, a way of understanding as well as a way of telling. Our own most accomplished regional novelist—though one with a worldwide readership—is perhaps Carl Hiaasen.

Hiaasen, a reporter for the *Miami Herald*, is one of the bestselling triumvirs of crime writing who built their craft upon a journalistic foundation, the other two being Thomas Harris and Michael Connelly. Journalism has long been linked with the novel, the very title of the genre suggesting something new, interesting, and strange. From the time of the form's inception novelists have focused on current phenomena and issues, and one could as easily make a case for Defoe's being the first novelist as for Defoe's being the greatest journalist of all time.

Journalists root out stories that contain implicit narratives and are driven by a search for the human conflict that is capable of undergirding such narratives. They come to specialize in certain areas and subjects. To a degree they are anchored in a community (we think of Mencken in Baltimore or Mike Royko in Chicago), and they often develop an affection for that community that manifests itself in constructive criticism.

This is certainly the case with Hiaasen, who has maintained his connections to Florida and his journalistic career despite his great material success as a bestselling writer. Charles Willeford once said that he moved to Florida because he was a crime novelist and he wanted to be where the crime was. Ed McBain has been doing a Florida series (the Matthew Hope novels) for some time now, and the state remains a favorite setting for Elmore Leonard. Edna Buchanan, a crime reporter for the *Miami Herald*, has written fiction as well as an important true crime book, *The Corpse Had a Familiar Face: Covering Miami, America's Hottest Beat.*

For Hiaasen, however, the comic depiction of crime serves principally as a platform for defending Florida against the depredations of developers and the tourists and snowbirds to whom they cater. The preservation of his novels' setting is Hiaasen's great theme, and in several of those novels the central consciousness is that of Clinton Tyree, the former governor who has tried to protect the state through rational discourse and the judicious use of public policy and has now turned to more basic and more violent strategies.

Hiaasen's most explicit treatment of the theme comes in *Double Whammy* (1987), the second novel in his comic series (his first, *Tourist Season*, having been preceded by three coauthored conventional crime narratives). The subject of *Double Whammy* seems unprepossessing enough: an elaborate attempt to fix a largemouth bass fishing tournament. It is Hiaasen's alternative to the studied, georgic efforts of Izaak Walton, the idyllic and heroic tendencies of Hemingway, and the spiritual inclinations of Norman Maclean's *A River*

Runs Through It. Double Whammy is what a literary critic would term chthonic. It is earthy, vulgar, commercial, plastic, and, as such, thoroughly American.

The novel contains one of the most memorable series of scenes in contemporary crime fiction. A contract killer from New Orleans named Thomas Curl encounters a pit bull owned by the neighbor of the protagonist's ex-wife (who left him for a time-share salesman turned chiropractor). The pit bull attaches itself to Curl's wrist. Curl disembowels it with a screw driver and cuts the body away from the dog's head with a hacksaw, but the dog's jaws stand fast and the head remains attached while Curl, eventually coming in and out of delirium because of the resultant infection, comes to see the pit bull as a pet and dubs it "Lucas." He goes so far as to attempt to feed it and is not put off by the fact that the kibble falls through Lucas's mouth and onto the carpet. We will return to this sequence later.

At the conclusion of the novel, after a vast number of plot developments, complications, and partial explanations, former governor Clinton Tyree ("Skink") is attempting to save the life of a huge bass—a twenty-nine pound "hawg"—named Queenie, with whom he is able to communicate. Next to the Everglades, which represents nature, life, and vitality, stands "Lunker Lakes," the site of the bass tournament, a housing development designed for fishermen that has been built upon a former landfill whose poisonous waters kill all of the fish that are placed therein within a period of some eighteen hours.

Tyree must save Queenie from Lunker Lakes and get her into the Everglades before she expires. Separating the Everglades from the development is a dike Skink describes as "the moral seam of the universe," with "evil on the one side, good on the other." The terms and stakes are as clear as those of any medieval religious drama, though the vehicle for their depiction is as distant as might be imagined.

Double Whammy includes approximately thirty major characters (counting "Lucas") who figure significantly in the plot. That plot is labyrinthine, the texture and detail endless. The novel is a comic but deadly serious morality tale, its point being that there are many people but only one Everglades, and if the Everglades and other such God-given features of the state are lost, the natural, moral, and ultimately human damage will be incalculable. The story is replete with exploitative liars and charlatans, not the least of which are such preachers as the Reverend Charles Weeb (president of the Outdoor Christian Network). The novel itself preaches, of course, but its messages are effective because they are subordinated to the plot, the characters, and especially the setting.

The setting is, in a sense, nearly invisible, since the landscape has been covered with plastic (theme parks, which bear a large share of the responsibility for this occurrence, come in for their share of Hiaasen's comic wrath in *Native Tongue*, 1991). Of course, we often now *choose* to substitute plastic for reality. Disneyland's three-quarter-size Main Street is far more manageable and certainly far more clean and safe than those in most of our towns and villages. One can visit the Georgetown section of White Flint Mall in suburban Maryland, with its pseudo-cobblestone streets and quaint shoppes, where one is far less likely to encounter broken glass, dog droppings, and street crime than at Thirty-fourth and Prospect Streets. Citywalk at Universal Studios has now been expanded, and one can have the safe "equivalent" of a Sunset Strip or Hollywood Boulevard experience without having to deal with the hookers, porn shops, and even stranger denizens of the latter.

The calculated confusions and cultural substitutions that now characterize our lives were chronicled by artists who were postmodern before we had the word (Thomas Pynchon or Donald Fagen and Walter Becker, for example); they are now one of the mainstays of Carl Hiaasen's fiction. The logical next step in the depiction of setting, of course, is to move toward science fiction and depict alien space as real. Many of our most distinguished crime writers are already there. One thinks, for example, of Joe R. Lansdale, Neal Barrett Jr., and, quintessentially, Jonathan Lethem.

We will return to these issues later. For now, it might be said that while setting is important in all fiction it is particularly important in crime fiction, where it can figure as a character in its own right, a subject of both journalistic and moral instruction, a determinant of plot points, and the embodiment of a culture or ethos. Most interesting, it can provide a context in which the deepest themes are most tellingly articulated.

The critic and novelist Frank McConnell once commented that we read crime novels for single lines. That is, we follow the plot, understand the characters, and immerse ourselves in the setting in order to feel the full resonance of a single statement. The literature of crime, at its best, is as searching as the finest investigative journalism, as simultaneously empirical and skeptical as enlightenment philosophy, as sadly wise as Sophoclean tragedy, and as deeply wounded as high Romantic verse. Its voice, however, is generally short and sad and to the point. How does one summarize, for example, the relationship between the lone individual and the institutions of power before which he or she is largely helpless:

> You hear the voice of the night captain. You receive him loud and clear. He puts you through your paces as if you were a performing dog. He is tired and cynical and competent. He is the stage manager of a play that has had the longest run in history, but it no longer interests him.
>
> Chandler, *The Long Goodbye*, chapter 8

> "No window, Hannibal. You'll spend the rest of your life sitting on the floor in a state institution watching the diaper cart go by. Your teeth will go and your strength and nobody will be afraid of you anymore and you'll be out in the ward at someplace like Flendauer. The young ones will just push you around and use you for sex when they feel like it. All you'll get to read is what you write on the wall. You think the court will care? You've seen the old ones. They cry when they don't like the stewed apricots."
>
> Harris, *The Silence of the Lambs*, chapter 27

> Dick and I met for dinner the next night. It was my forty-fifth birthday; I felt like I was standing at the bedrock center of my life.
> Dick played me a be-bop "Happy Birthday" on his accordion. The old chops were still there—he zipped on and off the main theme rapidamente.
> We split for the restaurant. I asked Dick if he would consent to appear as the hero of a novella and my next novel.
> He said yes, and asked what the book would be about. I said, "Fear, courage and heavily compromised redemptions."
> He said, "Good, I think I've been there."
>
> Ellroy, "Out of the Past"

Without the full exploration and depiction of their narratives' settings broadly conceived, these are simple commonplaces; within their settings their impact is given life and point and dimension. In some very special books by very special writers setting is far more than the generalized outline of time, place, and circumstance. It is the very source and foundation of the writers' work as moral agents.

The Fun House

One of the most pressing issues with regard to mystery and crime fiction is the function of humor. Humor must be distinguished from the comic, since the comic tends to refer to *form* rather than to the *ethos* of the "comical." Both comedy and tragedy can have humorous moments (we speak of "comic relief" in tragic drama, for example), but the function of that humor is generally different because of the demands of the form in which the humor is embedded.

Comedy, for example, often consists of material that is deeply painful. The comic form, however, can mute that pain in a number of ways. It can, for example, create distance between the pain and the perceiving audience by inflicting that pain on a character for whom the audience has relatively little sympathy, either because of the character's personality or because the audience does not know the character well enough to care about him. Alternatively, the suffering can be inflicted on an individual the audience knows only too well and whose suffering (often deserved) can be safely predicted.

Pain can be muted by stylizing it. As mentioned above, the suffering in *Candide* is presented with great rapidity so that its full effects are not permitted to be felt. This is akin to cartoon pain, another form of stylization, in which heads can blow apart or limbs elongate but somehow come back together a moment later. The visual cues offered and, more important, the expectations that inhere in the genre (as with formal comedy) provide assurances to the audience that the suffering will be temporary, that the forces of evil will ultimately fail and all, eventually, will be well.

As an example, one could take one of the Christmas episodes of *Frasier,* the episode in particular in which Frasier is visited by his son, Frederick. Frederick desires particular sorts of toys, while his father is inclined to buy him "educational" toys. Frasier appears at the mall just as the stores are about to close and finds himself in the toy store battle-to-the-death experienced by all parents when the hot toy of the season is not widely available and loving adults are thrown back upon such age-old devices as pushing, shoving, elbowing, and bribing.

The material itself is, on its face, extremely painful. Frasier's former wife, Lilith, has custody of Frederick. Frederick lives in Boston, a continent away from Seattle. Frasier sees him rarely. When he does see him he wants the experience to be perfect, but the fates never seem to cooperate in the process.

The pain is muted for a number of reasons. First, Frasier is insulated by wealth. Ultimately, he can always buy Frederick whatever Frederick truly needs. We also know his personality. He is type A and pompous, so that the very trip to a mall with a middlebrow crowd and a ticking clock assures the audience that certain things will happen that will bring him down a peg or two but not do lasting damage. He is fundamentally good, but his pomposity results in awkward, comic expressions of that goodness. We would be disappointed if he did not suffer to some extent, and we would be even more disappointed if he suffered deeply. In short, we know, from the genre and topoi (the last-minute gift, the pompous fish out of water in the middlebrow mall) that there will be humor based on conflict; at the same time we know that the ultimate resolution of the story will bring comfort rather than concern.

In mystery bookshops we encounter a panoply of genres, from thrillers, novels of espionage, and gothic writings to true crime narratives, English mysteries, and hard-boiled detective fiction. The thematic and structural lines between the principal forms—the English mystery and the Chandlerian crime narrative—have already been discussed, but so far we have said little about tone. One of the putative differences between the forms should be their level of seriousness, an important but slippery notion.

In still-Puritan America we use level of seriousness as a mechanism for distinguishing among novelistic narratives. We say of a given work that it is a "beach novel" or, more honorifically, a "summer novel." We speak of "escapist fiction" and of writing that is "diverting." Samuel Johnson defended what he termed "harmless pleasure," arguing not only that it was relatively rare but also that it served important purposes. We, however, continue to privilege materials that are judged "serious."

In that connection, traditional mysteries are likely to be considered less serious than crime fiction since comedy is commonly considered less serious than tragedy. Readers of mysteries are often associated with readers of romances: individuals who consume quantity rather than quality, who are more comfortable with the more predictable than with the less predictable. (This is, of course, often unfair. P. D. James, for example, is a writer of exceptional skill and makes significant demands on her readers, as does, for example, Dorothy Sayers.)

There is also some middle ground—the so-called soft-boiled detective novel, which traces its influence to Ross Macdonald rather than Chandler and whose current principal exemplar is Sue Grafton. Soft-boiled fiction maintains the outlines of the Chandlerian novel, but with slightly more genial characters and less violence. On the continuum of such narratives it tilts toward the traditional mystery rather than toward more gothic forms.

A good example would be the Lauren Laurano novels of Sandra Scoppettone. Scoppettone, a gifted New York writer, has written various forms of crime fiction along with fiction for young adults. Using the pseudonym Jack Early, Scoppettone wrote a series of violent crime novels, the best known of which is probably *Donato and Daughter*, which was sold and produced as a made-for-television film. Scoppettone's later series, to which she has just bid farewell, features a lesbian detective, Lauren Laurano, who lives in New York with her lover, a therapist named Kip who is reminiscent of Parker's Susan Silverman, though, of course, gay.

The titles of the novels are plays on classic song titles and hint at the fact that the novels will be more of a piece, lighter in tone and substance, and, like mainstream fiction, more focused on relationships: *Gonna Take a Homicidal Journey, My Sweet Untraceable You, I'll Be Leaving You Always, Everything You Have Is Mine,* and *Let's Face the Music and Die.* All of these novels are lower in intensity and lighter on violence than the Jack Early novels.

There are, however, a goodly number of contemporary crime novels that are populated with comic characters and filled with comic incidents but are nonetheless extremely violent. Hiaasen's novels are a case in point. Before discussing examples of such writing we should return to some points of definition.

Frye once commented that all humor is ultimately gallows humor: "Humor begins in the accepting of the limits of the human condition. The desire for knowledge may begin as a revolt against the consciousness of death, but being directed toward the conquest of the unknown and mysterious, and the ultimate unknown mystery being death, the goal of the impulse to know becomes the same as its source."

If tragedy is, as has been said, a provisional, interim explanation of life, one that flourishes when we are between settled philosophies, it might be associated with noir rather than mystery writing, since the latter conventionally solves questions and settles issues, while the former explores them, often with very mixed results. The noir narrative, like the tragic, sometimes brings final justice, but it often does so at a horrific price.

It can do so, however, with a considerable admixture of humor. Frye labels the combination of the tragic and comic the *grotesque,* and that is a fair description of a great deal of contemporary crime writing. Carl Hiaasen's *Double Whammy,* for example, is replete with grotesque characters who behave comically but often die violently. Bobby Clinch, who dies at the outset of the novel, is buried in part of his bass boat at Our Lady of Tropicana cemetery (a moribund citrus grove). He must be buried with his cap on in order to hide the damage inflicted by the ducks who had been feeding on his dead body. Ott Pickney, a newspaperman who plays the mascot for the local high school ("Davey Dillo"), is killed and put on a stringer. When Skink kills a character named Lemus Curl, he is added to the stringer holding Ott. Ben Geer, a character aspiring to play a role on the program *Fish Fever,* weighs 390 pounds and is rejected for the job because he continually coughs sputum into the microphone. Lou Zicutto, an insurance company executive with a shaved head, is described as resembling "a Tootsie Pop with lips." Bambi, Catherine Decker's poodle, is barbecued by Skink. We have already mentioned "Lucas," Thomas Curl's name for Decker's neighbor's pit bull, whose head is attached to Curl's wrist, causing an infection that results in delirium.

This is only a sample of the characters and events in the novel. Like all of Hiaasen's writings, the book is laugh-out-loud funny, but also violent and—when one stops to think of it—grim. The destruction of a state and a society *is* grim, after all, though Hiaasen is at pains to keep us from stopping to think about it for too long, lest he appear to be ponderous and preachy.

Following Horace, he is both teaching and entertaining, but the emphasis falls upon the latter. *Grotesque* is an apt term to describe his characters and plots. Unfortunately, the grotesque does not often translate well to a visual medium. *Strip Tease* (1993), an exceptional novel, was a less than exceptional film (directed by Andrew Bergman, 1996). This was not due to the fact that great liberties were taken with the narrative, but rather to the fact that the grotesque is sometimes more memorable when imagined than seen. Congressman David Dilbeck (played by Burt Reynolds in the film), for example, enjoys slathering himself in Vaseline when his libido is operating at full throttle. The mental image is amusing but the realistic on-screen image and the squishy sounds of bare, Vaseline-laden feet in leather cowboy boots are far less effective, since the camera makes real something that is humorous (in part, at least) because of its relative lack of reality.

Similarly, I am not sure that we would want to see Lucas's head attached to Thomas Curl's wrist or Ott Pickney with a stringer through his mouth. The Coen brothers have shown that something approaching this level of the grotesque can be attempted, as in *Fargo* (1996), but *Fargo*—even with the criminal partner being fed into the wood chipper—is far more muted and conventional than the average Hiaasen novel.

The comparison is a useful one, however, for the kidnapper / murderers in *Fargo* and the car salesman who employs them recall the Runyonesque tradition, one that is still common to much crime writing, though in *Fargo* it is eventually pushed toward the gothic. Damon Runyon's characterizations of criminals have long endeared them to readers and theatrical audiences. Genial, full of personality, but sometimes a bit thick, the Runyon characters are recalled in such later narratives as *The Gang Who Couldn't Shoot Straight* (1969) by Runyon's biographer, Jimmy Breslin, or in such recent films as *Happy, Texas* (directed by Mark Illsley, 1999) or *Out of Sight* (directed by Steven Soderbergh, 1998), both of which feature Steve Zahn, playing textbook examples of Damon Runyon figures.

The operational notion here is that criminals are dim enough to pursue a life of crime but interesting enough to hold our attention in the process. The contemporary master of the Runyon character is the author of the novel upon which *Out of Sight* is based, Elmore Leonard.

In a career that has spanned many decades and encompassed many forms, including highly skilled work in the western, Leonard has established himself as both a multiply talented and a multiply successful genre writer. Like Lawrence Block and Evan Hunter, he has always worked as a professional writer (Hunter worked very briefly as a teacher, the principal result of which was the writing of *Blackboard Jungle*). He has had far greater success than Block and Hunter, however, in selling projects to Hollywood. Moreover, these projects have sometimes been reasonably close to the original novel as well as commercially successful. Block's experience is probably more indicative of the fears felt by the writer in the face of Hollywood tendencies: *Eight Million Ways to Die* (directed by Hal Ashby, 1986) was set in Los Angeles rather than in New York; the film of Sandra Scoppettone's *Donato and Daughter* was set in San Francisco rather than in New York; and the film *Burglar* (directed by Hugh Wilson, 1987), based upon Block's character Bernie Rhodenbarr, featured a black woman rather than a white male in the protagonist's role (Whoopi Goldberg, actually, whose name was changed to *Bernice* Rhodenbarr).

Out of Sight is an excellent film, but Leonard's real triumph recently has been with the novel and award-winning film *Get Shorty* (directed by Barry Sonnenfeld, 1995). The novel and film demonstrate Hollywood's love affair with itself, even when the affair consists largely of good-natured satire.

As most are now aware, *Get Shorty* follows the career of a Miami loan shark named Ernesto "Chili" Palmer who moves to Hollywood and decides to become a film producer. His skills and talents as a loan shark prove to be a perfect fit for the challenges faced by those in his new profession of choice. The novel includes a horror-film producer named Harry Zimm and his featured performer, Karen Flores, whose Hollywood trademark is her unique ability to scream. The wiseguys (one played to perfection by Dennis Farina in the film) are less wise than they need to be, and what violence there is remains largely muted. The breathless narration and seamless, delicious plot show Leonard at the top of his powers.

Leonard's newest book, *Pagan Babies*, delivers a variation on both familiar and unfamiliar themes. A particularly dark comedy, the novel concerns "Father" Terry Dunn, who leaves Rwanda after exacting justice from several Hutu murderers who have slaughtered forty-seven Tutsis in his church. Dunn goes to Detroit, his hometown (and Leonard's), where he forms a relationship with Debbie Dewey, a woman who has just been released from prison, where she was serving time for aggravated assault. Debbie is currently beginning a career as a stand-up comedian. As he and Debbie raise money for Rwandan orphans (and become ever more intimately involved), one wonders whether Terry is actually a priest and whether the contributions will end up in Africa or in Terry and Debbie's pockets. Or just Terry's. Or just Debbie's.

Leonard is an ambidextrous writer. He can do the Runyonesque narrative (*Freaky Deaky* is another good example) and the more "serious," as in *Killshot* or one of his classic westerns like *Valdez Is Coming*. He can also do something in between, as in *Pagan Babies*, which even adds an overlay of romance. Whatever the form, the dialogue is crisp and spare, the language economical and pointed.

By way of contrast, one might look at the novels of George V. Higgins. His final work, *At End of Day*, provides an excellent example. As in his most famous novel, *The Friends of Eddie Coyle*, the business of the narrative is deadly serious. *At End of Day* gives us the dirty and dangerous Boston of Dennis Lehane, not the more comfortable and comforting Boston of Robert Parker. The novel concerns the long-standing interplay there between the mob and the FBI and the manner in which the entanglements that develop over time become difficult to sustain. The novel is written almost entirely in dialogue, and the passages are long, detailed, and sometimes convoluted. Where Leonard would give you nonce expressions that are clever but immediately clear (describing a loan shark's client as "a slow pay," for example), Higgins offers slang and dialect with spellings that force the voice in the reader's head to concentrate on less familiar pronunciations and sounds. This results in a far slower narrative, one that feels more weighty and appears to ask much more of its audience. If Leonard were to be compared with Hemingway, Higgins here feels much more like Joyce.

There is little or no humor in *At End of Day*, even in a form where some level of humor is traditional. Chandler, for example, offers a speaking voice that is arch and sardonic and, as Chandler would say, cracks wise. The inheritor of the Marlowe mantle here is doubtless Robert Crais's Elvis Cole. The humor of Chandler and Crais is often humor in the face of horror, the kind of byplay that occurs in an office of homicide detectives, a humor that comments wryly on reality or keeps it at arm's length by functioning as a defense mechanism. It is humor nonetheless, and it moderates the tone and subject in such a way as to raise the comfort level all around. In *At End of Day,* however, the only apparent relief that we receive is a small bit of sex, but that ultimately offers more discomfort than comfort.

Where Chandler offered us an occasional witticism (often with a somber edge), we are now accustomed to humor of the more raucous variety. Indeed, the "seriousness" of Higgins or Andrew Vachss is far starker than the narrative ethos many readers are coming to expect. In fact, laugh-out-loud humor often appears now to be in the ascendent. One of the most effective (and funniest) writers of paperback originals these days is a man named Norman Partridge (*Slippin' into Darkness, Saguaro Riptide, The Ten-Ounce Siesta*), who offers the Hiaasen-esque grotesque with a southwestern setting. His work recalls some of the work of Neal Barrett Jr., particularly in Barrett's wonderful Wiley Moss series. Hiaasen has recently been joined in the crime fiction business by a journalistic Floridian colleague, Dave Barry. Barry's novel *Big Trouble* lacks the finesse in its constituent elements that one would expect from Hiaasen or Leonard, and it nearly passes the limits of homage in its Hiaasen-like spirit, but it is very funny indeed. In this connection, one might mention *Naked Came the Manatee,* a novel consisting of chapters written by separate writers, including Hiaasen and Barry. Elmore Leonard's chapter stands out from the others, but the book is relatively seamless and another good example of the joining of the Runyonesque with the grotesque in a Florida setting.

A slightly darker version of the form would be Charles Willeford's *Miami Blues,* which translated well to the screen. As noted above, Willeford said that he moved to Florida because he was a crime writer and that's where the crime was. His Hoke Mosley series is often Runyonesque (on both sides of the law), and there one can also see something of the pulp origins from which Willeford began, with such delicious titles as *High Priest of California.* I have discussed his crime novel send-up of the art novel, *The Burnt Orange Heresy,* elsewhere. This book should be better known in academic literature departments, since it anticipates the ethos of the contemporary academy in a way that is frighteningly prescient, particularly given the fact that it was written some thirty years ago.

An interesting, recent example of the Hiaasen-bandwagon trend is David Martin's *Pelikan*. Martin began his writing career as a mainstream novelist. He then turned—with considerable success—to horror/thriller writing. Some of the titles of these novels suggest their nature: *Bring Me Children, Lie to Me, Tap, Tap,* and, most recently, *Cul-de-Sac.* These novels are generally southern Gothic, involving sleazoid family histories and the occasional deranged doctor in the woods. They are the kind of books that could be made into splatter movies, though I would hasten to add that they are also well-written, mature genre fiction. Martin is extremely popular in Britain, where readers, of course, appreciate an able use of the linguistic instrument as well as the instruments of psychological and physical torture. Where copies of Marcel Montecino's sometimes gory *The Crosskiller* filled the windows at Hatchard's, Martin has done far better. His novels appear in trade paperback form in airport and railway WHSmith shops, right up there with the novels of Jilly Cooper and Jeffrey Archer.

With *Pelikan,* however, Martin has taken a right turn. James Joseph Pelikan is a New Orleans pimp, hustler, and scam artist plotting a world-class burglary. He is joined by his nephew, Charlie Curtis, who has been sent to him by James Joseph's dying half-brother. Needless to say, Charlie is mentored by James Joseph, but not in the more conventional senses associated with the term. James Joseph's New Orleans is populated by, among others, ladies of uncommonly easy virtue, the homeless (who James Joseph regularly bathes), and a rather interesting assortment of nuns. The jacket copy explicitly acknowledges Martin's indebtedness to Leonard and Hiaasen and also offers the prior example of John Kennedy Toole's assemblage of curious characters in his novel, *A Confederacy of Dunces.*

I may be making too much of this, but I am struck by the fact that, with the publication of *Pelikan,* David Martin has now suddenly become (in large block letters) DAVID LOZELL MARTIN. My guess is that the author and his publisher are signaling some sort of Saul/Paul vocational shift here. (When Ruth Rendell tilts toward the darker side she writes as Barbara Vine; perhaps this is a reverse of that process.) Of course, he could have published *Pelikan* pseudony-mously; it is not unheard of for genre writers to select a new name in order to acquire some of the momentum associated with a "de-but" novel. Because Martin has already gathered a large audience, however, one that neither the author nor the publisher is anxious to lose, the name has been changed but remains recognizable (and the jacket photo remains the same). In lieu of the dark, gothic jackets usually associated with Martin's thrillers, however, we have a crowned pelican set against a shiny orange sun whose rays reach the cover's margins, all set against a bright, cheery yellow background. It almost looks like . . . Florida, though the setting is, as mentioned above, New Orleans.

The Hiaasen industry is flourishing. Witness the recent, accom-plished works of Tim Dorsey, for example (*Florida Roadkill, Hammer-head Ranch Motel*), which fit the Hiaasen template perfectly. What rea-sons might be offered for the industry's popularity and growing longevity? In the first place, the use of strange but recognizable char-acters has long been a formula for literary success. It was anticipat-ed in Roman comedy, long before the "humor" plays of the Renais-sance or the quirky, retro-baroque characters of Dickens. Indeed, the devil was one of the principal types (commonly a comic character) on the medieval stage. Dryden says that we create statues for public spaces that are exaggerated in their proportions so that they will look normal at ground and eye level. By the same token, narrative art ex-aggerates and distorts so that we can, in a sense, see more clearly, and few forms of art exaggerate and distort to the degree that satire does.

In short, Hiaasen is drawing upon a host of traditional elements that have stood the test of millennia, and one of these traditions is the satiric. Satire is often divided into two broad categories: direct and indirect. In direct satire, the satirist heaps abuse on a satiric tar-get in the presence of a sympathetic audience. It is assumed, always, that the audience shares the satirist's view of the target and enjoys observing the lashing the satirist administers. Such satire is some-times termed *punitive*, and it is associated with the work of such clas-sical satirists as Juvenal and Persius. It can be distinguished from more hortatory, *persuasive* satire, which attempts to correct and im-prove. In this form of satire, the satirist has not given up all hope for reform in the satiric target and is making a conscientious attempt to effect behavioral change. Persuasive satire of this sort is often associated with the work of Horace.

In indirect satire the satirist moves beyond the simple process of castigating and scourging the satiric target. Indirect satire involves the creation of some fiction (often an allegoric fiction) that offers greater challenges to the audience and may force upon them the necessity of making significant choices and risking association with the actions of the satiric target. Moral norms are often submerged within the narrative, and the thin line between detached amusement and complicit guilt is often highlighted. This is the form of satire in which, for example, Swift excels.

Hiaasen is writing indirect satire, in that he is using an established genre and subgenre (the novel, crime fiction) as an elaborate and lengthy vehicle for his satiric purposes. Alternatively, of course, he could simply write acerbic, accusatory newspaper columns about the scoundrels whose actions he deplores.

At the same time, his criticism of these targets is very direct. He is not so much attempting to persuade them to mend their ways and become contributing citizens to our society as he is identifying them for what they are and meting out the kind of punishment their behavior (in his judgment) deserves. To the extent that the degree of exaggeration in their portrayal approaches the extreme, we are less likely to feel empathy for them as fellow human beings. (For a cinematic example, think of Willem Dafoe's portrayal of the character Bobby Peru in *Wild at Heart* [directed by David Lynch, 1990], whose worst-teeth-of-all-time smile and unctuous sexuality enable us to see his head literally blown into the air without too many regrets.) The fact that these characters' behavior and appearance move them to the margins of humanity helps to insure that some of the more violent justice that is applied to them (particularly by Clinton Tyree) will be more easily tolerated. Those bothered by the fundamental injustice of all violence should be reminded, as C. S. Lewis notes, that satirists may be many things, but they are very seldom fair.

There is no question that, beneath the jacket photograph smile, Hiaasen feels very strongly about the social, cultural, and environmental issues that are at stake in his novels. However, he is a commercially successful writer, building a large audience for his views as well as his narratives, and he knows that satire closes on Thursday. Thus, he has stressed the humorous side of his narratives rather than the more caustic or explicitly punitive and violent sides.

It may be that his feelings run so deep that the use of humor is functioning as something of an ultimate and serious defense mechanism. Frank McConnell has offered such a reading, for example, of the work of Thomas Pynchon (with whom Hiaasen enjoys some commonalities), though "defense mechanism" is perhaps too crude a term for Pynchon's intention, as seen through the lens of McConnell's analysis.

In studying the work of great clowns such as Buster Keaton and Charlie Chaplin or our own contemporaries Mel Brooks and Woody Allen, McConnell notes the manner in which their putative suffering offers us reassurance. Slipping on a banana peel demonstrates the triumph of gravity over humanity, but the professional clown acts out our enslavement to gravity by falling and then rising, teaching us, in the process, both the nature of our limitations and the possibility of our survival. Thus, the task of the clown is a deeply serious one, and the potential for real sacrifice, over and above the ritual sacrifice, is always there. Not all make it; Richard Pryor barely survived, and Lenny Bruce succumbed.

"The technical term for the comedian's talent of taking upon himself the unpleasant aspects of chaos is *abreaction*," McConnell writes. We attempt to conquer that which would threaten us by confronting it in a way that is both comic and highly risky. I think it would be an exaggeration to characterize Hiaasen as employing abreaction in order to wage war, like Pynchon, against the lords of the night. For that matter, McConnell's view of Pynchon might have been altered significantly if it had been written after the publication of *Mason & Dixon* and, more particularly, after the publication of the kinder, gentler *Vineland*. Hiaasen as comic sacrificial lamb may be something of a stretch. In my judgment, however, it is not too great an exaggeration to see Clinton Tyree as a comic figure, warring against the forces of the night at great personal risk and often at great personal sacrifice.

Hiaasen's novelistic judgment that individual character and personal integrity have a greater likelihood of success than public policy and the channels in which it is developed and enacted would resonate with Chandler. (Erin Grant of *Striptease* is another casebook example. The quintessential Hiaasen heroine, Erin has an essential integrity and determination that enable her to rise above circumstance and all of the officials who constitute it.) Clinton Tyree's decision to abandon the governor's mansion and head for the trees (particularly in light of the regular successes of his labors) certainly reinforces Chandler's concern that we not invest our hopes in large institutions, particularly political ones. In that connection, Tyree's roadkill diet, shabby clothes, and missing eye create a stark contrast to the trappings and perquisites of officialdom and offer us something relatively unique in crime fiction: a character out of Beckett (the monosyllabic, nonethnic name *Skink* would work in a Beckett play), but one whose function is more that of the crusader than that of the commentator or wounded, innocent bystander.

This is all very modern and in a sense very postmodern, since there is a generic unreality to Hiaasen's world, whose representation may constitute a higher form of realism. One of the striking things about the Pynchonesque is that the seemingly comic or odd names for people and the comic, seemingly exaggerated industries, splinter sects, and political movements that populate Pynchon's and Hiaasen's novelistic worlds all have their real-world counterparts in our daily lives.

Tabloid culture is often characterized as exaggerated and sleazy if not blatantly false. However, despite all of the protestations concerning the extremism of tabloid representations of experience, there seems now to be no doubt that the current Prince of Wales has actually expressed a wish to be a tampon for his mistress, and no real challenge to the authenticity of the photographs depicting the Duchess of York's toe sucking. Space constrains us from listing all of the details of William Jefferson Clinton's now acknowledged escapades as well as those of his political model, John Kennedy. We have gone from seeing our fallen president as one who enjoyed Robert Frost and Pablo Casals and presided over Camelot to one who looked forward to nude ménage-à-trois afternoon swims in the White House pool. In his representation of a world of comic knaves where the bizarre has become the expected and, hence, accepted as reasonably commonplace, Hiaasen may be described as simply recording what all of us regularly encounter (or read about in the *Washington Post*).

In interviewing Roman Polanski about *Knife in the Water*, Charles Champlin asked if Polanski had shot in black and white because he wanted to achieve a more intense realism than would have been possible with color photography. Polanski responded by reminding

Champlin that the world is in color, not in simple black and white. Of course, that was somewhat disingenuous, since the black and white of the great noir films constituted a vast set of visual cues whose ultimate goal was to seek and represent what might be called a realism of assessment if not a realism of color tone. On the other hand, if one compares the remakes of noir classics with the originals the use of color can prove to be far more gritty than the more stylized black and white. Compare, for example, John Garfield's first encounter with the goddesslike Lana Turner in *The Postman Always Rings Twice* (directed by Tay Garnett, 1946) to Jack Nicholson's with the sweaty and dusty Jessica Lange (directed by Bob Rafelson, 1981).

When we read conventionally dark fiction with conventionally dark characters we sometimes mistakenly believe that we are encountering "gritty" realism. In a certain sense, we may be doing so. Thus, more gothic crime fiction and gothic true crime writing may point to the ultimate heart of darkness of mankind by depicting the deepest and foulest (when acted upon) of human urges. However, the likelihood of our being murdered by a serial killer or having our blood drained by a figure such as the "Sacramento Vampire," Richard Trenton Chase, does not carry with it a high degree of statistical probability. On the other hand, the likelihood of our encountering (and being exploited by) a corrupt politician, a greedy television preacher, an avaricious businessman, a crooked union official, a political spin doctor, or a libidinous boss remains quite high.

Thus, it might be argued that where the putatively realist crime novelist offers us "realistic" convention—the realism of harsh language, dark shadows, turned-up collars, and unremitting rain—the true realist shows us the sort of individuals and events we encounter in our daily lives, lives that are more likely to be the subject of tabloid journalism and tabloid television than of film noir. There is a bit of exaggeration (appropriate to satire) to be expected, for our daily lives *as lived* lack the interest and conflict that are requisites for fiction. Hence, "reality television" shows such as *Survivor* or the *1900 House* are heavily edited and decidedly shaped, lest the audience lose interest. Each forty-four-minute episode of *Survivor*, for example, is the end result of the selective editing of more than 130 hours of film.

Similarly, if Santayana was correct in his judgment that the characters found in Dickens are the same as the characters routinely found in London streets, then the characters found in comic crime fiction are also to be found in the streets of America. From the reflecting-pool amours of Wilbur Mills to the dress collection of J. Edgar Hoover, from the lachrymose Jimmy Swaggart to the smiling, nattily dressed mobsters of Gotham, from the moralistic Darva Conger in *Playboy* to the topless Dr. Laura on the internet, from the travails of Ivana to the travails of Elian, we do not lack real-life counterparts to the people and events of contemporary crime fiction. Indeed, at times it appears that the most real figure for contemporary readers is a young boy with a lightning scar beneath his black hair who is adept at riding on brooms and is in training to become a wizard, a figure who, by turns, seems to indicate both the kind of reality we seek and the kind of reality we seek to escape.

Live and Learn

Chapter VIII

The other half of the Horatian dyad, teaching, has not been neglected by crime writers. Indeed, given the journalistic dimensions of this craft, the teaching may sometimes come easier than the pleasing. Richard Price's above-mentioned *Clockers*, an account of the details of urban drug dealing (do they really drink Yoo-Hoo to calm their nervous stomachs?), is a good example of the practice. Both Mitchell Smith's *Stone City* and Tim Willocks's *Green River Rising* are extended meditations on penology, with many reflections on both the sociology of the maximum-security prison and the theoretical underpinnings of particular penological experiments. Ellroy's "L.A. Quartet," with its meticulous attention to correct details and its intercut clips from *Hush-Hush* magazine, the *Times, Mirror-News*, and *Examiner*, recalls Dos Passos's *U.S.A.* trilogy and its journalistic approach to historiography.

There is overlap here between crime fiction and the English mystery. In fact, some collectors assemble books based on subject rather than author, period, or genre. For example, there are collections of books involving murders employing poisons from specific geographical areas. A number of mystery series focus on historical periods and personages and offer details concerning the daily life and material culture of those periods. (This is rarer in crime fiction, though the work of Caleb Carr is a good counterexample. His success is encouraging others, and we can expect to see the historical crime novel become a major growth area.)

The procedural is a subgenre that focuses on detection techniques and technologies. The Mystery Writers of America association sponsors seminars and issues materials on such matters, so that its members can display the erudition expected by their readership. Real-life connections with actual practices and practitioners are points of discussion for jacket copy. Patricia Cornwell's experiences in this regard are often noted (and somewhat exaggerated), while Carl Hiaasen's, Edna Buchanan's, Thomas Harris's, and Michael Connelly's journalistic backgrounds are duly mentioned. Jonathan Kellerman, like his protagonist Alex Delaware, *is* a child psychologist, and Andrew Vachss *is* a practicing attorney, specializing in cases of abuse and, hence, looking into the abyss on a daily basis.

The endless semesters spent in the school of hard knocks often serve writers well when they finally break free of their daytime jobs. James Lee Burke, for example, worked on the oil rigs he often describes, and Charles Willeford (who worked as a painter, prizefighter, and soldier, among other things) had a rich enough experience to fill two volumes of autobiography (and those dealing only with his early life). Chandler's life did not include detective work, but it did include a gothic family history, military service, British education, and work in the oil industry (all very ably charted in an excellent recent biography by Tom Hiney).

Joseph Wambaugh was a police department insider as well as a chronicler of department experience, and Gerald Petievich worked for the secret service, which has responsibility for the forgery cases of which Petievich has written. Hammett was a Pinkerton operative, and Steve Martini was originally a trial lawyer, experience that is evident in his accounts of courtroom procedure, particularly in the ways and means of cross-examination. John Grisham and Scott Turow, of course, have also worked as attorneys as well as become highly successful crime novelists. Parenthetically, one of the few areas of crime writing in which supply falls short of demand is courtroom drama. This is a popular subgenre, and fanzines sometimes report on the percentage of a given novel devoted to actual courtroom scenes and procedures.

We have recently been treated to two exceptional novels that depict aspects of criminal experience in professional detail. The first is by Don Winslow. Winslow began his writing career with a series character named Neal Carey. Carey is, interestingly enough, a Columbia University graduate student. The challenge of getting such a protagonist out of the library and onto the crime scene offers intriguing opportunities for plotlines. In 1997 Winslow published his breakout book, *The Death and Life of Bobby Z*, a switched-identity-scam narrative that found a wide and appreciative audience.

In 1999 Winslow followed *The Death and Life of Bobby Z* with *California Fire and Life,* an elaborate tale of arson and the investigation thereof, featuring a protagonist named Jack Wade. Winslow knows whereof he speaks, for in addition to working as a private investigator both in Europe and in America he also worked as an arson investigator in Los Angeles for more than fifteen years. The film *Backdraft* (directed by Ron Howard, 1991) may have stolen a bit of Winslow's thunder, but *California Fire and Life* is a strong novel built upon strong facts and a professional knowledge of authentic techniques.

Robert Crais has followed this course with his recent novel, *Demolition Angel,* an elaborate account of explosives and their detonation and defusing, complete with accounts of air pressures, shock waves, detonation rates, and countermeasures. The acknowledgments section includes a statement expressing the concerns of Crais's technical consultants, who were worried that the book could prove to be instructional. As a result, Crais altered certain facts and procedures and included fictional elements, lest the criminals among his readership understand the full range of techniques and equipment at the disposal of modern law enforcement.

As the title suggests, *Demolition Angel* is a departure from Crais's Elvis Cole series, one featuring a female protagonist named Carol Starkey, one of the more memorable followers in Clarice Starling's wake. One might also mention in this regard Merci Rayborn, the excellent protagonist of T. Jefferson Parker's *The Blue Hour* and more recent *Red Light. Demolition Angel's* movie rights brought top dollar, suggesting that there is still the occasional good role for women actors and an abiding audience interest in procedural detail.

The master here, on both counts, is Thomas Harris, and Harris's masterpiece is *The Silence of the Lambs.* While this is not the first novel dealing with a serial killer, it is the most prominent of such books. It is also the most prominent book to capitalize on the expertise of the FBI's profiling unit, particularly the expertise of the individual who coined the phrase *serial killer:* Robert K. Ressler. It was Ressler who introduced Harris to the sole female agent then in residence and Ressler who discussed cases with Harris such as that of Ed Gein, the terribly disturbed resident of Wisconsin upon whose activities *The Silence of the Lambs* is partially based.

Gein's name has passed into the realm of legend in Wisconsin, where stories à la those of the urban legend "hook man" are still told. (James Ellroy has acknowledged a particular interest in Ed Gein, given the fact that his mother, Geneva Hilliker Ellroy, was originally from Wisconsin.) Ressler also profiled such well-known individuals as Richard Trenton Chase, the Sacramento "Vampire Killer," William Heirens, Charles Manson, Richard Speck, Ted Bundy, John Joubert, Gerard Schaefer, John W. Hinckley, Duane Samples, Harvey Murray Glatman, John Wayne Gacy, Edmund Kemper, Monte Rissell, and Jeffrey Dahmer.

To date, Ressler has written three true crime books on his efforts, the most important of which is *Whoever Fights Monsters,* which he wrote with Tom Shachtman. This book contains the accounts of the above-mentioned cases and includes a summary of Ressler's profile of the archetypal serial killer and of his meetings with Thomas Harris. (Ressler admires Harris's work but objects to specific details; an agent-in-training such as Clarice Starling would never, Ressler says, be given the responsibilities that she was given or be put in such a dangerous position.)

While Evan Hunter, writing as Ed McBain, may be the master of the police procedural, Harris was shrewd enough to realize that an FBI procedural would offer greater range and opportunity. The FBI operates across state lines, has bigger databases and better toys, and provides the film director the opportunity for lush Washington establishing shots and cuts between them and the stark settings in "the field." Each of Harris's four novels has resulted in a movie *sale* as well as a successful *movie,* and he is closely attuned to cinematic opportunities.

In addition to the use of FBI profiling procedure, Harris includes other technical details. He explains how one takes the fingerprints from a corpse that has spent a great deal of time in the water. He instructs us as to the substance used by the FBI to counter the smells of rotting corpses (Vicks VapoRub). We receive a tour of the Anthropology and Entomology section of the Smithsonian, learn how to position a body when conducting a recreational flaying, and, of course, gain an appreciation of the difficulties involved in making a garment of human skin.

Even some of the novel's best jokes involve scientific detail, such as the chemical formula for bilirubin. For all that, however, the use of technical detail is handled with a very light touch. This is not an elongated class; it is a novel with characters and plot, both of which stay firmly in the narrative foreground. Harris realizes the risks of allowing these elements to be subsumed by procedure and maintains the balance neatly. He does so, in part, by building his narrative upon a time-honored structure.

First and foremost, *The Silence of the Lambs* is a beauty-and-the-beast tale. In finding leverage in Madame Le Prince de Beaumont's 1756 classic, Harris has ridden a tidal wave of contemporary beauty-and-the-beast stories, including the Disney animated film, the Catherine and Vincent television series, Andrew Lloyd Weber's *Phantom of the Opera,* and such film and television titles as *Darkman, Swamp Thing, Terminator II,* and *Twin Peaks.*

The best-known, eighteenth-century version of the tale (and its faithful cinematic reproduction by Jean Cocteau in 1946) is part of a larger category of fairy tales—the animal-groom story. The de Beaumont rendering tells of a merchant with three daughters, one of whom is especially lovely. The merchant suffers financial reversals, loses his wealth, and undertakes a voyage in an attempt to recoup. While his other daughters request expensive gifts upon his return, Beauty asks for nothing beyond a single rose.

The journey fails, and in the course of the return voyage the merchant's ship is lost in a storm. He stumbles upon a magic palace, sees a rose in the palace garden, and plucks it for his daughter Beauty. This angers the beast who inhabits the palace, who demands either the life of the merchant or the hand of one of his daughters in marriage.

Beauty reciprocates her father's love by volunteering to serve as his substitute. However, once inside the palace of which she is now mistress she develops respect for the beast who is its master. Missing her father, who has become ill, she returns to his home but stays too long. Then, missing the beast, she returns to find him at the brink of death, grieving over what he has taken to be her loss. When Beauty tells the beast of her love for him he is turned into a prince and the two marry.

The Disney version also focuses on the relationship between Beauty (Belle) and her father (Maurice) and forces her to come to terms with the nature of loyalty as well as the nature of fear. The rose figures in the story, but in a different way than in the de Beaumont version. Instead of functioning symbolically as an emblem of Belle's virginity, the rose here is a magic one, given to the prince by an enchantress who he turned away in a storm and who punished him for his selfishness and meanness of spirit by turning him into a beast. Unless he finds love before the last rose petal falls, he will remain a beast forever. There is also a subplot involving a rival suitor, a handsome but oafish village figure named Gaston, and of course the requisite Disneyisms (talking objects and such) suitable for sale as merchandising tie-ins.

One of the Disney studio's clear intentions in the project is to present a very contemporary Belle, one who represents a conscious departure from the characteristics of earlier Disney heroines. Belle is an intellectual, bored in her small French village. She is also curious and independent and fully capable of charming, taming, and managing the Beast. She is also drawn with a woman's body, unlike, for example, her immediate predecessor in the Disney animated pantheon, Ariel of *The Little Mermaid.*

The Disney version's moral is made explicit in the lyrics of the title song, whose shelf life has been immeasurably extended now that Celine Dion has covered it on a "best of" record. The song indicates that love occurs when each lover is prepared to "bend" and realize that each has been wrong. That takes us several steps beyond the realization that beauty and beastliness are only skin-deep; there is also the need for cooperation and compromise and a willingness to relinquish control. Again, this is noticeably contemporary.

This is quite different from the *Beauty and the Beast* television series, which plunges us into melodrama with the romantic saga of Catherine and Vincent, the professional woman in Gotham and the lion-faced man in medieval garb who dwells within the tunnels below the city. Whenever called, Vincent leaves his idyllic world to protect Catherine in hers. He also has a tendency to pop in for soulful, seemingly endless chats. Vincent is the confidant extraordinaire, the man who will talk and share and love without ever posing a sexual threat. He demonstrates the cultural acceptance of Deborah Tannen's view of men, women, and communication by representing something approaching the female ideal—an extension of the best friend from a woman's youth, that special person with whom she bonded while the boys were busy establishing dominance relationships and playing contact sports.

"Although we can never be together we will never be apart,"

Catherine says, suggesting that the ultimate source for the program is not an animal-groom story but rather something like *Wuthering Heights*, that most passionate and violent of sexless love stories. If the Disney story answers Freud's question by saying that what women want is a man who will defend them from wolves but also take them dancing, the television story adds, "and talk, emotionally and endlessly."

The Silence of the Lambs is quite different. It plays off the key notion in the de Beaumont tale by focusing on the relationship between a young woman and her father. (There are no mothers in these stories.) Clarice Starling has become an FBI cadet out of loyalty to the memory of her father—a policeman killed years earlier in the line of duty. Her career is advanced by Jack Crawford, chief of the behavioral sciences unit at Quantico, but also by a psychotic psychiatrist, Dr. Hannibal Lecter. This is a modern story about a career woman in search of a mentor. This particular career woman has two.

In the de Beaumont story the plot is precipitated not by the appearance of the beast but by the separation from the father. It is an account of human development susceptible to an aggressive Freudian reading. Beauty cannot mature without leaving home and hearth and embracing a man who at first appears beastly but who turns out to be rather princely. The rose represents Beauty's sexuality, and what Frye would term the mythos of the tale is a battle with demons that are far more psychological than bestial. The id—as frightening as it might be in its early manifestations—is still a terrible thing to waste.

In giving his story a professional-woman spin, Harris also avoids the "girly men" princes who turn up in these fairy tales, looking like they have just come from either central casting or the stage of a Sigmund Romberg operetta. He offers us instead a sweet but hardened FBI agent, whose wife is dying (this gets far more attention in the book than in the film), and a cannibalistic serial killer.

He has, in short, departed very far from our conventional sense of the prince beneath the beast, but still leveraged some of the initial energy and point of the tale. He has also leveraged some parallel aspects of the beast figure. Looking more closely at Dr. Lecter we see some familiar traits and trappings. Both Disney's Beast and Cocteau's (like TV's Vincent) sport capes, as does that other most famous of beastly mentors, the Phantom of the Opera. The Phantom (like Dr. Henry Jekyll with his Mr. Hyde) represents the monster as aesthete, the ur-figure here being, perhaps, the aristocratic aesthete, Count Dracula. (Certainly the academic version of the aesthete who has passed over to the dark side is Professor Moriarty.)

Hannibal Lecter is a great aesthete, using nothing less than the Goldberg Variations as background music for two of his murders. His cell is decorated with personal artwork—not of naked women or previous victims, but rather of the Duomo and Florence, the city in which we encounter him in the first section of the sequel, *Hannibal*. He is an individual with impeccable manners. He is, indeed, quite courtly in his behaviors. After some initial tilting he systematically treats Clarice with respect. He also pays her the supreme compliment in telling her that the world is a more interesting place with her in it. He wants to understand her and her experience; the high point in the arc of their relationship (in *The Silence of the Lambs*) is Clarice's account of the episode in her own life that is the basis for the novel's, and the film's, title. The moment of high intimacy, in effect, is one of extended, soulful talk.

I have spent some time on this particular novel to highlight the nature and effectiveness of Harris's strategy. His putative intention is to inform, and to inform with regard to a matter of great contemporary interest: serial killers and the complex procedures used by law enforcement agencies to bring them to justice. The lessons taught and learned, however, are embedded in the most primal of forms, the traditional fairy tale, but a fairy tale given the most contemporary of spins, with the focus on the modern career woman, her need for assistance, but also her need for independence and respect.

Neither Clarice nor her close friend and fellow cadet Ardelia Mapp has time for any significant social life. Their places in their academy class are prized above all else. These are modern women. At the same time, the novel's values are exceedingly traditional. The post-Hoover, post–Patrick Gray FBI is presented as a successful organization whose members function as a coherent, cooperative team. In contrast to the Chandler loner, Clarice has individuals and resources at her disposal, and her celebratory graduation (in the film) proceeds without any irony or cynicism, just as her meeting with Crawford (in the novel) and his final words, "Starling, your father sees you," are uttered with total seriousness and carry all of the emotional freight that Crawford intends.

In short, this novel brings together old and new, the traditional and the contemporary, and it does so with an excellent sense of setting, though it is exceeded in this regard by *Hannibal*. The sequel novel has brought mixed reactions, though it has been a great commercial success. For one thing, the sequel is far closer in genre to the horror novel than to the crime novel; this has not been appreciated by all readers, some of whom have seen it as a simple extension of *The Silence of the Lambs* that seems too violent and too graphic. *Hannibal* is actually the kind of book that David Martin (not David Lozell Martin) has been writing.

There is general consensus that the Florentine section of the novel is brilliantly realized, but there have been concerns expressed about later sections and particularly about the book's ending. The fact that Jonathan Demme passed on directing the film and Jodie Foster passed on reprising the role of Clarice has suggested to some that the book is too violent, the facts of the ending and some of its details legitimately too difficult to accept. While the meal shared by Hannibal and Clarice at the end of the novel (and designed to be shared by them at the end of the film) presents directorial challenges when depicted in a visual medium, it flows naturally from all that we know of the characters. This is, after all, the woman who caught Buffalo Bill and earned the respect of Hannibal Lecter, not some frail flower. Moreover, the romantic relationship between the two (established in the novel, but altered for the film) flows not just naturally but absolutely from the beauty-and-the-beast tale. "Read Marcus Aurelius," Hannibal is fond of saying. "Read Madame Le Prince de Beaumont" is the proper rejoinder to Harris's critics.

The two books are simply different. The plot of *Hannibal* is looser and more episodic than that of *The Silence of the Lambs*, but the same can be said of the novel preceding *Silence*, *Red Dragon*, which is also a very fine book. Also, Clarice's travails in the bureau in *Hannibal* restore some of the Chandlerian distaste for large organizations and are sufficient to mute any criticism of *The Silence of the Lambs* as being too trusting or even sentimentally patriotic.

We should remember that Harris is an innovator. He does not take ten years writing a book in order to give us just what we expect. In *Hannibal* he gives us just what we would expect if we only knew where to look—the beast rushing to beauty's defense and then embracing her as his mate. Since that apparently was not expected, he has succeeded in the most difficult of the crime writer's tasks: surprising and outsmarting the reader after honestly giving that reader all of the clues required to solve the case.

Of course, he does that brilliantly in *The Silence of the Lambs* as well. It is striking to the point of embarrassment to realize how obvious and consistent the clues are, and still the narrative unfolds with great suspense along with ruthless logic. That is not easy to do, and making it look easy is harder still.

Harris's skill and success raise the whole issue of the level of quality we might reasonably expect from the form and the extent to which these works' subject matter can contribute to or detract from that quality. It is a fact, for example, that many individuals go to mystery and crime fiction to learn of exotic details and technical procedures. These matters can take precedence over the usual expectations of the novel reader: strong plots, rounded characters, significant themes, fully realized settings, and solid prose.

One hears great praise, for example, for Tony Hillerman and his ability to secure the trust of Native Americans, trust that runs sufficiently deep that these individuals will divulge secrets (for example, concerning tribal ceremonies) that no white man has ever known. The cynic might ask how trustworthy the material is if its confidentiality compromises our ability to confirm its accuracy, but that is not the point. The point is that Hillerman is being praised as a researcher rather than as a writer and that in valuing the facts in particular we are turning his mystery novels into anthropology texts.

One can, of course, have both: highly polished novels that also convey unique information. That is the desire, but with an audience that can sometimes fixate on the quality of the fact over the quality of the narrative there are potential dangers. Many of the most interesting crime novels have been crossover books—the subject of our next chapter—and they have been able to reach far broader audiences than conventional category fiction. Fresh and expansive views of the genre are, in my judgment, to be encouraged. At the same time, the stress on subject over craft can narrow the sights of writers and result in pap for the undiscriminating. We all know readers of shlock mysteries and romances who read them purely to pass time or feed an undernourished fantasy life. There are people, for example, who read Regency romances in order to "understand England during that period," people for whom the essence of the English seventeenth century is captured in *Forever Amber* or that of the American civil war in *Gone with the Wind.*

It is not the case that bestselling books must be pitched to a middlebrow audience, but it is the case that lowered expectations often result in the publication of commercial writing geared to those expectations. In this regard there is something of a disconnect between writers and readers. In one poll of crime writers, for example, the individual chosen as the contemporary master of the form was James Crumley, a wonderful writer, but one with a small and scattered output and a relatively small audience, certainly compared with that of writers such as Turow and Grisham. Many mystery and crime readers are not familiar with all of his work, and the vast majority of readers of bestsellers will not have heard of Crumley at all.

The writers of bestsellers are often scorned by the crime fiction fanzines. I was probably not the only reader to make audible sounds of disappointment at the ending of *Presumed Innocent.* As the master says, "When you have eliminated the impossible, whatever remains, however improbable, must be the truth." The ending was thus telegraphed from the very beginning. My pat quotation in cases such as these is, "Elmore Leonard would never do this."

Turow, however, is a far better writer than some who have achieved commercial success. The author of a book on the first year of law school, *One L,* he was a publisher's dream for the writing of courtroom fiction. Here, the argument would go, is an individual who is both a practicing attorney and the author of a book on law school. Hence, his legal audience will follow him and support him in his new endeavor.

Some of this thinking mirrors Hollywood's. Readers will recall the buzz concerning Johnny Carson's successor and the touting of Pat Sajack as a logical choice. Since Carson's prior role was as a successful game show host with *Who Do You Trust?* the logical person to succeed him would be the host of a currently successful game show. Talk shows are different from game shows, however, and books about law school experiences are different from novels, but then the publisher was right after all and *Presumed Innocent* was huge, both as a novel and as a film. John Grisham's *A Time to Kill* has been criticized as a knockoff of *To Kill a Mockingbird,* but very few would turn down Grisham's royalties.

The fact is that mainstream novelists often plow very familiar territory, while writers of category fiction (social melodrama, for example, à la Arthur Hailey) are expected to take on grand subjects and instruct as well as titillate and divert. The development of strong plots, vivid settings, compelling characters, and substantial themes is already a tall order; to ask for unique material as well is asking a lot. As readers we are often forced to compromise.

One of the writers whose work I always read is Steve Martini. Martini's plots often stretch credulity. His most recent book, *The Attorney*, for example, features an individual named Jonah Hale who is raising his granddaughter because her mother—Jonah's daughter—is a drug addict. Jonah has the good fortune to win millions in the state lottery, whereupon his daughter attempts to trade the custody of Jonah's granddaughter for a big-money payoff. She enlists an obnoxious feminist activist named Zo Suade to help her. Zo turns up dead; Jonah is arrested, and Martini's series character, Paul Madriani, is called upon to defend him.

It is not quite as preposterous as it sounds in a brief summary, but the sentence-by-sentence writing is crude and often clichéd. Steve Martini, however, understands courts, he understands trials, and he understands California statutes. The legal material in his books is exquisite, and his depiction of lawyerthink and courtroom strategies is masterful. Other writers do everything at a slightly higher level of skill (J. F. Freedman, for example, Stephen Hunter, Peter Blauner, Robert Ferrigno, Lawrence Block, of course, or T. Jefferson Parker) and I read (and would recommend) them as well, but you can't always get all that you want in a form that makes such varied demands.

Genre writing enjoys a ready audience, but it also brings with it constraints. The last great age of such writing—the English eighteenth century—offers readers an uncommonly high level of average writing, but few peaks and masterworks. In our own time there are few writers on a par with Ellroy, Harris, Burke, and Leonard, but there are still many writers of uncommon competence. One writer, for example, who delivers bestsellers that include interesting characters, solid plots, and a highly developed sense of setting is Michael Connelly.

Connelly began as a crime journalist and turned to full-time novel writing after a series of early successes. His setting is Los Angeles and his series protagonist a crusty figure named Harry (short for Hieronymus) Bosch. The implicit notion that Harry's Los Angeles bears some striking similarities to the subjects of his namesake's paintings is frequently reinforced. His novels often deal with contemporary subjects; in *Angels Flight*, for example, he takes us to a Los Angeles landmark and offers us a murder victim who is suspiciously similar to the prominent local attorney Johnny Cochrane.

Connelly may, however, be overly constrained by his series character. His very best books, in my judgment, have been *The Poet*, a freestanding book written on a very broad canvas, and his most recent novel, *Void Moon*. The latter has an effective female protagonist named Cassidy "Cassie" Black and pivotal scenes in that most American of crime-novel settings, Las Vegas.

This young writer has all of the right tools, and he uses them in all of the right ways. He demonstrates that writers of true craft can also produce bestsellers for a broad audience. In this regard he may be compared with Jonathan Kellerman, who has been demonstrating that ability for years. Kellerman also occasionally writes freestanding books that do not focus on his series protagonist, Alex Delaware. An early and effective example is *The Butcher's Theater*, a serial-killer novel set, interestingly, in Jerusalem. Kellerman's masterpiece, however, is the more recent *Billy Straight*, a novel about a young boy who witnesses a crime that recalls the O. J. Simpson case. He then must protect himself from those who would do him harm and, as an unfortunate side result, from those who are actually seeking to protect him. Billy is the quintessential survivor in the contemporary urban jungle and acquits himself well.

Alex Delaware makes a brief appearance in the book; the setting, after all, is Los Angeles, and he is a top (if fictional) child psychologist there. However, the center of the stage belongs to Billy, an exceptionally well developed character, and LAPD detective Petra Connor, another effective female character, who investigates the case.

Just as the presence of constraint does not insure failure, its absence does not guarantee success. Conventions have a way of freeing writers as well as circumscribing them, since they offer a host of tools and a set of prior agreements recognized by the audience. Hence the frequent desire on the part of publishers for both a recognizable genre and a series character. At the same time, however, publishers seek books that "transcend genre." While this may seem a difficult or even contradictory ideal, writers such as Kellerman and Connelly are able to flourish within its terms.

Cross Over

William Goldman once pointed out that the problem with Hollywood is that no one really knows what actually works. This results in a sense of guardedness with regard to anything that appears to be fresh and new. However, once someone takes a risk and produces something new, one of two things can happen. If the project flops, prejudices with regard to newness are reinforced; if the project succeeds, we get a succession of imitations of that project the following season.

The same is largely true of category fiction, though the vocabulary for characterizing the situation is different. There is a sense of "what works," and "what works" is encouraged, so long as the constituent elements (plot, theme, setting, characters) have not been "done to death." Thus, there is a desire for the fresh and new so long as the resulting book is likely to work—in other words, not be too new. Bets are hedged by describing the ideal in terms of a desire for category fiction that "transcends genre," in other words something tried and true that is simultaneously fresh and new.

The transcendence of genre implies the inclusion of mainstream elements, but the more proper implication is that the work will find an audience beyond those who read category fiction exclusively. In other words, editors are not looking for, for example, coming-of-age stories that involve mysteries; they are looking for mysteries that will also appeal to the readers of coming-of-age novels and / or other types of fiction.

There is nothing wrong with this; this is the way in which genre writing proceeds. In fact, the practice is built specifically on a strong critical foundation, the best expositor of which is Samuel Johnson. Basically, Johnson asks of a work of literary art that it be both just and new. By *just* he means *natural*, by which he means that the work

127

squares with generally accepted views of human psychology. In short, the just work represents life as it is. It is, in other words, humanly realistic in the broad sense of the term.

Johnson also asks for novelty, for freshness and newness. A work that is *just* but not *novel* recapitulates old pieties, telling us old things in the same old ways. A work that is *novel* without being *just* is simply weird. The challenge is to say something profound in a new way, to embody an existing insight in a fresh vehicle, to present the truth in a unique way so as to move us to rethink it and, hopefully, gain a richer and deeper understanding of it.

There is, obviously, a great deal of room here for outraged disagreement when we get down to cases. Thomas Gray's Eton College Ode, for example, which Johnson thought trite and banal, transported other readers, including Boswell. Johnson's judgment of Sterne's *Tristram Shandy*, that it was new but not just ("Nothing odd will do long. 'Tristram Shandy' did not last"), has obviously not been sustained by later commentators or, indeed, by literary history.

The basic framework, however—the justness/novelty dyad—is quite useful as a device for framing discussions, and it is particularly useful with regard to genre writing. The critical method that follows from the foundational principle, one Johnson both supports and practices, is the assessment of the individual work through a process of elaborate comparisons and contrasts with cognate examples. That is the way one assesses what is just and also what is new. The process one would follow in an attempt to understand and appreciate *Hamlet*, for example, would be to look at other examples of Jacobean revenge tragedy and trace the commonalities and, most important, the differences between Shakespeare's play and other examples of the type.

The result would be an understanding of what a writer might be expected to do and what a writer of the order of Shakespeare actually does. *Hamlet* is a genre piece, but one that transcends genre, satisfying a contemporary audience expecting a certain type of play but reaching out, then and now, to a far wider audience.

Part of the underlying assumption here is commercial. It was Johnson who said that no one but a fool would write, except for money. The work that reaches the widest possible audience is the one that has achieved an important form (though not the only form) of success. In terms of contemporary crime writing, the transcendence of genre can occur in a number of ways. Not all, unfortunately, guarantee commercial success. One can, for example, produce a work that is so skillfully rendered and so compelling in its constituent elements that it reaches a wider audience than does a more mundane work. One can produce a work that involves the conscious overlap of genres, so that the result is comparable to a Venn diagram in which the shaded area represents elements from multiple forms that more often remain discrete. One can also, if one is very skilled, develop a voice that is sufficiently unique that the author's name becomes a brand name. Stephen King, for example, sometimes laments the fact that he has become a brand name, though many would envy that position and the success upon which it is built.

The dangers here are obvious, and they are the dangers articulated by Johnson. The slightest tilt in the balance between justice and novelty, a tilt judged by the individual reader, whose experience may or may not be adequate to the task, can result in the labeling of a work as either trite or odd, the assumption being that neither will be commercially successful.

When one looks at the market, however, it becomes difficult to gauge that tilt. Some of the most successful writers appear to be fairly conventional (Robert B. Parker) or somewhat odd (Stephen King). How far would an unpublished young novelist get with the Parker formula or with a book about a love affair between a man and an automobile? (The answer is: not very far nearly all of the time, but very far once in a very great while.)

The frequent result of this challenge is a fairly conventional story line with a unique protagonist. For example, April Smith's new novel, *Be the One*, a nice follow-up to her debut crime novel, *North of Montana*, features a woman baseball scout and former player named Cassidy Sanderson. Cassidy has a new prospect, fresh from the Dominican Republic, who has great hands, great eyes, great moves, and a growing pile of blackmail notes. This is a distant cry from the story of a private investigator in a tiny office with a shabby desk and a half-full, heavily fingerprinted pint of Rye.

Frank McConnell (*Murder among Friends, Blood Lake, Liar's Poker, The Frog King*) imagined just such an investigator, but one whose boss dies, leaving the agency to his daughter, a Sister Mary Godzilla nun with a taste for jazz. The investigator has an uneasy relationship with the nun, who, of course, calls him "dear" and solves all the cases.

One of my favorite unique protagonists is Tom Bethany, the creation of the Washington writer Jerome Doolittle. Bethany, a Vietnam veteran, is a wrestler who qualified for the Olympics but was kept from competing by Jimmy Carter's boycott. He continues to carry a grudge as a result of the experience, and he continues to use his athletic skills in the pursuit of criminals. He is one of the few memorable wrestlers in literature since Beowulf, the nature and success of whose techniques with Grendel were once the subject of a Modern Language Association convention session.

Another clever creation, this one by Bob Sloan, is NYPD detective Lenny Bliss (*Bliss, Bliss Jumps the Gun*). Lenny's wife is a stand-up comedian who uses his experiences and foibles as the principal grist for her act. Add to this New Yorkness and Jewishness, and you get recognizable pieces brought together to form a very novel amalgam. The Bliss novels manage to be lighthearted and humorous but at the same time gritty and realistic, a sort of hard-boiled, soft-boiled fusion. The narrative is crisp, the dialogue funny, the details realistic. Sloan writes with a light touch, making it all look easy, something that is, of course, extremely difficult to do. *Bliss* was an excellent book, but *Bliss Jumps the Gun* is even better. This is a very bright and promising new talent.

To rise above the mass of genre material, writers seek distinction, knowing the attendant risks. Work that is relatively safe, work that minimizes risk, can be either quickly forgotten or extremely successful, as Patricia Cornwell has demonstrated. Some have taken risks and received strong critical plaudits but not reached a wide audience.

Neal Barrett Jr. is an excellent example of a risk taker. Barrett works in multiple forms and has developed a strong and unique voice. His science fiction novel *Through Darkest America*, a postapocalyptic narrative, was very well received. It is an engaging, realistic book, effectively capturing a sense of the landscape, both human and natural, at eye level. I would contrast it with an equally impressive novel, William Brinkley's *The Last Ship*. Where Barrett's book is a polished genre piece, Brinkley's aspires to be an epic, and—in terms of size, scope, and breadth of canvas—it comes close.

Barrett has written expert short stories and a series of crime novels (*Bad Eye Blues, Dead Dog Blues, Pink Vodka Blues, Skinny Annie Blues*) that are Hiaasen-level hilarious, with lightning-quick plots and quirky, fascinating characters. Barrett offers the humorous alternative to the more "serious," dirty-white-boy novels of Stephen Hunter. Barrett's most interesting book is perhaps *The Hereafter Gang*, the tale of a man named Doug Hoover who longs for the sweetness of the past and eventually finds it, realizing in the process that he has had to die to do so. The book is part mainstream narrative, part sci-fi, part fantasy, part magic realism. It was published by a small but important California press that issues a handful of books a year and described in the *Washington Post* as "one of the great American novels." Such is the world of genre writing and risk taking.

A compatriot of Barrett and of Andrew Vachss, Joe R. Lansdale has had a writing career similar to Barrett's, publishing multiple stories and paperback originals, while moving in and out of the world of hardcover publishing. Lansdale's world is darker than Barrett's, with stronger horror elements and a greater degree of violence. His short story "Night They Missed the Horror Show," for example, begins with the kind of redneck world depicted by Stephen Hunter and then proceeds to push it far beyond the realm of nightmare. Lansdale, like Barrett, is the kind of writer other writers read. He is never dull, and he never fails to surprise. His work, however, is likely to be far too strong for mainstream readers.

Brinkley's *The Last Ship* is horrific in its own way. The novel imagines the world following a nuclear exchange in which a single ship cruises the oceans in search of life. All of the landmarks of our cultural heritage are either gone or shattered. (Ultimately, I believe, the book is an extended reflection on the culture wars raging at the time it was written in 1988 and the importance of preserving our cultural traditions and the artifacts that embody them.) Gibraltar no longer exists; the Thames valley consists of charred architectural skeletons. A few living humans are seen, dying of radiation poisoning and waving frantically from beaches. Suddenly we learn that a Russian ship has survived also, and when it is encountered new relationships must be established between what is left of America and what is left of Russia. Land is found that is sufficiently clear of radiation to support life. Agriculture must be developed, de novo. Moreover, there are women sailors on the American ship. The relationships between men and women, all desirous of repopulating the planet, must be completely renegotiated. A few remnants of civilization in the form of books and tapes are found and protected.

You get the idea. While I find the book very moving in its elements and very interesting in its issues, students have found it somewhat tedious because the canvas is so broad, the details so plentiful, and the narrative so weighty. I keep threatening to require some Joe R. Lansdale instead, but I don't want to see the letters from parents that might ultimately lead to a test of the limits of academic tenure.

A book that I admire suggests the possibility of crossover from another direction. Where Brinkley takes a fairly conventional sci-fi concept and turns it into a mainstream epic, other more mainstream writers have capitalized on successful genre elements and topoi. Steven Spielberg's *Raiders of the Lost Ark,* for example, was inspired by the great wartime serials, in particular the Rod Cameron chestnut, *Manhunt in the African Jungle* (1943). This is a story of Nazis in the jungle, though there are (oops) no jungle scenes in the serial. Duncan Renaldo, famous for his role as the Cisco Kid, plays a Frenchman (he was born in Romania), and Rod Cameron engages in a succession of "fistic encounters" with the Nazis, a permissible form of violence then. The airport in Berlin from which Rod—an American secret agent—escapes has prominent palm trees in the background and is clearly the Burbank airport.

The notion of Nazis in the jungle, however, is a powerful one, including the notion of Nazis hiding there after the fall of the Reich. George Steiner took that notion and the mystery/adventure elements inhering therein and created an interesting mainstream novel, *The Portage to San Cristóbal of A. H.* (1981). In Steiner's story, Israeli Nazi-hunters find the ultimate prize in the rain forest. Hitler is alive, though ninety years old, and living in the Amazon jungle. Much of the novel consists of an exploration of the flora and fauna of the Amazon and the difficulties of transporting Hitler through this landscape. The book builds to a climax in which A. H. finally speaks, offering an extended apologia based on the notion that it wasn't he who developed the concept of the master race but rather the Jews themselves. A. H.'s voice is, of course, an exceedingly dangerous and effective instrument, as Steiner is at pains to demonstrate. For all of the genre and pop culture elements, the novel is ultimately a moral reflection on the nature and power of language.

Steiner's book is an interesting one and demonstrates how a mainstream novel can capitalize on genre elements. The inside-out version of the process is represented by a book such as Allan Folsom's *The Day After Tomorrow*, a guilty pleasure and tremendous commercial success. Folsom's novel is a Nazi hunt that aspires to the level of international epic and ends, literally, with the schlock-fest conclusion, "they stole Hitler's brain!" Most who have read it have been unable to put it down. Here we have some of the same sorts of awkwardness of *Manhunt in the African Jungle* mixed with the international-thriller formula and turned into a huge bestseller. Folsom's logical next subject: the Vatican. I cannot resist quoting the summary for *Day of Confession* from Amazon:

> This massive thriller pits a scheming prince of the Church who believes he was once Alexander the Great against the Addison brothers—Harry, a Hollywood lawyer, and Danny, a Vatican priest. It seems that Danny had the bad luck to hear another cardinal's confession outlining a heinous plot to poison China's water supply in order to win the Vatican bankers a multi-billion-dollar contract to rebuild it—and of course to take advantage of the opportunity to convert a quarter of the world's population and ensure the Church's world domination into the next century. Spanning the globe from Vatican City to Beijing, from Los Angeles to Switzerland, the action never stops. And whenever it seems to falter for more than a paragraph, someone among Folsom's picaresque cast of minor characters (a nun, a dwarf, a CIA station chief, a beautiful television journalist, and an African poet, among others) turns up just in time to give it a nudge. The narrative is not as fluid as it could be, and the plot might have been devised by a conspiracy theorist with a taste for chaos physics, but fans of Folsom's intense novel *The Day After Tomorrow* won't be disappointed.—Jane Adams

It is comforting to note that there are successful novels with more fluid but far less tangled plots. Robert Clark's *Mr. White's Confession* won the 1998 Edgar Award for best novel from the Mystery Writers of America. This was an interesting selection for several reasons, the principal being that *Mr. White's Confession* comes very close to being a mainstream novel. Set in St. Paul, Minnesota, in the 1930s, the story concerns the death of a dime-a-dance girl and her relationship with the individual eventually convicted of the crime.

Herbert White is an exceedingly shy and reclusive individual whose hobby is photography. The fact that he has taken pictures of the victim helps to incriminate him. White is innocent, however; he has been successfully framed for the murder. Nevertheless, he spends years in prison for a crime he did not commit. The case is investigated by a police lieutenant who is hard but decent. Essentially the novel is an exploration of loneliness and fantasy, the fragility of the law and the tenuous nature of what passes for justice. There are but a few characters, and, as Johnson said of Richardson, if you were reading the book for the plot you would become so frustrated as to wish to hang yourself. It is, in short, a psychological study but not a psychological thriller. It is also a period study that conveys a sense of the vulnerability of individuals and the power of institutions. In that regard it is Chandleresque, but the atmospherics are delicate and touching and, hence, more shattering in their effects. *Kirkus Reviews* described the book as "a gently, powerfully moving demonstration of the ways, as White concludes, that 'we are but a memory enfleshed by love.'" That is an excellent description, but it hardly seems to be the description of a crime novel. The fact that the book was singled out for the Edgar suggests the breadth of the category for this particular type of fiction and the fact that the particular types of excellence represented by the book are recognized by the association and its review panel.

Another significant St. Paul writer (Clark was born there but now lives in the Pacific Northwest) is Steve Thayer. Where Clark includes journalistic excerpts à la Dos Passos and Ellroy, Thayer focuses on a set of journalistic heroes, utilizing them in intriguing ways.

Thayer himself might be something of a hero to crime writers. His first book, *Saint Mudd,* was declined by forty publishers. Thayer published it himself, selling some ten thousand copies over four years before it was picked up by Viking. Nearly every successful writer has such a story to tell. James Lee Burke went for a decade without a hardcover sale, his mainstream masterpiece being published by the Louisiana State University Press (and then short-listed for the Pulitzer Prize). Jonathan Kellerman went through similar travails with the publication of his first novel, *When the Bough Breaks,* which promptly became a bestseller and went on to become a made-for-television movie featuring Ted Danson.

Grover Mudd, Thayer's protagonist, is a writer for the St. Paul *Frontier News.* A World War I veteran who survived a severe poison-gas attack, he fights against Depression-era villains on both sides of the law. Real-life characters such as John Dillinger, Baby Face Nelson, and Ma Barker appear in the narrative as Mudd works with the incipient Federal Bureau of Investigation to bring them to justice.

Thayer's second novel, *The Weatherman*, is more conventional. This is a serial-killer novel featuring two new newspeople, Andrea Labore, a TV anchorwoman, and a news producer with the rather unlikely name of Rick Beanblossom. The latter wears a mask because his face was destroyed by napalm in Vietnam. The culminating novel of what, for now, is a trilogy appeared in 1999 and is entitled *Silent Snow*. It demonstrates the elasticity of the crime novel form and the interesting uses to which that form can be put.

Where Thayer's first novel presents itself as historical documentary, with a great deal of local color and detail, the second is more conventional, though the narrative is ambitious in its length and in the strategies it uses to narrow the range of possible killers and then identify the actual killer. The cat-and-mouse game with the reader manages to be both stark and quite engaging. The third novel, however, is truly unique.

In *Silent Snow*, Rick Beanblossom and Andrea Labore are now married and have a son. The son is kidnapped on March 1, the date of the kidnapping of the Lindbergh baby in 1932. In order to solve the crime with which he is presented (he is now the city's leading investigative reporter), Rick must immerse himself in the past. In doing so he studies the investigative writings of an individual covering the Lindbergh kidnapping more than sixty years earlier. That figure, of course, is Grover Mudd, who here functions as a kind of alter ego for Rick.

The plot, in short, mirrors that of Sydney Kirkpatrick's *A Cast of Killers*. Rick, living in the present, is investigating the same case as Grover Mudd. As he struggles to see concrete connections between the 1932 kidnapping and that of his infant son, the clock is ticking in the back of his and the reader's mind. Thus, we get the historical/documentary elements of *Saint Mudd* with the narrative operating on two time levels. At the same time, the Lindbergh case is a very real one, so that any connections that Thayer is able to draw between the events in New Jersey in 1932 and possible events in contemporary St. Paul must be reasonably plausible or the architecture of the book will collapse in a heap. He is, in short, allowing himself to be held to some of the same standards of accuracy that must be met by writers of true crime books.

There is some melodrama here, but it is balanced by Thayer's willingness to take novelistic risks. Like Thayer, Marcel Montecino, particularly in *Sacred Heart*, allows a strong imagination sufficient rein to expand our sense of the capacities of the crime novel form. Montecino's novel sounds like a Folsom project in its outlines, but it manages to work on the page. *Sacred Heart* deals with two brothers, one a priest in Mexico, the other a gangster in New York. The gangster goes to Mexico in order to hide out and does so by masquerading as a priest. In the face of the oppression of the church at the hands of the Mexican government, his pious brother resists and the two begin to exchange roles, with powerful results on both sides.

Using that most conventional of genre pieces, the pastoral elegy, Milton writes in *Lycidas*:

> Yet once more, O ye Laurels, and once more
> Ye Myrtles brown, with Ivy never-sear,
> I com to pluck your Berries harsh and crude,
> And with forc'd fingers rude,
> Shatter your leaves before the mellowing year.

Milton's subject is death, and the form he has chosen for depicting it will not contain his feelings. This is the challenge of the crime writer—to expand the form without wholly shattering it or to shatter it in such a way that our sense of it is reconfigured as a result. Fortunately we have writers who do not hesitate to make the attempt. One of the most compelling is Jonathan Lethem.

To date Lethem's writing career has been bounded by two quite different crime novels, the first a sci-fi crossover. *Gun, with Occasional Music* appeared in 1994. It concerns the investigation of the wife of a rich urologist by a conventionally rumpled detective with the classical name of Conrad Metcalf. The difference is that *Gun, with Occasional Music* is set in the future and contains too-quickly-developed humans named babyheads and a cast of evolved, talking animals, including a particularly nasty kangaroo. Like many successful books, it is one that it is very difficult to imagine ever being published. Sci-fi has devoted readers, but the field is dominated by a small number of writers. Crime fiction has a wider readership, but the market is glutted. Nevertheless, *Gun, with Occasional Music* made it and it did so in style.

Lethem followed this futuristic, Chandler–meets–Philip K. Dick crossover with three books of science fiction and a collection of short stories, *The Wall of the Sky, The Wall of the Eye*. *Amnesia Moon* is a post-something novel set in Hatfork, Wyoming, Vacaville, California, and San Francisco. Lethem presents a fully realized world without any explanations and lets the action proceed, the action consisting principally of the search for meaning in a confusing world by an individual known as Chaos who lives in the projection booth of an abandoned cineplex. Certain things are realized and understood, but there are no "keys" offered to the narrative, no Colonel George Taylors suddenly encountering the remains of the Statue of Liberty on a lonely beach on the Planet of the Apes and finally understanding everything.

Lethem is a bit more forthcoming in his short stories, where the terms are established more clearly. "The Happy Man," an exploration of the nature of hell, does offer the reader some explanations for the experiences of the protagonist, as does, for example, "Vanilla Dunk," a futuristic view of basketball in which players are endowed with the skills of previous athletic superstars.

In 1997 Lethem published a novel entitled *As She Climbed Across the Table*, a sci-fi / mainstream crossover concerning the love of an anthropologist named Philip Engstrand for a particle physicist named Alice Coombs. Alice and her colleagues have created a physical void they call Lack. Lack has the curious ability to absorb certain household objects (apparently of his own conscious choice) while rejecting others. It is Alice's desire to be chosen and somehow merge / mate with Lack (hence the title of the novel), and this is putting a strain on her relationship with Philip. A writer like John Barth would turn this into an elaborate commentary on the academic world, as in *Giles Goat-Boy*, but Lethem does not. He presents a straightforward love story with plot complications resulting from the scientific capabilities of the near-future physicist.

Lethem's *Girl in Landscape* (1998) is straightforward sci-fi with strong western elements. We are presented with another post-something world in which past inhabitants of earth move freely between planets. Pella Marsh loses her mother at the age of thirteen, and her family moves to a place called the Planet of the Archbuilders (that is, builders of arches). The planet is inhabited by a few long-term set-tlers, some native archbuilders, and some new arrivals. Some of the plot points one might expect in a western are used, but, again, the narrative is presented very straightforwardly, without comment or interpretive keys.

With Lethem's most recent novel, all of this changes. In *Motherless Brooklyn* (1999) he returns to the noir ethos of *Gun, with Occasional Music,* but without the sci-fi elements. We are in (more or less) pre-sent time. We are in Brooklyn, and we have a straightforward group of human beings with straightforward problems. With one excep-tion: the protagonist, a man named Lionel Essrog, suffers from Tou-rette's syndrome.

Lionel is an orphan. He and several of his compatriots have been enlisted by a man named Frank Minna to accomplish various tasks. These tasks take them away from their normal, constrained world and open up a host of new, if illegal, possibilities. Minna is a small-time criminal, and he uses the boys for such activities as the loading and unloading of trucks carrying stolen goods. The group is called the Minna Men. When they grow up they form a seat-of-the-pants detective agency and limo service. When Frank turns up dead, Li-onel must function as a real detective and find Frank's murderer. He must even do something he has never done in his life: leave Brook-lyn (for the Maine coast actually, a change he handles very well).

Lethem offers no cheap shots with the Tourette's (in contrast, for example, to the repeating *L.A. Law* figure who blurted out embar-rassing comments). Lionel's most severe statement is a recurring "Bite me." Instead, the syndrome is represented through painful, compulsive attention to detail and a need to touch people around the neck and shoulders. Lionel must continually struggle to resist the syndrome. When he enters a room, for example, his automatic im-pulse is to begin counting things.

Of course, many of the elements of Tourette's that constitute an affliction also serve the quintessential needs of the detective. Li-onel's challenge is to keep these things in balance. He is known as "The Human Freakshow" by some of the people he encounters, his affliction providing both the occasion for ridicule and the basis for redemption.

This is very, very clever. The predicted response to the supreme Johnsonian merging of the just with the new is, "Why didn't I think of that?" The idea that seemed so preposterous prior to its embodiment seems so natural after. Lethem handles all of this with superb delicacy. Further, as a longtime Brooklyn resident he can present the details and atmospherics with a light touch and a sure hand.

This is extremely impressive work. It is also work that emerges from a career (short, but very successful) in genre writing that has embraced sci-fi, the western, noir, and a touch of the mainstream. Lethem has always handled the crossover points well, but this, his best book to date, is the one that is most faithful to a single genre. The instrument is fully refined and exceedingly effective. *Motherless Brooklyn* is, as they say in Hollywood, very high concept. At the same time, it is very character-driven. The constituent elements were all there in his previous writing, but the final result is exquisite. It is no small matter for a crime novel to receive the highly coveted National Book Critics Circle Book Award, but Lethem accomplished that with this fine novel.

Standard definitions of the concept of *genre* generally involve two elements—structure and ethos. Sonnets, for example, are fourteen lines in length and consist of an octet and sestet (Italian version) or three quatrains and a couplet (English version). The subject and tone are those of romantic love, though writers such as Milton and Wordsworth have used the sonnet form for political commentary.

With a novelistic subgenre, however, things are far more complicated. The most protean of literary forms, the novel is also the least amenable to formal definition. At various times it has assimilated the elements and characteristics of a host of other forms of writing: the essay, the letter, the memoir, the religious or revolutionary tract, the etiquette book, the travel account, the history book, and the personal history book, whether in the form of biography or of autobiography.

There is no official agreement concerning the novel's length. One sometimes hears forty-five thousand words as a minimum, but the form includes among its examples books that are slightly longer than so-called novellas and books such as Richardson's *Clarissa*, which is longer than all of Thomas Wolfe's novels combined. The novel's subject matter can encompass something as broad and traditional as heroic legend (in the case of *Don Quixote*) or as specific and contemporary as modern journalism (in the case of *In Cold Blood*).

Novels have been categorized in a variety of ways: by method of narration (omniscient, first person, epistolary), by length (novellas, novelettes, "short novels"), by structure (the roman-fleuve, the picaresque, the "road novel"), by level of seriousness ("escapist" fiction, the summer novel), by theme (the bildungsroman), by setting in time (the historical novel, the period novel), and by setting in place ("local colorism," the regional novel, the "California novel").

Novels have been discussed vis-à-vis other narrative forms in terms of the relative positioning (either through ability, morality, or social rank) of the characters (a good Fryeism). Thus, pastoral romances feature characters slightly above us, aristocrats and such; the chivalric romance concerns characters with abilities far in advance of our own; while the jest book, criminal biography, and satiric piece deal with characters (morally) below us. The novel—the argument goes—deals with characters more or less like us, though the addition of such techniques as magic realism can destabilize the categories.

In some cases there is the danger of confusing the novel (*Jane Eyre*, for example) with a work that is closer to romance (*Wuthering Heights*, for example). The abbreviated version of the novel would be the "short story," while the briefer version of the romance would be the "tale," the sort of thing Kafka and Karen Blixen ("Isak Dinesen") write. The tale has connections with the gothic as well as with science fiction.

Novelists who hope to see their books turned into films realize that the standard film script is a far more constrained genre, with strict expectations with regard to length (plus or minus 120 pages) and strict expectations with regard to plot points (coming generally at pages 25–27 and pages 85–90). The success of *L.A. Confidential* (a sprawling novel that was part of a tetralogy, but one resulting in a tight screenplay) is heartening in this regard, indicating that novelists can continue to enjoy the freedom and latitude offered by the form without giving up all hope of a film sale.

Discussions of subgenres within crime writing broadly considered tend to be quite fuzzy at the edges. What is the difference between a "thriller" and a novel of "suspense," for example? Spy fiction or espionage fiction is more easily identified, as is the techno-thriller, but how much crime need there be to separate crime fiction from mainstream fiction? And what of the social melodrama that includes a healthy dollop of criminality? Booksellers and publishers sometimes list their biggest names (Elmore Leonard or Thomas Harris, for example) among their mainstream offerings, since these authors have attracted broad audiences, just as bookstores put the works of these authors under fiction as well as under crime (or even under classics, in the case of Hammett, Chandler, or James M. Cain).

Thus, both scholarly commentary and the nature of the marketplace reinforce the fact that the novel and noir writing, broadly conceived, are extremely elastic with regard to formal requirements. At the same time, readers of the latter bring a set of relatively firm expectations to each book. The result is that those who work this particular territory are both liberated and constrained at the same time. Their achievements come, in part, through an appreciation of the balance between the liberation and the constraint and the degree to which that balance can be adjusted. This is a more difficult task than it at first appears to be, but we are blessed that so many writers are able to accomplish it so often and so well.

The difficulty of the challenge and tenuousness of the accomplishment can be illustrated by James Ellroy's newest novel, *The Cold Six Thousand* (2001), the second volume in the "Underworld, U.S.A." trilogy. The book is drawing very strong responses, both pro and con. Ellroy has again refined his stylistic instrument, giving us— through most of the novel—successions of parallel, sometimes alliterating declarative sentences:

> He trashed. He tidied. He worked fast. He worked fastidious.
> He tossed the medicine chest. He restacked the shelves. He debuilt and rebuilt the toilet. He tapped the walls. He pulled up rugs. He laid them back straight. He slit-checked the chairs. He slit-checked the sofa. He slit-checked the bed.
> No slits. No stash holes. No duplicates extant. No stash of loose clips.
> He popped some Bayers. He chased them with gin. He dredged up some guts. Queers overkilled queers. It was standard cop wisdom. All cops knew it.
> He got a knife. He stabbed Jim Koethe ninety-four times. (p. 277)

Even positive reviewers are confessing to a certain degree of frustration with the narrative, comparing it, in some cases, with *Finnegans Wake*. This is a very odd comparison for a number of reasons, but it points up the conflicted nature of the reviews. Readers so want to enjoy and praise Ellroy, and they somehow feel betrayed. Some have responded in kind. The following is from an online review on Amazon's website:

> Ellroy wrote LA Quartet. Ellroy wrote noir. Ellroy gained fans boo-coo. Ellroy got plaudits. Ellroy wanted MORE. Ellroy got serious. Ellroy wrote Tabloid. Ellroy eschewed crime writing. Ellroy took White Jazz style. Ellroy did it MORE in Tabloid. GQ loved it. Time loved it. Ellroy got press. Ellroy got praise. Ellroy shook and shimmied. He did the Wah-Watusi. Ellroy wanted MORE. Ellroy wrote Cold Six Thousand. Ellroy said crime fiction is done. Crime fiction is passé. Noir is moribund. Dig it: Ellroy says he writes historical fiction now. New book has triad of mob goons. New book scopes drugs / murder / mob hits / sleaze / corruption. New book warps White Jazz style. New book overdoes style. Style gets confusing. Style too staccato. Style too dense. Style eschews character. Style eschews depth. Ellroy wants to write historical fiction. Ellroy eschews history for conspiracy. Ellroy eschews 60s ambience. Ellroy gives us Mob epic. The Mob ran the country. The Mob called the shots. Ellroy calls it: private nightmare of public policy. Ellroy eschews public policy. Ellroy deals only with private mob plots. The 60s gets bogged down. The 60s gets lost. The 60s gets washed out by mob plots / phone transcriptions / noir violence / Hughes / Sal Mineo / Hoover fixations. Call it: Cold Six vintage Ellroy. Thug triad / noir dames / mob plots / gore / fatalism. Cold Six not historical fiction. Characters shallow / period ambience shallow / plot byzantine. Call it: Read it for Ellroy. Read it for new spin on Noir. Still the best crime fiction. But as historical fiction? Bad juju.

The reviewer is correct that this is not unalloyed historical fiction, despite any protestations to the contrary. The ethos is clear. The novel studies the effects of big government (embodied principally in Hoover's FBI but also in Robert Kennedy's actions as attorney general), big business (Hughes Aircraft), organized crime, the Las Vegas Police Department, and other institutions on the lives (usually doomed lives) of a set of individuals. This is pure Chandler on the large scale.

What is missing in the criticisms of Ellroy's style, I believe (and in some of the criticisms of an absence of incident), is an appreciation of the challenges in writing a trilogy. The second volume is perforce transitional, and since very few writers write trilogies, we are not as adept as we need to be in describing them.

American Tabloid ends with the death of John Kennedy in Dallas. Martin Luther King and Robert Kennedy fall in the second volume, but their deaths are almost afterthoughts within the rhythms of the novel. How will the trilogy conclude, assuming that it ends, as promised, in 1973? With Watergate? With the death of Lyndon Johnson? With Henry Kissinger's receipt of the Nobel Prize for peace? With a single great crescendo or a multilayered, multileveled one? And who will create that crescendo and what will we know and feel when we experience its details and learn its mysteries?

We do not know, but the effectiveness of the final crescendo will be affected by the groundwork that precedes it. The second movement of a symphony is perforce different from the last movement. Ellroy is preparing us. The stylistic instrument, which has been criticized as opaque, is, on the contrary, clear in the extreme. The relative absence of incident (criticized by many) is countered by that very instrument. In a sense, the novel is all plot and breathless action, since the chief rhetorical device that undergirds the narrative is parataxis, the endless stringing together of statements without the usual connectives.

This is not history or a historical novel so much as it is the purest crossover between historiography and crime narrative. The historian seeks connections between events. The crime novelist seeks connections between certain institutions and the impact of their actions upon individuals. Ellroy's stylistic instrument floods our imagination with actions and impressions, eschewing the connections, for the moment, since he is drawing us in as readers of fictional narrative, forcing us to absorb facts and impressions as they appear, before they have been historically digested. At the same time, he is leading us toward the ultimate connections, connections that are likely to be shattering in their impact, even though we might be able to anticipate some of them through the use of historical hindsight.

In this context, transitional volumes are not pointless passages through wastelands but journeys toward something unspeakable and inevitable. The ability to create such a transition—in this case a novel of nearly seven hundred pages—utilizing the language of the street and the rhetorical devices of the Greeks, while embodying those words and forms in a crossover narrative that bridges historical fiction and crime fiction, is impressive indeed. We should not be disappointed. At the same time we should not yet experience a sense of closure. We are shuffling in the aisles, absorbing the impact of the first two acts, and looking toward the final act with a sense of impending doom. That is precisely where Ellroy wants us to be.

Afterword

The current panoply of crime writing includes a vast amount of material in a growing number of formats. It is clear that we are seeing a second renaissance of this form of category fiction. The writers of stories for *Black Mask* would be impressed with the output (and the audience reception) of their current colleagues' work.

The systems through which this material is distributed are becoming increasingly complex. The number of New York publishing houses has shrunk just at the time that the internet has made possible new forms of distribution. Online magazines such as *Nefarious: Tales of Mystery* are thriving, and such work is increasingly becoming available in handheld electronic form (by, for example, Victoria Esposito-Shea's *HandHeldCrime*). XC Publishing distributes its materials in multiple formats: ebook, diskette, cd, download, hard copy, and audio. At the same time, a number of regional presses are publishing the mysteries and crime novels for which New York lacks space, and a small number of university presses have entered the market.

This is all part of a larger set of publishing patterns. The conglomerates are less and less interested in midlist titles, and the university presses, which have been struggling, now have access to material that offers what for them are large sales. This, combined with electronic commerce, is a boon to readers, who can enjoy both a wide choice of reading material and the prompts, updates, and other marketing aids / devices utilized by Amazon, Barnes & Noble, and other companies. The publishing picture has never been more complex; at the same time it has never been more easy to access.

Despite this flurry of activity and this range of options, there is a striking degree of commonality in the themes and topoi that repeat across the genre. The instances offered in the foregoing chapters

could easily be expanded with multiple examples. There is also a no-
table degree of continuity with regard to these matters across the
years. Chandler was summarizing much of what he saw in contemporary practice, but his generalizations still largely apply today as
we survey current writing.

If one were to take a cultural inventory of our concerns and desires based on a broad reading of crime writing, the result would be
something like the following. As a nation we imagine a society that
is still marked by frontiers and borders. These serve a multiplicity
of functions. They invite us, offering adventure. They help us form
a conception of our society that both defines and delineates that
society's history and serves to characterize its members. Individuals are measured by landforms and divided by imaginary borders.
Such a society offers great promise, but in a context that has often
proved violent (physically, socially, and economically). We cherish
and lament these features simultaneously, and our ambivalence gen-
erates narratives rooted in those twin perceptions.

After a century of war and a succession of revelations concerning
public leaders, our concept of divinity, like our concept of heroism,
has been shaken. We long for evidence of that divinity but do not regularly expect it. Religious institutions have been subjected to searching examination and have not always fared well in the process. Graham Greene once said that he had never been a believer but had never
lost his faith. That is as good a description as I can offer of much contemporary feeling. Santayana said that he held a pious view of the
universe but was an atheist of the sort represented by Spinoza; he
would not worship gods fashioned in the image of men, particularly
by men seeking to exploit their creations for personal gain.

The treatment of public figures at the hands of an increasingly
tabloid press has eroded our sense of heroism, not because the
tabloids have been incorrect, but because they (and the full range of
electronic and print media paralleling their practices) have all too often been accurate. Thus, the distrust of institutions and of some of
the individuals who lead them, combined with a heightened sense
of their callous self-interest (exacerbated by their public protestations to the contrary), has been a constant in our fiction as it was in
Chandler's.

In the broader society, issues of race have sometimes been confronted and problems have, to some degree, been ameliorated, but an open and honest discussion has not yet occurred. Injustice remains, and there has been more posturing and politicization (on all sides) than wisdom. While popular culture can still indulge in stereotyping for the purpose of humor, it has also more often understood the importance of humor in achieving understanding than have our political leaders and opinion makers. If our fiction is any guide to our attitudes, we desire justice and brotherhood without a sacrifice of individuality or of the ability to laugh at ourselves.

Our crime fiction suggests that we are concerned about our society's fundamental sanity. While the likelihood of being murdered by a serial killer is extremely remote, the continual presence of such figures in category fiction suggests an ongoing set of real human concerns. In this case it is probably a displaced concern for the loss of sanity, or at least civility, in general. At a time when our economy is regaining strength and we are increasingly united as a people we are still seeing ongoing incidences of rage of various sorts. Some of this is traceable to the fracturing of the social contract in business and industry and some is traceable to new electronic media and the fact that we are now working around the clock.

Deborah Tannen has described what she terms our "argument culture." Part of the coarsening of our society can be blamed on television programming (Jerry Springer, Jenny Jones) that serves as both symptom and cause. Viewers are exposed to individuals who lead disordered lives and who resort to abuse and violence as a first step in dispute resolution. This serves viewers both as entertainment and, in a sense, as instruction. It can add to our current rage or slake it when we see deserving individuals become the target of anger and physical violence. It can also provide solace, in that our own condition, no matter how desperate, is better than that of the figures appearing in this sort of programming.

Single-issue voting and the resulting political litmus tests and divisiveness are part of the problem, as is the ongoing spectacle of litigators who see themselves as hired guns rather than as servants of justice or representatives of the court. Increasingly, our concept of news analysis is reduced to the sound of two extreme voices screaming at and interrupting one another. The recent concept of the president as the country's chief executive officer rather than as a national leader (never mind hero) and, hopefully, figure of dignity is a contributing factor, reducing the office to purely utilitarian rather than moral or spiritual norms.

It may not be so much the violence of crime writing that attracts us as its relative purity. In "The Simple Art of Murder," Chandler describes the sexual morality of the detective. "I do not care much about his private life; he is neither a eunuch nor a satyr; I think he might seduce a duchess and I am quite sure he would not spoil a virgin; if he is a man of honor in one thing, he is that in all things." As Marlowe says in *The Long Goodbye*, "I'm a romantic, Bernie. I hear voices crying in the night and I go see what's the matter. You don't make a dime that way." It is a very different image from that of a president being fellated by an intern next to the Oval Office.

The fact that our society is sometimes compared with Christopher Isherwood's Berlin is a growing cause of concern. The decadence is clear in something as simple as television wrestling. Where it once offered a touch of ritual and ballet, it is now nothing more than vulgar, commercial spectacle. To see opponents thrown onto piles of steel tacks or mounds of feces bespeaks an appetite for "entertainment" that consciously reduces our sense of human dignity.

Whatever the etiology, the increase in incidents of road rage, airline rage, school shootings, and individuals going "postal" is palpable. The border between sanity and insanity, it is clear, can be crossed and is being crossed frequently while the edges of society have grown progressively more jagged.

This may be indicated in part by the rebirth of interest in the work of the 1950s pulpmaster Jim Thompson. Dark and brooding, Thompson traces the niches and corners of the heart of darkness and the hollow universe in which it beats. Filmgoers will remember Pat Hingle's portrayal of the gangster Bobo Justus in *The Grifters* (directed by Stephen Frears, 1990, with screenplay by the great mystery writer Donald Westlake), terrorizing Anjelica Huston's Lilly Dillon with the prospect of being beaten with a towel full of fresh oranges. If the beating is done properly it can be used for insurance scams—marking the body with ugly bruises. If it is not done properly there can be permanent damage: "You never shit right again."

Thompson's masterpiece is *The Killer Inside Me* (1952), an account of a homicidal deputy sheriff in a small town in Texas. His name is Lou Ford, and he thinks and talks like this:

I've loafed around the streets sometimes, leaned against a store front with my hat pushed back and one boot hooked back around the other—hell, you've probably seen me if you've ever been out this way—I've stood like that, looking nice and friendly and stupid, like I wouldn't piss if my pants were on fire. And all the time I'm laughing myself sick inside. Just watching the people.

"If you've ever been out this way" does not refer to Texas. It refers to the valley of the shadow of death just outside the door of your home or local church. Our fiction suggests a collective sense that the number of Lou Fords in our midst has multiplied significantly.

Our crime fiction suggests that we long for a sense of place, perhaps for a new sense of *places*. We long to laugh. We long to learn. Most of all, we long for justice of all sorts—justice that is administered swiftly and fairly; justice that is built upon fact and evidence, not upon judicial or jury bias or whim.

English mysteries have been positioned to offer us such a sense of justice, but our deeper selves understand that what may be temporarily comforting is not always realistic. Our desires and longings are tempered by experience and the skepticism it breeds, but that does not mean that we end our efforts.

Finally, the success of crime writing suggests that its readership and viewership seek supple, imaginative art, art that can exploit the conventions of genre without being shackled by them, art that can borrow from other forms and, in the process, expand our sense of the possibility of the form itself. We are blessed in having so many writers producing so much work of a high order for that audience.

For Further Reading

Rather than provide a bibliography or a list of footnotes I am including this essay. I hope it will suffice. The background reading for this book includes the works of more than seventy authors, and those works can be identified more easily and effectively in this format than through a lengthy bibliography. The card pages of the newest novels by prolific authors list their works to date, and electronic booksellers such as Barnes & Noble and Amazon offer lists of all the authors' books in print as well as links to secondhand copies available from individual booksellers.

Moreover, the electronic booksellers provide a host of information not available in conventional bibliographies: illustrations of the cover art, "reviews," lists of other authors favored by the buyers of the author in question, sales rankings, links to author biographies, links to interviews, and other material. Amazon, for example, has a separate Mystery and Thrillers page. It lists bestsellers, the current and next month's releases (in hardcover as well as paper), features, and a column by Otto Penzler, the dean of American commentators on mystery and crime writing and the world's preeminent bibliographer of crime and mystery-related genre fiction.

Readers may be struck by the output of some of the writers discussed here. Lawrence Block, for example, has written more than one hundred novels, not all listed on his various volumes, and Evan Hunter has written close to that number. Some of the authors' work is not really cataloged, for example the script doctoring of James Crumley or Gerald Petievich. In order to develop a sense of the writing lives of these individuals one must follow the often ephemeral material appearing in fanzines and on the internet. There is rich interview material, for example, on James Ellroy on the internet and endless speculative material on matters that have sparked curiosity.

151

Still photographs from shoots for the film version of *Hannibal*, for example, were appearing on the internet seven months before the film's scheduled release.

Mystery bookshops frequently carry fanzines such as *Armchair Detective* and *Mystery Scene* as well as other relevant materials. For example, bound proofs of forthcoming books (known as advance reader copies, or ARCs) are often issued to reviewers and to bookshops. Some booksellers sell these (though they are not supposed to), so that an active curiosity can be satisfied before the actual publication date. These materials often contain information on the size of the initial print run and other matters, designed to hype the project and catch the bookseller's attention. While that information can be exaggerated, it offers some insight into the status of a project and the anticipated dimensions of the expected audience.

One anecdote might suggest the level of interest on the part of fans and offer some insight into editorial interest in critical issues. When James Ellroy's *White Jazz* (the final volume in the "L.A. Quartet") was completed, Ellroy had moved from Mysterious Press to Knopf. The French rights were sold and the French edition issued. At Knopf, however, Sonny Mehta had reservations about the breathless, phenomenological narrative, feeling that sections of it were simply too tight to be followed. Thus, he asked Ellroy to make some changes in the text. Ellroy did, and the American edition appeared. By that time many of the Ellroy faithful, anxious to see the final volume of the quartet, had secured the French version and already read the book. This is an example of the kind of information that can be secured only by combing through relatively ephemeral publications or postings or by talking to insiders in the trade.

The lore of crime writing—publishers' plans and expectations, agents' interests and expectations—can be obtained through the newsletters issued by the Mystery Writers of America and from a between-the-lines inspection of *Literary Market Place*, which is generally available in the reference collections of academic libraries. Such material also finds its way onto the internet, though the publishing industry is still relatively conservative with regard to electronic media.

Given the signing circuit, owners of mystery bookshops are excellent sources for information, lore, and gossip, particularly with regard to local writers who frequent their establishments. These individuals are nearly always fans as well as merchants. They also frequently possess a professorial knowledge of bibliography and can direct readers to little-known materials, materials that have appeared under multiple titles, and so on. For all of the violence and conflict in the books these individuals sell, they are generally a convivial and congenial lot, happy to take the time to discuss their passion with their customers.

Introduction

On "narrative" criticism, see Tzvetan Todorov, *The Fantastic: A Structural Approach to a Literary Genre*, trans. Richard Howard (1973), p. 98.

Chapter I. Frontiers and Borders

Northrop Frye's thesis statement is *Anatomy of Criticism: Four Essays* (1957), one of the masterpieces of modern criticism. The heavy influence of Jung dates the book somewhat, but the current work in sociobiology should return Frye to a position of prominence. On comedy, see his frequently anthologized essay, "The Argument of Comedy," or a piece such as his introductory essay to the Pelican edition of *The Tempest*. A center dedicated to Frye has been established at Victoria College of the University of Toronto, and a complete edition of all of his work is planned.

L. J. Potts's little book *Comedy* (1948) remains useful. For a sense of the "interim" readings of life offered by tragedy, see Robert Ornstein, *The Moral Vision of Jacobean Tragedy* (1960). Many of the conflicts and instabilities of the Renaissance are discussed by Michael McKeon in *The Origins of the English Novel, 1600–1740* (1987). See also the very interesting hypotheses of Stephen Toulmin in *Cosmopolis: The Hidden Agenda of Modernity* (1990).

George Santayana felt that the characters encountered in Dickens's novels had their everyday counterparts in the streets of London. His essay on Dickens (1921) is reprinted in Norman Henfrey, ed., *Selected Criticism of George Santayana*, vol. 1 (1968).

The happy villagers are introduced at the outset of David Lynch's *Blue Velvet* (1986) just as the protagonist, Jeffrey Beaumont, stumbles upon a severed human ear. What first appears to be the world of comedy is revealed as the world of noir, a world in which a parallel universe of evil exists side by side with one of good, a world of evil that exists preeminently in the human heart. The same sorts of parallels appear in Lynch's television serial, *Twin Peaks*, which is, interestingly, set on the American / Canadian border.

See John Cawelti's *Adventure, Mystery, and Romance: Formula Stories as Art and Popular Culture* (1976). This is the most important study of category fiction to date. Cawelti is a sympathetic reader, conversant with all manner of category fiction as well as classic literary texts. See also Robin W. Winks, ed., *Detective Fiction: A Collection of Critical Essays* (1988). The Winks collection includes important pieces by Winks, George Grella, Cawelti, Jacques Barzun, and others, plus the famous essay by Edmund Wilson, "Who Cares Who Killed Roger Ackroyd?" See especially the two essays by George Grella, "The Formal Detective Novel" and "The Hard-Boiled Detective Novel." A fanzine in book form is the much reprinted *Murder Ink: The Mystery Reader's Companion* by Dilys Winn (1977). Howard Haycraft's *Murder for Pleasure: The Life and Times of the Detective Story* (1984) is a history up to World War II. Haycraft's *The Art of the Mystery Story: A Collection of Critical Essays* (1983) can also be recommended. In addition to pieces by G. K. Chesterton, Dorothy Sayers, Joseph Wood Krutch, and others, it includes a piece entitled "The Professor and the Detective" by the great intellectual historian Marjorie Hope Nicolson, which addresses the attractiveness of detective stories for academics. Horror writing, which has a significant overlap with noir, is surveyed in Edward J. Ingebretsen, S.J., *Maps of Heaven, Maps of Hell: Religious Terror as Memory from the Puritans to Stephen King* (1996).

The literature on category fiction is voluminous. A few suggestions for further reading can be offered. For additional differentiation between the detective novel and the crime novel, see Tony Hilfer, *The Crime Novel: A Deviant Genre* (1990). Dennis Porter, *The Pursuit of Crime: Art and Ideology in Detective Fiction* (1981), offers interesting material on the history of crime literature with some judicious applications of poststructuralist theory. For points of contact between westerns and detective fiction, see Marcus Klein, *Easterns, Westerns, and Private Eyes: American Matters, 1870–1900*. R. Gordon Kelly's *Mystery Fiction and Modern Life* (1998) can be paired with Jon

Thompson's *Fiction, Crime, and Empire: Clues to Modernity and Post-modernism* (1993) for links between genre fiction and the modern, modernist, and postmodern contexts. Heta Pyrhönen's *Murder from an Academic Angle: An Introduction to the Study of the Detective Narrative* (1994) studies detective stories as literature and discusses the manner in which the academy has approached them. Kathleen Gregory Klein's *The Woman Detective: Gender and Genre* (2d ed., 1995) provides a learned treatment of the subject. For an interesting account of the relationships between fictional narrative and the history of forensic science, see Ronald R. Thomas, *Detective Fiction and the Rise of Forensic Science* (1999). LeRoy Lad Panek, *New Hard-Boiled Writers, 1970s–1990s* (2000), examines ten writers, half of whom figure prominently in *Nice and Noir*. Panek's book pays more attention to the writers and their works to date than to the larger themes that emerge in those works.

The Newgate Calendar or Malefactors' Bloody Register is available in a modern paperback edition (ed. Sandra Lee Kerman, 1962). This edition reproduces earlier illustrations, many of them lurid. For other examples of nonnovelistic prose narrative see Charles C. Mish's collection *Short Fiction of the Seventeenth Century* (1963). For the influence on novelistic fiction of prenovelistic forms, see J. Paul Hunter, *Before Novels: The Cultural Contexts of Eighteenth-Century English Fiction* (1990).

Sydney Kirkpatrick's subject is the death of William Desmond Taylor, the second most famous Hollywood murder case after that of Elizabeth Short, the so-called Black Dahlia. The third most famous is perhaps that of Thelma Todd, which has also resulted in an excellent true crime book: Andy Edmonds, *Hot Toddy: The True Story of Hollywood's Most Sensational Murder* (1989). The Thelma Todd case is perhaps less interesting than the other two, since they (like the Jack the Ripper case) have not been definitively solved, whereas the Todd case is explained conclusively. The Todd case does have the advantage of having been perpetrated in a location that drivers of the Pacific Coast Highway pass daily, while the other two sites are visited infrequently.

The standard account of *Black Mask* is by William F. Nolan, *The Black Mask Boys: Masters in the Hard-Boiled School of Detective Fiction* (1987). See also Peter Haining, ed., *The Fantastic Pulps* (1976), and Erin A. Smith, *Hard-Boiled: Working-Class Readers and Pulp Magazines*

(2000). Note that Nolan's book includes samples from the writings of the contributors, for example some of the deliciously hard-boiled writing of Carroll John Daly, one of the principal prototypes for the language of the detective as understood by Raymond Chandler. Copies of *Black Mask* are available through such mystery bookshops as John Mitchell's on Washington Boulevard in Pasadena. Those containing stories by Chandler are more expensive. The cover art is generally lurid and fun. There is a complete run of *Black Mask* at the UCLA research library, which also contains interesting Chandler materials (first editions, shooting scripts of films, and contemporary material culture items such as restaurant menus). See also E. R. Hagemann, *A Comprehensive Index to* Black Mask, *1920–1951,* with brief annotations, preface, and editorial apparatus (1982).

Chandler's essay "The Simple Art of Murder" is available in a paperback collection with the same title (1972). There is fascinating critical material in Chandler's letters. See Frank MacShane, ed., *Selected Letters of Raymond Chandler* (1981). This book frequently turns up on remainder shelves; it remains an exceptional bargain.

For Frye on romanticism, see *A Study of English Romanticism* (1968). A small paperback original in a Random House series, this is one of Frye's most interesting and valuable works. It also contains important material on humor and the grotesque.

On Gilkes and Dulwich, see Tom Hiney's excellent new biography of Chandler, *Raymond Chandler: A Biography* (1997), now available in a paperback edition (1999).

For Las Vegas see Robert Venturi, Denise Scott Brown, and Steven Izenour, *Learning from Las Vegas: The Forgotten Symbolism of Architectural Form* (rev. ed., 1993).

For Henry David Thoreau see Sherman Paul, *The Shores of America: Thoreau's Inward Exploration* (1958). F. O. Matthiessen's overreading of *White Jacket* is discussed by Bruce Harkness, "Bibliography and the Novelistic Fallacy," *Studies in Bibliography* 12 (1959): 59–73.

Camille Paglia's major work is *Sexual Personae: Art and Decadence from Nefertiti to Emily Dickinson* (1990). A second volume is expected. See also her essay collections: *Sex, Art, and American Culture* (1992) and *Vamps and Tramps* (1994).

Philip Rahv's "Paleface and Redskin" essay was reprinted in *Image and Idea: Fourteen Essays on Literary Themes* (1949).

On realism, see the article by George J. Becker and Monroe Beardsley in Joseph T. Shipley, ed., *Dictionary of World Literature: Criticism, Forms, Technique* (rev. ed., 1962). This remains one of the best guides to literary terms, with individual articles—in some cases essays—by leading figures.

T. E. Hulme's "Romanticism and Classicism" was written in 1913 and first appeared in Herbert Read, ed., *Speculations* (1924). It was reprinted in Robert Wooster Stallman, ed., *Critiques and Essays in Criticism, 1920–1948* (1949). The course of Romanticism and its interplay with both category fiction and contemporary literary theory is one of the principal subjects of my *After the Death of Literature* (1997).

For a discussion of the connections between Aristotelian theory and category fiction, see Dorothy L. Sayers, "Aristotle on Detective Fiction," in Winks, ed., *Detective Fiction: A Collection of Critical Essays.*

John Milton's comments on Spenser's Bower of Bliss appear in *Areopagitica*, pp. 728–29, in Merritt Hughes's *John Milton: Complete Poems and Major Prose* (1957).

On the city of nets see the excellent book by Otto Friedrich, *City of Nets: A Portrait of Hollywood in the 1940's* (1986).

On the aristocracy simply "being," see Jürgen Habermas, *The Structural Transformation of the Public Sphere: An Inquiry into a Category of Bourgeois Society,* trans. Thomas Burger, with the assistance of Frederick Lawrence (1989).

The account of the vote in the Pacific Northwest appears in Stephen Ambrose's *Undaunted Courage: Meriwether Lewis, Thomas Jefferson, and the Opening of the American West* (1996).

Chapter II. Eternal Vigilance

A noteworthy, semi-paperless character who has recently emerged on the thriller / suspense scene is Lee Child's Jack Reacher. Reacher (*Killing Floor, Die Trying, Tripwire, Running Blind, Echo Burning*) is a former Military Police investigator who has left the service early and who travels from place to place with little more than the current set of clothes on his back. While there are connections established with his past, particularly in Child's more recent work, Reacher is internally riven and almost viscerally incapable of connections and permanence. He happens upon troubling circumstances, is drawn in, and attempts to right wrongs. Child's creation merges the wandering American figure set against an often bleak horizon with the traditions of both the police procedural novel and the thriller. The most recent book in the series, *Echo Burning*, is very nicely plotted and represents something of a departure from the unremitting suspense of the first four novels in the series; all five are highly recommended. Child, a former screenwriter for British television, is another British writer—like Tim Willocks—who is haunted by America and depicts it expertly.

For Leslie Fiedler's discussion of malleable characters, see his *What Was Literature? Class Culture and Mass Society* (1982).

The leaders in the "return to aesthetic concerns" movement have been Emory Elliott and Elaine Scarry. Scarry's recent *On Beauty and Being Just* (1999) has received polarized reviews.

Chapter III. The Never Ending Story

Ellroy's *Dick Contino's Blues* appears in his book *Hollywood Nocturnes*, but it was separately published in *Granta* 46 (winter 1994), an issue devoted to crime. The *Granta* version of the novella includes a rich set of illustrations, most dealing with Contino's life, but a number featuring such individuals as Mickey Cohen and Spade Cooley, who figure in Ellroy's tetralogy, the "L.A. Quartet."

Mike Davis's *City of Quartz: Excavating the Future in Los Angeles* (1990) is not to be missed. A former truck driver turned academic, Davis knows the City of Angels intimately. He approaches it from the point of view of urban planning, but in the context of deep cultural history. He is, for example, fully cognizant of the noir literature and brings it into play in this study. His most recent book, which can also be recommended, is *Ecology of Fear: Los Angeles and the Imagination of Disaster* (1998).

Wayne Booth's classic study of narrative, *The Rhetoric of Fiction* (1961), influenced a generation of readers and remains worth reading today.

On pseudo events see Daniel J. Boorstin, *The Image: A Guide to Pseudo-Events in America* (1987). One of the most thoughtful books on political correctness is Russell Jacoby's *Dogmatic Wisdom: How the Culture Wars Divert Education and Distract America* (1994). One can also recommend Jacoby's *The Last Intellectuals: American Culture in the Age of Academe* (1987), which discusses the historical events that eroded the opportunities for writing careers beyond the academy.

Chapter IV. The Avenging Angel

A segment from Vachss's unpublished novel, *A Bomb Built in Hell*, was included by Matthew J. Bruccoli and Richard Layman in their series "A Matter of Crime: New Stories from the Masters of Mystery and Suspense" in the late 1980s, but the titles in that series are now, regrettably, out of print. Amazon, however, has recently serialized the novel; see http://www.amazon.com/exec/obidos/tg/feature/-/65277/102-4131547-6261751. The site also includes comments by Vachss on his early writing career and his agent's attempts to sell his first novel.

Milton's view that without freedom of choice we would be either puppets or automata is articulated in *Areopagitica*, p. 733 in the Hughes edition. I have discussed the problem of evil and the various interpretations applied thereto in *Samuel Johnson and the Problem of Evil* (1975).

Chapter V. Together in the Wilderness

Woo's film *Face/Off* (1997) ends this way, for example, and note the clever echo in Jackie Chan's amusing *Shanghai Noon* (directed by Tom Dey, 2000). See Eliade's *Cosmos and History: The Myth of the Eternal Return*, trans. Willard R. Trask (1954).

Fiedler's masterpiece is *Love and Death in the American Novel* (rev. ed., 1966).

For a digest of Johnson's views, see Joseph Epes Brown, *The Critical Opinions of Samuel Johnson* (1926). The best guide to Johnson's criticism remains that of Jean H. Hagstrum, *Samuel Johnson's Literary Criticism* (1952). See also Leopold Damrosch Jr., *The Uses of Johnson's Criticism* (1976), and R. D. Stock, *Samuel Johnson and Neoclassical Dramatic Theory: The Intellectual Context of the Preface to Shakespeare* (1973). See especially W. R. Keast, "The Theoretical Foundations of Johnson's Criticism," in *Critics and Criticism, Ancient and Modern*, ed. R. S. Crane (1952), and Keast's "Johnson's Criticism of the Metaphysical Poets," *ELH* 17 (1950): 59–70. My book *After the Death of Literature*

(1997) looks at the culture wars and contemporary academic theory and criticism from Johnson's inferred point of view.

For Jane Tompkins, see *West of Everything: The Inner Life of Westerns* (1992). This is an engaging book with an interesting thesis.

There is an interesting merger of the western and the crime novel in Parker's recent *Potshot*, the title referring to a town in Arizona to which Spenser is called (and to which he brings his own posse). The novel adopts one of the classic western plots: the tale of the town bedeviled by corruption in the face of ineffectual local authority. The standard approach is to make that authority part of the corruption, so that the hero is perceived as an isolated "outsider." This plays to a number of noir themes. Parker modernizes the story, however, by showing that the gang of grubby ne'er-do-wells suspected of the principal evils are small fry compared with the moneyed interests lurking in the background. *Potshot* is interesting in this regard because it is enjoying great commercial success. This is Parker's best-selling book to date, with a first printing of 170,000 copies (*Publishers Weekly*, April 2, 2001, p. 16). The story of the big city PI in the corrupt small town is a television mainstay, one used, for example, in every Quinn Martin series. Parker's success suggests the extent of the reading public's appetite for a new version of an extremely conventional story.

In his just-released *Gunman's Rhapsody* Parker takes the ultimate step—not just penning a bona fide western, but rewriting the story of the gunfight at the OK Corral. This is sacred territory, and the resulting novel consists of material that stretches Parker and forces him to come to terms with elements of history and period details far in advance of anything he has yet attempted. Interestingly, he includes contemporary newspaper clips à la Ellroy to further ground the narrative and constructs characters more distant from Spenser and Hawk than any in his previous works. His version of the story depicts the political divisions and machinations of the time and focuses on Wyatt's triangular relationship with Josie Marcus and Sheriff Johnny Behan (a significant subtext in George P. Cosmatos's masterful *Tombstone* [1993], which principally stresses Wyatt's efforts to eradicate what amounts to an organized crime family). Parker has Wyatt kill Johnny Ringo, while Cosmatos has Doc Holliday do it. There is some historical basis for an earlier contretemps between Holliday and Ringo, but the current wisdom is that Ringo committed suicide. For Cosmatos, Holliday serves as consumptive avenging angel, the ultimate partner in the wasteland. For Parker he is principally an alcoholic who consistently masks the effects of drink while effectively wielding a gun.

The successor to *Homicide: Life on the Streets* for best writing for television is HBO's franchise series, *The Sopranos*. A mafia soap opera, it combines the best of both traditions: culture, language, and lore with a set of characters whose endless problems are the source of equally endless fascination. The difference between *The Sopranos* and representative examples of the traditions from which it springs lies in its quality. As with *Homicide*, the dialogue is all, and the dialogue is as studied and nuanced as the most discerning might demand. Each word is weighted, and each episode repays repeated viewings. This is not so much Godfather Knows Best as it is the Godfather as Everyman, running a New Jersey crime family while simultaneously coping with what my freshman English teacher (on tiptoes) called the quotidian vicissitudes of banal existence. These vicissitudes, however, are presented with more edge, more blood, and more skill than the normal garden state variety.

One indication of the success of *The Sopranos* is the space devoted to it on HBO's website. There are constant tie-ins: web chats, "live" webcams, merchandise offers, character files, episode summaries, reprises, and teases. This is the sole program for which many pay the HBO subscription fee, the program often described as "the only show on television I regularly watch." At its heart lie two twinned conceits—the degree of criminality that can inhere in the "normal" personality and the degree of normality that can inhere in the criminal. The world of the series is an enclosed one—culturally, geographically, ethnically, morally—but it is a world that manages to feel very familiar. It is a world with vows of silence, but one in which the dialogue is endless and continually engaging.

M. H. Abrams's description of the pragmatic tradition is in *The Mirror and the Lamp: Romantic Theory and the Critical Tradition* (1953).

For Russell Jacoby, see his *Dogmatic Wisdom: How the Culture Wars Divert Education and Distract America* (1994).

Chapter VI. The Electric Mist

I have discussed the high/low eighteenth centuries in *Daily Life in Johnson's London* (1983).

Harry Berger Jr.'s piece, "Naïve Consciousness and Culture Change: An Essay in Historical Structuralism," appeared in the *Bulletin of the Midwest Modern Language Association* 6.1 (1973) and is discussed by Cawelti in *Adventure, Mystery, and Romance,* p. 16.

While narratives are often set in major media markets, there are a number of important writers who locate their stories elsewhere: Earl Emerson (Seattle), Loren Estleman (Detroit), Kent Anderson (Portland), Wayne Dundee (Rockford, Illinois), Patricia Cornwell (Richmond, Virginia, and environs), and Peter Blauner (Atlantic City and elsewhere). Chicago, of course, has Barbara D'Amato, Sara Paretsky, and the late Eugene Izzi. On setting and the procedural, see Gary J. Hausladen, *Places for Dead Bodies* (2000).

The same sorts of encounters appear throughout the Billy Bob Holland series. Billy Bob accidentally killed a friend, L. Q. Navarro, during a Ranger operation in Mexico. Forever after, the ghost of L. Q. appears to him at crucial plot points, expressing opinions, offering advice, and providing painful reminders.

Burke's most recent novel, *Bitterroot,* is a solid Billy Bob Holland book that reprises a number of the themes and situations from *The Lost Get-Back Boogie.*

"Out of the Past" appeared, in different form, in *GQ* (1993). The quote is from the later version, which appeared as a prelude to the novella *Dick Contino's Blues* in Ellroy's *Hollywood Nocturnes* (1994).

Chapter VII. The Fun House

For Frye on gallows humor, see *A Study of English Romanticism* (1968), p. 62. The discussion of the grotesque begins on p. 60.

The odd image of damage inflicted by ducks also appears in *Nibbled to Death by Ducks,* from Robert Campbell's Jimmy Flannery series. The Flannery series, dealing with a Chicago ward heeler who works for the sewer department, is soft-boiled, as opposed to Campbell's more hard-boiled "La-La Land" / Whistler series.

The discussion of *The Burnt Orange Heresy* is in *After the Death of Literature,* chap. 4.

C. S. Lewis's discussion of satire occurs in his treatment of the master Elizabethan satirist Thomas Nashe: *English Literature in the Sixteenth Century, Excluding Drama* (1954), p. 413.

For Frank McConnell on Thomas Pynchon, see *Four Postwar American Novelists: Bellow, Mailer, Barth, and Pynchon* (1977), chap. 4.

I owe the *Postman Always Rings Twice* observation to my colleague Nancy West and her student, Bryan Crockett. See also Alain Silver and James Ursini, *The Noir Style* (1999).

Chapter VIII. Live and Learn

Three other historical novels worthy of mention (treating the fourteenth, sixteenth, and eighteenth centuries respectively) are Umberto Eco's *The Name of the Rose* (1983), Iain Pears's *An Instance of the Fingerpost* (1998), and David Liss's *A Conspiracy of Paper* (2000).

Willeford's *Something about a Soldier* and *I Was Looking for a Street* have recently been reissued (2000) in a single volume. Both are highly recommended.

See Deborah Tannen's *You Just Don't Understand: Women and Men in Conversation* (1990).

Whether Harris will follow the plot line established at the conclusion of the novel *Hannibal* or instead follow the direction established by the film is a most interesting question at this point. While the novel brings the two central characters together, the film splits them apart, maintaining the outlines of the original relationship between Clarice and Hannibal rather than envisioning them as a retired couple or active duo. There are ways out of this narrative box, but Harris's perfectionism is likely to be tested by them. At the same time, the pressures generated by the film's vast commercial success may prove overwhelming. At this point Harris's audience has in effect become split between those who know the novel and those who know only the film. The manner in which he eventually sustains his novelistic integrity without ignoring commercial blandishments should prove to be a textbook case for those studying the relationship between art and commerce in contemporary society. A remake of Harris's *Red Dragon* (shot earlier by Michael Mann under the title *Manhunter* with Brian Cox playing Lecter) is now in preproduction with Brett Ratner directing and Hopkins playing Lecter.

Holmes's comment on the far-fetched truth appears in *The Sign of Four* (1890), chap. 6.

Chapter IX. Cross Over

For Goldman, see *Adventures in the Screen Trade: A Personal View of Hollywood and Screenwriting* (1983).

Sometimes the allegorical dimensions of contemporary fiction are less clear. Stephen King, for example, has argued (in public lectures) that Cormac McCarthy's horrific and suitably bloody *Blood Meridian: Or, The Evening Redness in the West* is actually a book about Vietnam.

Where Folsom pushes the novelty side of the justice/novelty dyad to extremes, another writer has maintained the balancing act (but just barely). Frederick Schofield's *A Run to Hell* (1999) combines two actual stories: the death of Princess Grace and the capture of Manuel Noriega. These will appear to be unrelated, but Schofield manages to bring the two together, with the Philadelphia mob as linchpin. The writing is just a tad under the over-the-top line and uses historical events to create conflict and suspense—the protagonist is on a mission to secure Manuel Noriega, but we know how Manuel Noriega was actually secured, so we worry over the fate of the protagonist and his love interest. At the end of the book (this has to be a first) the author gives us a fifty-page epilogue detailing the lives and times of Grace Kelly and Manuel Noriega, "for you, my dear readers who find A&E's 'Biography' is their favorite television show." The novel is a combination of sex, violence, constant conflict, and heavy-duty suspense. It has also resulted in a six-figure movie sale. Schofield's other novels, *Megasino: The Thirteenth Casino* and *The Boardwalkers*, can also be recommended.

In contrast to the genre-bending writing of Robert Clark, the succeeding year's Edgar winner was far more conventional. Steve Hamilton's *A Cold Day in Paradise* (1998) plays riffs on very conventional themes and topoi. Alex McKnight, a former Detroit police officer with a bullet lodged near his heart, is now working as a PI on the Upper Peninsula. Dead bodies begin to turn up along with messages that appear to be from the individual who shot Alex (and killed his partner) more than a decade earlier. That individual, however, is in a maximum-security prison. How can this be? The writing is very effective, and the suspense is sustained expertly. The novel's interest lies in the author's fresh handling of an old template rather than in a dramatic departure from conventional expectations. *A Cold Day in*

Paradise received the Shamus award from the Private Eye Writers of America as well as the Edgar.

In the prefatory material to his most recent novel, *Silent Joe* (2001), T. Jefferson Parker acknowledges the importance of Lethem's work and says that his "writing inspired me to try this book" (p. vii). *Silent Joe* concerns a young man (eventually) named Joe Trona whose infant face was scarred by acid. Joe is adopted by Will and Mary Ann Trona, grows to manhood, and follows Will into law enforcement. By now Will is a successful politician in Orange County, and when he is violently murdered young Joe is suddenly forced into the role of investigator. As some compensation for his physical mutilation Joe possesses an eidetic memory that, obviously, materially aids him in this task. While the debts to Lethem's work are clear, the novel—among Parker's very best work to date—should be considered more homage than imitation.

A standard beginning point for the discussion of genre is René Wellek and Austin Warren, *Theory of Literature* (1942), chap. 17.

In addition to the above-mentioned books on the novel by Hunter and McKeon, one should mention Ian Watt, *The Rise of the Novel: Studies in Defoe, Richardson, and Fielding* (1957) and A. D. McKillop, *The Early Masters of English Fiction* (1956). The following are still read: Dorothy Van Ghent, *The English Novel, Form and Function* (1953), Arnold Kettle, *An Introduction to the English Novel*, 2 vols. (1951), Percy Lubbock, *The Craft of Fiction* (1957), Walter Allen, *The English Novel: A Short Critical History* (1954), and F. R. Leavis, *The Great Tradition* (1948).

On the demands and constraints of screenwriting see Syd Field, *Screenplay: The Foundations of Screenwriting* (expanded ed., 1982), Wells Root, *Writing the Script: A Practical Guide for Films and Television* (1980), and John Brady, ed., *The Craft of the Screenwriter: Interviews with Six Celebrated Screenwriters* (1981). Brady's interviewees are Paddy Chayefsky, William Goldman, Ernest Lehman, Paul Schrader, Neil Simon, and Robert Towne.

Afterword

Nefarious: Tales of Mystery can be found at http://www.thewindjammer.com/nefarious. For XC Publishing, visit http://www.xcpublishing.com.

Garry Wills has summarized the feelings of many with regard to the church in his recent book, *Papal Sin: Structures of Deceit* (2000). Wills traces the philosophic absurdities of key doctrinal positions and demonstrates how the church's behavior has resulted in an erosion of its moral authority. One of the most striking aspects of contemporary Catholicism is the extent to which some theologians have kept their beliefs and conclusions from the laity. While many academics have produced trade titles that attempt to elucidate the points under dispute within their fields, theologians have been comparatively silent. Their misguided loyalty has contributed to the erosion of the laity's faith, for the laity is led to believe that putative intellectuals are as naive and / or self-interested as the Vatican.

See Deborah Tannen, *The Argument Culture: Moving from Debate to Dialogue* (1998).

The "Simple Art of Murder" quote is in *The Simple Art of Murder* (1972), p. 20; the quote from *The Long Goodbye* (1953) is on p. 280 of the Vintage edition (1988).

The only thing darker than Thompson's books is Thompson's own life. See Robert Polito, *Savage Art: A Biography of Jim Thompson* (1995).

Index

167